Loch Down Abbey

About the Author

Beth Cowan-Erskine is an American expat who married into a mad Scottish family with their own tartan and a family tree older than her home country. Using them as inspiration, she wrote her first novel during the coronavirus lockdown, hoping it would be enough to get her disinvited from the annual family walking holiday. Sadly, it backfired and led to long discussions of who would play whom in the film. When not writing, she owns an interior architecture and design studio in the Cotswolds.

Loch Down
Abbey

BETH COWAN-ERSKINE

HODDER

First published in Great Britain in 2021 by Hodder & Stoughton
An Hachette UK company

I

Copyright © Beth Cowan-Erskine 2021

A CIP catalogue record for this title is available from the British Library

B format ISBN 978 1 529 37099 7
eBook ISBN 978 1 529 37097 3

Typeset in Plantin Light by Palimpsest Book Production Limited,
Falkirk, Stirlingshire

Printed and bound in Great Britain by Clays Ltd, Elcograf S.p.A.

Hodder & Stoughton policy is to use papers that are natural, renewable
and recyclable products and made from wood grown in sustainable
forests. The logging and manufacturing processes are expected to conform
to the environmental regulations of the country of origin.

Hodder & Stoughton Ltd
Carmelite House
50 Victoria Embankment
London EC4Y 0DZ

www.hodder.co.uk

For my mother, Teresa, who always
said I was a born storyteller.

Loch Down Abbey

Introduction

Loch Down Abbey is a grand house near the village of Inverkillen, which sits on the shores of Loch Down, deep in the Scottish Highlands. On the Estate runs the River Plaid, source of Plaid Whisky, but it is the salmon fishing that makes it famous. It is April, somewhere in the 1930s. There is rumour of a mysterious illness spreading throughout the country. It is highly contagious, and hundreds have already died, but they were mostly English, and we are far from concerned.

List of Characters

The Ogilvy-Sinclair Family

The Matriarch

Lady Georgina – The Dowager Countess of Inverkillen

Her Children

Lord Hamish Inverkillen – The 19th Earl of Inverkillen, son of Lady Georgina. Married to **Lady Victoria**
The Honourable Major Cecil Ogilvy-Sinclair – Second son. Widower of the **Marchioness of Drysdale**
Lady Elspeth Comtois – Married to **Philippe, Marquis de Clairvaux**

Her Grandchildren

Lord Angus Templeton – Heir to the Earldom, married to **Lady Constance**
The Honourable Fergus Ogilvy-Sinclair – Engaged to **Lady Eva Zander-Bitterling**
Lady Annabella (Bella) Dunbar-Hamilton – Married to **the Honourable Hugh Dunbar-Hamilton**

Also

The Family Ward – **Iris Wynford**, parentage unknown
The Family Dogs – Grantham, a German short-haired Pointer and Belgravia, a black Labrador
The Great-grandchildren – One stroppy teen, three petit French and three wee Scots

Servants

Butler – **Hudson**
Head Housekeeper – **Mrs MacBain**
Valet – **Mr Mackay**
Lady's maid – **Miss Maxwell**
First Footman – **Ollie**
Nanny – **Miss Mackenzie**
Chauffeur – **Lockridge**
Cook – **Mrs Burnside**
Gamekeeper – **Ross McBain**
Distiller – **Old MacTavish**
Various other staff too numerous to name

Other

Mr Andrew Lawlis – Lawyer
Imogen MacLeod – His assistant
Reverend Malcolm Douglas – Vicar
Inspector Jarvis – Loch Down Police Force
Thomas Kettering – London Art Historian

April

It was a long ride home from a fantastically boring ball and the morning's journey was made worse by the whisky from the night before. Lady Annabella Dunbar-Hamilton, daughter of the Earl and Countess of Inverkillen wondered, not for the first time, why they bothered to go. The McIntyre Spring Ball was a family tradition, yes, but she and her brothers were married. Well, her youngest brother was finally engaged, and the wedding was in a mere five weeks.

Why they had been compelled to bring the children to the ball was another mystery. It was difficult to enjoy herself with the little ones running wild. Not that Nanny didn't have a firm grip on them normally, but after catching them hiding under the midnight-breakfast tables stealing sausages, she suspected that Nanny had rather helped herself to the overflowing whisky. She had no proof, of course, but that didn't bother her; it was widely accepted by her set that staff helped themselves when the family was not watching closely. Should she discuss it with them? She needed a bath before tea was served and would decide then. *When will we be home?* Travelling was so tiring.

At long last, they arrived, and Bella, as she was called, looked up impassively at the house she had lived in her whole life. The Abbey lay on the shores of Loch Down and had been home to the Ogilvy-Sinclair Clan for six centuries. The staff were standing in line in the entrance forecourt to greet them.

Bella wafted past and spoke vaguely to the line of house-maids, not focusing on any particular one. 'Nanny's not feeling well. Please see the children to the Nursery for her and then unpack my trunks.' Then, spotting the head house-keeper, she said, 'Ah, Mrs MacBain, I think the hem of my ballgown needs tending to. Strip the Willow got a bit out of hand – you know what Lord Neasden can be like. I heard a distinct tear. Hopefully nothing serious; it's only just come from Edinburgh.'

The housemaids curtsied and waited for the rest of the family to drift through the large stone archway and into the house before they dared to move.

The family never looked at the staff directly. It didn't do to be too personal with the household staff. Those that attended to them directly, who helped them dress and so forth, were called by their names. But the rest were simply interchangeable pieces in the house. Like chess. Maisie, Daisy, something . . . Lazy? Bella could never quite remember. She was the daughter of an Earl; she didn't need to remember.

Bella walked into the Armoury, which was the central space of the house. Built in the early 1500s, it was a long, double-height room lined with an impressive display of ancient family armour and weaponry. She proceeded up the oak staircase – left one for the family, right one for the guests – to the first floor and passed over a carved timber walkway, which proudly displayed the Inverkillen coat of arms surrounded by the broadswords and axes of their conquered enemies. While the collection was sought after by many museums, it was the ceiling of the armoury that people coveted most. The Abbey was one of the only houses in Scotland to have a barrel vault roof with hunting scenes painted on it. It was rumoured to have been done by Holbein himself when Henry VIII mentioned he wanted this as a hunting lodge one season. He never travelled to Scotland, of course, given the enmity between the two countries, but the 7th Earl of Inverkillen was an idiot and nearly bankrupted himself readying the house for the royal visit that never came. Luckily, the 8th Earl was quickly wed to a minor Danish princess with questionable paternity and an overly generous dowry. The 7th Countess had arranged it. The women were often the heroes in the family, but it was the men who had their portraits on the walls.

Not that Bella had ever looked at the portraits. She had grown up surrounded by them and they were simply a blur on the way from one room to the next. The art, the tapestries, the objects, all collected over the centuries . . . what was there to see? Everyone lived this way, didn't they? Everyone she knew did.

Bella turned back as she reached the arched entrance to the hallway. She could see a housemaid and two footmen herding the children towards the back of the house, the little voices ricocheting through the Armoury, piercing her already sore head. They could be such loud creatures. She couldn't wait to sink into her bath.

As she turned down the dark panelled hallway towards her rooms, Bella nodded at her mother's lady's maid, who bobbed a quick curtsey. Maxwell never travelled with the family to the ball, a decision neither Bella nor Maxwell understood. Not that Maxwell minded. She was happy for a night off and a bit of a lie-in the following morning. She waited for Lady Bella to pass her and then scurried towards the servants' stairs. She had been hoping to use the main staircase but now that the family was entering the Armoury, there was no chance of that. She ducked behind the green baize door and wound her way down to the main floor.

Appearing from behind a hidden door, she paused to let Lord Inverkillen and his sons walk past. Lord Inverkillen doesn't look particularly happy, she thought.

'Angus, Fergus, come with me.' It was a barked order more than a request. He strode off towards the Map Room, without looking to see that either son had heard him. The brothers exchanged an uncertain look and followed after him, Angus sighing loudly. Maxwell fleetingly wondered what had happened at the ball, and then hurried through the Armoury. She slipped out of the front door and took her place beside Mrs MacBain. Together they watched as Lady Eva, Fergus's fiancée, was handed out of a car. There was far too much ceremony in it, in her opinion; the footmen were overly enamoured with the girl and she milked it every chance she had. She had arrived from London some days ago and had spent that time largely alienating the household. They were used to difficult guests, difficult family even, but Lady Eva seemed to believe that it was she who would become the Countess when they married, and she was issuing orders left and right. The maids were exhausted. Maxwell thought of the staff Eva had left back in London; their lives must be much quieter now. A surreptitious smile crept on to her face.

The thrill of driving up to a full complement of staff was something Eva felt sure she'd never tire of seeing. But she did wonder if she was doing the right thing in marrying Fergus. Rather unfortunately, Fergus was the younger of Lord Inverkillen's two sons. The spare, not the heir, as Eva's father had pointed out when Fergus had asked for her hand. And only the best would do for his only child. But Lord Zander-Bitterling was a pragmatist, above all else. His companies supplied seafood to the Palace and other smart businesses in London. When it was explained to him, over dinner at White's, that it was Fergus who oversaw the family's salmon fishing enterprise, Lord Bitterling thawed, sensing a hefty family discount could be brokered for the famed salmon.

Eva had been swiftly dispatched to Scotland, where she was installed in what she felt were rather cramped rooms, on the second floor, to supervise the wedding planning. The cream of London society would be coming to Scotland for the wedding. It would be in all the papers, and *Tatler* if she could get it, so she was not going to leave the planning to a provincial household staff, most of whom had never been farther than the village. Having been in residence for some days now, she could see she had been right to come early. Tartan at a wedding? Honestly. Yes, it was Scotland and yes, it was tradition, but even their dress tartan was horrific. No, it was good she had come early. 'Mrs MacBain, could we please meet in the Morning Room to review the preliminary guest list? I'm quite concerned we have it finalised by Thursday, so we have time for the engraved invitations to be made. I'll just take off my hat and freshen up a bit.' She walked on without waiting for a reply.

Mrs MacBain froze, stunned, for a moment, then recovered, nodded her head, and replied, 'As you wish milady.' She turned to see the thirty or forty suitcases and trunks being driven into the delivery yard, the family dogs, Grantham and Belgravia, barking and jumping as they trundled by. Since there is nothing else for me to be doing just now, she thought.

Maxwell shot Mrs MacBain a sympathetic look and said quietly, 'Four days here and she thinks she owns the place.'

'Well, that's the English for you,' replied Mrs MacBain. She headed for the front door, saying to the housemaids, 'You'll have to look after the luggage for me. I'll join you as soon as I can. Just be sure the footmen bring it all inside at once. No smoking breaks. The dogs are out, and I'll not have a repeat of last year!' It had taken them weeks to remove the smell of urine from His Lordship's favourite travelling trunk.

Mrs MacBain reached the Morning Room first and as she closed the doors behind her, the noise of the Armoury faded. Out of habit, she glanced around the room to see all was in order, then smoothed her dress and looked out the window as she waited for Lady Eva. She had always hated this room. The carpet had been woven in the family tartan, colours that always gave her a headache. It had taken her several years to convince Lady Inverkillen to meet in her private sitting room to review the weekly arrangements. She would have to mount a similar campaign with Lady Eva, but had the unpleasant feeling that it might be tougher to convince her. She made a mental note to find another room as a study for the girl. Maybe the Wedgewood Room would do.

Alice MacBain was well aware that she was a supremely competent woman. If she had been born a man, she would have been a head butler, she often felt. But as a woman, she'd had to enter service as a housemaid. She had worked her way up to Head Housekeeper quickly and had been running the Abbey for nearly fifteen years. She was the youngest head housekeeper anyone knew, and it was always remarked upon with a bit of awe. There was nothing in the household she did not know about and she ran it like an Admiral of the Fleet.

Moving from the window, she glanced at the mantle clock. It had been ten minutes already. She needed to get tea ready and check the linen cupboard for towels. Now that the entire family was back in residence, they were going through them at an alarming pace. Fifteen minutes now. Where was she? It was going to be a long afternoon.

Mrs MacBain opened the door and looked out to the Armoury. The noise hadn't quite settled yet. Coats were being removed; orders given to housemaids. On the guest staircase, she spotted the Major. She'd have to remember to tell the maids to keep an eye out. He liked to rummage when he visited, and things always went missing. She still couldn't find the Regency silver egg cups from last year.

Major Cecil Ogilvy-Sinclair was looking forward to a hot bath. He sighed wistfully, thinking of his copper tub at home, in Stronach Castle. But here, in his ancestral home, he was relegated to the guest floor and a shoddy bath he barely fitted into. Buck up, he told himself, it's only temporary. An old bitterness filled Cecil. He would have made a much better Lord, in his humble opinion, than his older brother, Hamish. As he made his way up the stairs, he thought back over their childhood. Hamish had always run around the grounds with no shoes and torn clothing, befriending the servants – positively feral, Cecil thought disdainfully. Cecil, in contrast, had been a model gentleman, devoted to the family and the finer things in life. It was he who learned about art, books and culture; all the things that mattered. He mastered piano by the age of twelve. He had an encyclopaedic knowledge of French wines. And he could recite most of Byron's poems by heart when he was fourteen. He was clearly more suitable to be a Lord, not his dirty, ragged brother who wouldn't know a Manet from a Mozart. In the end, his father had packed Cecil off to the military, getting an old regimental buddy to agree to take his son on. He had worked only hard enough to rise to major, hoping that the income would help supplement his monthly allowance. His father could be so miserly. When his tastes quickly outstripped that, he had turned to his only other talent: cards.

It was at the cards table he had made his fortune. Not winning – he was an appalling player – but in who he lost to. It was in Lord Elsmere's games room that he was introduced to the Marchioness of Drysdale, only child of the late Marquess of Bertach. She was slightly older than he, a bit plump and quite plain, but elegantly dressed and far richer than his father. Cecil lost more to her than he could afford, but made up for it with a whirlwind courtship that was the talk of London. She financed it, of course. They married three months later in sumptuous fashion at Stronach Castle, her Estate in Scotland. They lived in her London house on Regent's Park during the season, summered at her French Estate in Bordeaux, and had various little houses around Europe in all the places that mattered. But he had returned to Loch Down each spring for the ball.

Just before he reached his room, he heard his name being called behind him. He turned to find a footman panting at the top of the stairs. 'Excuse me, sir, but the Dowager Countess would like to speak with you.'

'What, now?' Cecil sputtered, irritated. The last thing he needed was a chat with his mother. He sighed heavily, his hand on the oak balustrade. Slowly, he retraced his steps and descended the staircase, much to the relief of the footman, who had no wish to inform the Dowager her request had been denied.

As Cecil walked through the front door, he saw his mother's car waiting, the door opened for him. 'Mother,' he said wearily as he entered the car, 'why do you insist on being driven home? It is a two-minute walk between the front doors.' Drummond House was indeed very near to the Abbey, standing on the opposite side of the circular drive. Angus had once served a tennis ball from the Abbey into the front door of his Grandmama's home. She hadn't been pleased; he had broken a vase of flowers. Just as unfit to be a Lord as his father, Cecil thought. There really was no justice in the world.

'A lady simply does not walk home, especially when she's already seated in the car. Thank you, Lockridge.' She allowed the chauffer to hand her out of the car, as Cecil exited the other side.

The dower house was a beautiful ivy-covered manor that had been built in the late 1840s after a fire ravaged the Abbey. At the time, fingers of blame had been pointed at many, but in the end, it landed with the servants, in spite of the fact the fire had been started in the 13th Earl's bedroom. There had been no discussion of why his freshly dismissed mistress had been there at the time.

Given the size of the Inverkillen family in those days – they were a fertile bunch – the entire first and second floors of Drummond House had been given over to the family bedrooms but only His Lordship had a dressing room and sitting room. That had caused quite a row amongst the family, which ended with a rather valuable vase through the window of the Drawing Room. Shrubs had subsequently been planted at the base of each window.

The ground floor housed only four rooms: a Drawing Room, a Morning Room, a Dining Room, and a Library. It had been cramped, but they had managed. After the family had moved back into the Abbey, Drummond House was given to the dowager countesses and used to house the lesser guests, which never sat well with Lady Georgina. She hated being relegated to hosting second-tier guests, but thankfully, the Olgivy-Sinclairs rarely entertained.

As mother and son settled into the Drawing Room, she

instructed tea to be brought for them. 'I'm simply parched after that long drive. Why do we insist on going? It's so far to travel for one night. And they are such frightful hosts. Honestly, who doesn't serve a cheese course at dinner?'

Cecil shrugged and lit a cigarette, playing with a crystal match striker on the fireplace mantel. Quite a pretty thing. He wondered if it was particularly valuable.

'Now, what did you find out from the solicitor?' she asked, peering intently at her son. She had an unnerving way of staring at people when she spoke.

Cecil grimaced and said in a rather defeated tone, 'There is no way around it, I'm afraid. It's iron clad and that rake in London is the rightful heir!'

Lady Georgina was shocked. 'You mean there is nothing he can do? Nothing at all? No hidden codicil or . . . I don't know. It happens all the time in Dickens. There must be something.'

Cecil's wife, the Marchioness, had died suddenly that very winter, and while exceedingly wealthy, she had lived only on an allowance from the family fortune. The principal was tied up with the land and property in a family trust. And since she and Cecil hadn't any children, the Estate, the title, and more importantly, the money, all reverted to a distant male relative in London upon the Marchioness's death. It had come as quite a shock to Cecil when her will was read.

'So, you mean to say,' Lady Georgina went on, 'that she left you with nothing but the castle in Orkney and a small lump sum? I've never heard of anything so mean-spirited. Imagine if your father had taken care of me that way . . .' She tutted for a bit. Lady Georgina was fond of tutting. 'Poor Cecil. What will you do?'

Cecil didn't know. The small lump sum was nearly gone and the castle in Orkney was a ruin, if memory served, with only a few finished rooms. Restoring it had been a pet project for the Marchioness's father, but he had died from Spanish influenza in 1919 before it was completed. Cecil had once suggested to his wife that they finish the restoration and use it as a fishing cottage, but the Marchioness had batted the idea away – how could they possibly use it? It only had five bedrooms – so no more work was done to it. How Cecil was supposed to live there, and with so little money, he knew not. In the days after the will was read, he had convinced himself that it was some sort of joke, or mistake. There had to be something else for him. He had engaged the family solicitor, Andrew Lawlis, to check into it for him, but that had come to nothing but legal fees.

'There isn't a thing more for me from that woman,' Cecil confirmed. 'I have a ruin in Orkney and some stranger is now lawfully living in my houses.'

'Do we know who he is? Who his people are? Perhaps we can speak with them,' Lady Georgina prodded, never one to give up where family pride was at stake.

'Lawlis says it's a great-great-grand-nephew or something. I can't find him in Debrett's. I believe he's a librarian; it had to do with books, I seem to remember. My lord, he has a job. What does that tell you?'

Lady Georgina shook her head in sympathy. It was a distasteful thought, being displaced by a tradesman.

Cecil traced the outline of the marble fireplace with his finger, staring at his signet ring. 'And he is now in possession of my fortune. I earned that fortune, Mummy! I should at least have the house in France. It's tiny, really.'

Lady Georgina recalled the house. She'd been forced to visit one summer shortly after Cecil and his bride returned from honeymoon. Yes, it was tiny, by the Marchioness's standards: only fourteen bedrooms, the dining room seated a crowded eighteen and the grounds were mostly given over to a rather steep cliff down to a beach. A private beach, but still, all that sand and untidy seaweed . . . 'No, it's not really a crown jewel, is it? Perhaps Hamish can help? You're brothers, after all. Oh, I'll never understand why your father left you out of the will.'

Cecil glanced uncomfortably at his mother. Lady Georgina was unaware of her son's gambling problem, something neither the Marchioness nor Lord Inverkillen, past and present, had missed, and he had always been kept on a tight leash by them. Cecil appealed to Hamish for help, shortly after his wife's will had been read: property, money, anything. Hamish offered to cover the legal costs of the investigation but no more. They had quarrelled for months about it and Cecil had come to make peace in a last-ditch effort for a handout. And to be sure Hamish paid Lawlis's final invoice. Lord, what that man charged! Cecil had been living on the generosity of friends, travelling between their houses, but without the Marchioness by his side, he was tiresome company. And when word leaked out that he had been left with no fortune, no land, and no house, those doors stopped opening. So he had come home to the Abbey. He pushed aside all these horrid thoughts.

'That's why I'm here,' he said.

'I thought as much. What did he say?'

'That he's paid for Lawlis and that's as far as he'll go. "Not another sou," he said. He can be so cruel!' Cecil flopped down violently on the sofa, scaring the dog. 'At least I'm still in his will.'

'Yes, but that doesn't help you now, does it?'

'No,' he replied grimly, staring at Loch Down Abbey across the lawn. 'It doesn't help me now at all.'

★

Back in the Abbey, Fergus was stepping into the Map Room behind his father and brother.

'Close the door.'

That, Fergus thought, was not a good sign.

For months, the men had been locked in an argument about the future of the Estate. The family distillery was losing money rapidly. Angus, heir to the Earldom, oversaw the Distillery and he wasn't much for business, but what concerned Fergus most was the fact that it was terrible whisky. Fergus wanted to make changes, bring in a new distiller, but his father and his brother were dead set against it, and Fergus was growing less and less optimistic. It seemed that if there was one thing the Earl hated more than change, it was being told to change – and even more so when the command was coming from his own children.

Lord Inverkillen opened a book on the desk and flicked a few pages. 'It's been a long journey today and I'm tired, but we need to discuss the Distillery.'

Fergus had worked hard on a strategy to return the Distillery and the Estate to profitability. He'd given it to both his father and his brother several days before the ball, hoping against hope that at least his father would read it. He took a deep breath and said a quiet prayer.

'Did you read my proposal?' he asked, hoping he didn't sound eager.

Angus sat down roughly in a chair and started to light a cigarette. He shook his head and grimaced. Domestic. I have to raid Philippe's stash today. That was the good thing about having a French uncle: he never left France without several suitcases of Gauloises. 'No, Fergus. I have things to do with my time.'

Fergus snorted. 'Like what? Hiding in the Tennis Pavilion with Hugh?'

The Honourable Hugh Dunbar-Hamilton was the second son of a favourite neighbour and married to Bella, their sister. Hugh and Angus had been in the same house at school, and the two were inseparable. When Hugh's parents had announced he was to marry a girl from Yorkshire – some wool heiress or other – a plan was hatched between the two men to have Hugh marry Bella instead. While Hugh had never spent much time in Bella's company, he had been overjoyed when she accepted his proposal. He'd read the Brontë sisters; he had no desire to spend time on the wind-swept moors.

'Your plan is seventy-five pages long, Fergus! Who has time for that?' Angus picked a bit of tobacco from his lips and flicked it into the air. Why did English cigarettes have to taste so bad?

'What exactly do you do all day that you can't find the time to help save the family from bankruptcy?' asked Fergus. Angus was never in the Distillery if he could avoid it. MacTavish, the distiller, ran things with an alarming autonomy.

'Enough.' Hamish said it quietly, but Fergus and Angus instantly stopped squabbling. The Earl was a man of few words but those he did use could be vicious instruments if he chose.

Hamish sighed. The truth of the matter was that he knew Plaid Whisky was not doing as well as they had hoped that quarter. In fact, it had not done as well as he had hoped in any quarter and he knew it was the salmon sales – Fergus's part of the business – that was holding up the family. Hamish hated the idea of sending his salmon to others, but he allowed it, because new roofs were expensive. But what Fergus was proposing was reprehensible.

Fergus wanted, among other ideas, to use Drummond House as a lodge, taking paying guests for stalking or fishing.

Only the right sort of people, naturally, but people who would pay handsomely for a day of sport on the Estate followed by a dinner and whisky tasting that evening. Hosting shooting weekends was nothing new to the family, although it had been some time since they had done so. But now, it needed to be a commercial venture, or they would slip into bankruptcy. Hamish hated the entire idea of it. Honestly, what was the point of belonging to the aristocracy if one had to work for a living?

But Hamish knew the Estate was costly. His own father had struggled to keep the ship afloat. Wages had skyrocketed after the war, even in the Highlands. It was harder and harder to find staff to work for the pay they offered. Hamish and Lady Georgina knew only too well what it cost to keep up the standards of Loch Down. Something had to be done, he agreed, but to allow strangers on to his Estate, and then to expect His Lordship to be trotted out for entertainment? No, thank you. There were other, more traditional ways to fund the Estate.

And this is where they had circled for months. Modernisation on one side, tradition on the other. But today, Hamish was determined to settle the matter once and for all.

'I suppose you still feel replacing MacTavish is the right thing to do?' Hamish still did not turn to face his sons.

'He's been the Master Distiller here for nearly fifty years,' cried Angus, who had been fighting Fergus on this point for some months. Not that he cared; he just didn't want Fergus to be right. Fergus was often right, and that irritated Angus.

Fergus tutted. 'He's not a master distiller, Angus. He's an old codger who knows how to make whisky. We're in the Highlands, for god's sake; everyone knows how to make whisky. Some of them even make good whisky.'

'What's that supposed to mean?' snapped Angus. He had moved to the sofa and was petting the family dogs, who were nestling down for their afternoon nap. It was their favourite place to sleep.

'It's terrible whisky and you both know it,' Fergus said loudly. Both his father and his brother glared at him. 'Do either of you drink it?'

Hamish considered his son. The boy had a point. The whisky decanter he was holding was filled with another's blend. He'd never been able to put duty above his favourite whisky, but it only bothered him when Fergus brought it up, which he did frequently these days.

'And what would you have me do?' asked Hamish quietly. 'Throw open the doors to the Estate for any paying monkey?' Fergus could hear his anger mounting and braced himself for it. 'My god, they could be anyone. Can you see your Grandmama sitting at table with, with . . . Italians? Or, god forbid, Americans?'

Fergus shook his head. 'No. That is not how it works. Grandmama is not involved. If you'd read it—'

'I have!' He hadn't. Not really. He'd stopped when Fergus proposed moving Lady Georgina back into the Abbey. Hamish had no desire to share a roof with that woman again. He loved his mother, but there were limits. 'Well, it doesn't matter any longer. It's out of our hands.'

'What?' Fergus felt slightly unsteady but wasn't sure why. He looked to Angus, who looked equally confused.

'The Distillery has been sold.' Hamish turned his back and was silent.

Angus gasped. Would he be expected to take over the salmon now that he would no longer be managing the whisky? That looked like a lot more work than the Distillery. He rounded on Fergus – this had to be his doing.

But Fergus was looking just as stunned as he felt. 'What? To whom? When did this happen?' he blustered. Angus was satisfied with the confusion, and took a long drag on his cigarette. Yes, I definitely need to raid Phillipe's stash after this, he thought.

Hamish shrugged slightly, his back still to his sons. 'Lawlis handled it.' He took a sip of whisky and moved to stare out the window.

Fergus couldn't take it in. He knew that Lawlis had been pushing Hamish to sell the Distillery for several months, but he hadn't realised his father was considering it seriously. Without the Distillery, his proposal fell apart completely.

But as he took in the set of his father's shoulders, he realised it was no use questioning him any further. When Hamish was finished, he was finished. Fergus stood and looked at his brother for a moment. Angus merely shrugged. Fergus walked swiftly to the door and tried not to slam it on his way out. He was so upset he didn't see Iris standing in the hallway. He barrelled into her and then apologised brusquely and carried on. *What is that girl doing in the hallway?*

'That girl' was rubbing her shoulder as she retrieved the book she'd dropped. *Why does everyone keep running into me? I'm hardly invisible.* Straightening her skirt, she went back to looking at the painting on the wall.

Iris Wynford was the family ward, and invisible was exactly what she was to the family. Lady Georgina had brought her to live at the Abbey twelve years ago. No one knew why – Lady Georgina didn't like to be questioned – and they accepted her, mostly, but not warmly. While she took her meals with them, her bedroom was on the guest floor, clearly marking her as 'not family'. Not that she minded; she had the entire floor to herself. And she preferred it to the orphanage. Here, at least, she could spend her days curled up studying art and history in the Reading Room. It was there had she found *The Inventory*, which she'd just dropped.

Hamish's great-grandfather had been the last collector in the family and had commissioned a book of all the artworks in the Abbey. There was a sketch of the object accompanied by a history of the work, the artist, and sometimes a bit about how the piece came into the family. It fascinated her, and she tried to study one piece a week, which is why she'd been in the hallway when Fergus nearly knocked her over.

She had been looking for months for this particular painting, a portrait of the 10th Countess of Inverkillen, which had been done sometime in the 1600s. She was the only countess to have been painted, but no one could remember why. Iris was shining a torch on the painting, comparing it to the book. None of the artworks had been restored in decades from what Iris could see, and she often needed a torch to view them properly. This one, however, looked nothing like the sketch in the book. She was puzzling over the pattern of Lady Morag's dress when Fergus bumped into her. The tartans didn't match. Lady Morag's is almost tasteful, she thought. It could never be said that Inverkillen tartan was tasteful. Had the family changed it sometime in their history? Or had the tartan been repainted? It was very curious.

The grandfather clock struck four and Iris hurried to the Library for tea. As she entered the room, something felt different. They were all silent. The Ogilvy-Sinclairs were rarely silent. She walked quietly to the tea tray, helped herself and then settled into a chair on the far side of the room, wondering what had happened.

'I told you Nanny wasn't drunk,' Angus taunted his sister, looking strangely jubilant.

'Now is not the time, Angus,' Elspeth scolded her nephew.

Lady Georgina swept into the room. 'I've just heard the news,' she breathed, perching herself on a chair. She waved away a cup of tea, peering intently at her daughter in law. 'Is this true, Victoria? Nanny's dead?'

Iris gasped. No wonder the room was quiet.

'Yes, I'm afraid so.' Lady Inverkillen was so quiet they all leaned forward to hear her. 'The doctor is with her now.'

'But how on earth did it happen?' the dowager asked. 'I thought she just had too much whisky at the ball. Is this anything to do with the rumours of illness that I've heard around the village?'

'The rumours are just that: rumours,' an unfamiliar voice said from the doorway, making them all jump. It was the doctor. 'Bored women with nothing else to occupy their minds.' He fidgeted with his medical bag. It irritated him greatly to have his opinion undermined by gossips in the village. 'There have been some illnesses, yes, but nothing to suggest this is anything out of the ordinary. And Nanny was old. It was simply her time.'

'She wasn't old,' snapped Bella. 'Was she?' Suddenly uncertain, she looked round at the others. Angus shrugged and turned to light his cigarette. No one really knew how old Nanny was.

'Nearing seventy-eight,' said the doctor. 'I think that counts as old. I'll look in on Archie tomorrow afternoon but ring me if anything changes.'

They all looked at him blankly. 'Archie?'

'Your footman.' Nothing registered on their faces. 'Bit of a cough, slight fever. Nothing serious, I should think. Until tomorrow, then.' He left swiftly, before they could think of anything to ask.

'I'd had no idea Nanny was that old,' murmured Elspeth, moving to sit on the sofa.

'And just who is going to look after the children until we find a new nanny?' Bella asked sharply. 'I'm certainly not watching them! I have things to do.'

Bella hated children. Sticky, germy, nonsensical things. And she resented them for the havoc they had wreaked on her body. While she still had an enviable figure, the compliment was always accompanied by 'after three children' or 'for your age'. Barbs and stings where once it had been admiration and envy. She dearly missed admiration and envy.

While she could never have been described as beautiful, she was by no means unfortunate looking. Bella alone had inherited the pale blond hair and cornflower blue eyes of her Danish ancestors, which made her the envy of every girl in the county. But she was also the daughter of a wealthy father, so when she had come of age, invitations had poured in for her: balls, shooting parties, dinners. Not that she went to any, but still, it's always nice to be asked. But after the war, many of those boys never came back, and when she turned twenty-one, her parents had been desperate to marry her off. A spinster they would not have.

Thus, the marriage between Hugh and Bella had been accepted.

They had quickly produced three children, and then Hugh moved into his dressing room. Bella went about her business, although no one was sure what that was. Hugh turned his hand to writing and spent most of his time in the Tennis Pavilion, which he used as a study. Nanny took charge of the children, and they had all gone on happily like this for some years. But with Nanny gone, someone needed to watch them. And now with the French cousins visiting, it really was a substantial job.

The room turned and pointedly stared at Iris.

'Oh! Um, I'm happy to do it,' Iris stammered, blushing as she found herself the object of their hard, entitled scrutiny. 'I don't know how strong my French is, though,' she said, glancing at Elspeth, 'so it might—'

'That's settled, then.' Lady Georgina cut her off. 'I'll ring and place an advertisement straight away. With luck, it will be in the morning papers. Now, I must return home, I have letters to write. So many invitations to refuse.'

With tea finished, Elspeth was in the Boot Room, selecting a walking stick for her evening outing. As she chose her old favourite, she heard shouting in the service yard. Leaning out the door to investigate, she saw Hamish. He was holding his fishing gear but had a thunderous look on his face. A moment later, Fergus came into view, chasing after his father. Fergus was doing most of the shouting – Hamish rarely raised his voice – but then, Hamish turned on his son and was in his face two steps later, shouting as Elspeth had never heard her brother do before.

Not wishing to intrude, Elspeth shut the door quietly and made her way to the kitchens. Guess I'll have to use the servants' door tonight, she thought. Glancing into the yard on her right as she slipped out the door and across the drive, she could just see Fergus, still shouting at his father. *What on earth can that be about?* she wondered. She pushed it out of her mind; she had other things to think about.

Minutes later, she was walking away from the house and into the woods. Swiftly and quietly, she made her way to the bothy. She had been coming to the hidden cottage since she was girl. It was buried in a thick dark wood past the fishing spot, just at the base of the crag on a border of their

Estate. Who had built it, she could not say; it wasn't on any map of the Estate, but it was dry and comfortable and, crucially, very difficult to find. She doubted anyone else knew it existed. She had certainly not, until Ross had showed it to her all those years ago.

Ross MacBain was the love of her life. He was a third-generation gamekeeper on the Estate and had grown up with her brother, learning to shoot and stalk, and to sneak whisky from the Distillery. Elspeth had been a late-in-life surprise for her parents, and Hamish, then eleven, absolutely doted on his baby sister. When Elspeth turned five, she started tagging along after the much older boys on their outings, begging to learn how to shoot and stalk. She excelled quickly at everything sporting they taught her, but fishing was her true genius. She somehow always knew where they were rising, and they never went hungry when she was with them.

It wasn't until Elspeth returned from Paris during her year out that things changed for Ross. Elspeth was no longer a little girl, stealing away from Nanny. In her smart gowns, speaking perfect French, Ross could no longer see the bratty little thing he taught to stalk a deer. She was a woman, and he was smitten.

When the romance blossomed between them, they were shrewd enough to keep secret. It was one thing for them to grow up together, but Ross was not gentry and marriage between the two would never have been accepted. Elspeth had managed to stave off being married until she was twenty-seven, which was quite a considerable feat. Her parents eventually grew tired of waiting, though, and one evening, at dinner, announced her engagement to Philippe, Marquis de Clairvaux, resident in Champagne. Stricken, Ross and Elspeth had stolen away to the bothy and exchanged vows.

Ross had declared he would never marry, and he hadn't; Elspeth had declared she would never love another, and she didn't. She married ten days later and moved to France.

Ever since, Elspeth had made a point to return to Loch Down each year for the Spring Ball, exaggerating the importance of it to her new husband. Philippe respected tradition greatly, but hated visiting Scotland and generally spent the trip smoking and whining. 'The weather is abysmal. The food is abysmal and there is never any coffee. Only tea! And the cheese, don't get me started. No, the only delight is bringing my own wine.'

Some years she arrived with her husband. Other years, gloriously without him. It was no coincidence all her children had birthdays in January and February.

The rain was finally starting to let up when Elspeth's foot slipped on some wet leaves. Swearing softly, she grabbed a tree instinctively, taking a moment to steady herself. She could hear shouting again. What on earth had happened? She'd never seen Fergus so worked up. Setting off again, she arrived at the stone hut a few minutes later.

Letting herself in, she was greeted by a warm fire. Two glasses of whisky stood on a little table between the armchairs.

'That better not be Plaid,' she said, removing her boots, knowing full well from the sight of the pale amber liquid that it was Ross's whisky, not her family's. Ross had been distilling whisky for years, having spent much of his childhood with old MacTavish up at the Distillery. It was MacTavish who had encouraged him to study science at university, hoping to turn his young protégé into a Master Distiller. Ross made very good whisky.

He leaned around. 'Are you trying to provoke me?'

Elspeth took off her jacket. 'Maybe.'

He stood and crossed the room in three quick steps, swept

Elspeth into his arms and tossed her onto the double bed, the only other piece of furniture in the room. Elspeth laughed and helped him take off his shirt.

The dressing gong at Loch Down Abbey was rung promptly at half past five every day. The children had always begged to be allowed to strike it and in the thirty years he had served the family, Hudson, the butler, had only capitulated once, giving it as a reward. Giving a small child a mallet and a gong was never going to go well, and Hudson had regretted it immediately. It had been a vicious attack until he managed to disarm the little beggar, but not before the 17th century artefact had been heavily dented. It had rung a slightly discordant tone ever since. Hudson had moved the mallet to a locked cupboard in his office and none had rung it since but him, and today was no exception.

Dinner was a sacred tradition at Loch Down, and they still observed the old ways. The family was expected to gather in the Library for an aperitif; any time between seven and eight o'clock was acceptable, but one must arrive before Hudson came to seat them for dinner. Much to Lady Eva's dismay, no modern cocktails were served – only sherry for the ladies, and whisky soda for the men. At eight o'clock sharp, Hudson would enter the Library and escort the family across the Armoury to the Dining Room. The first course was always consommé, then came the fish, followed by meat – game when in season, of course – then sorbet, cheese, and finally fruit and other puddings. It never varied. They still dressed formally for dinner and when the meal was finished, the women moved to the Drawing Room – the Blue in the summer, the Red in the winter – to play cards and gossip; the men moved to the Library or the Billiards

Room for whisky and cigars. They occasionally came together for whist before bed. Lady Inverkillen, without fail, retired promptly at eleven o'clock. Hudson locked the front door and retired at midnight. Anyone awake after that was on his own.

As usual, then, the family was in the Library before dinner, sipping and chatting. Lady Georgina was tutting about her lady's maid.

'She asked for leave to go to her parents. Can you believe it? Her packed bag was sitting in the hallway as we spoke. Worried about this illness, she said. As if this is truly a matter of life and death. And if it were, not a care in the world for me. No, no. Off to her sick parents.'

Hudson coughed quietly in the corner.

'How does one even manage without a lady's maid? Hm?' She looked round the room to find all but Bella in sympathy with her. Bella was rarely in sympathy with anyone who had a lady's maid while she did not.

'Perhaps I can give you Maxwell until she returns, Mama,' said Lady Inverkillen. 'She can come to you after she draws my bath, if it's not too early in the morning for you?' Lady Inverkillen famously rose early each morning and spent the first half of her day in the Glasshouse, cultivating anemones. After luncheon she could be found in the Music Room – she was a gifted pianist – until tea.

'Oh, that's very kind of you, dear. Tell me, how is she with hair? Can she do the more traditional styles? I will not have one of these new waves. It's just too modern and vulgar.' Involuntarily, she glanced at Lady Eva, who noticed. 'Tell me, dear, how go the plans for the wedding? I do love a summer wedding. The flowers are so very colourful.'

Before Lady Eva could draw breath to speak, Bella jumped in. She had heard quite enough about the plans for the wedding, and how nothing was up to London standards. 'How long will your maid be away, Grandmama?'

'No idea. I shall have to find a replacement. If she thought she could simply come back in her own time, she has another think coming. Oh, I do hate finding new staff.'

'I can place an ad in *The Lady* for you. I know the editor quite well,' Eva offered. She was always mentioning who she knew in London; famous this, prominent that. It rankled the family, not that she cared. She was well connected, and they should be thankful for that. The only important people the family knew were Scottish, and they hardly mattered in the real world.

Lady Georgina looked shocked. 'Our staff have always been Highlanders.' She shook her head and continued the conversation as if Eva didn't exist.

When the grandfather clock struck eight, they stood to be led into dinner. Rank and importance determined where one was seated and served to let everyone know their place. Hamish and Victoria sat opposite one another in the centre, rather than at the ends of the table. It was a very modern arrangement that placed the Countess close to the fire. It hadn't escaped anyone's notice that the lesser guests were literally left out in the cold.

Upon entering the room, they took up their places at the table. But it was only when they had all gathered that they realised Hamish was missing.

'Hudson, where's Lord Inverkillen?' asked Lady Georgina. The butler stared back at her uncomfortably for a moment. Clearly, he hadn't noticed the absence either. 'Then perhaps you should send someone to his rooms.' She was grouchy when hungry.

A footman was dispatched to his dressing room and the family stood behind their chairs awkwardly. No one wanted to sit down; they would be an uneven number. It was one of the few things the family noted instantly: odd numbers at dinner. It spooked them, and they went to great lengths to avoid it. Odd numbers at breakfast, however, seemed perfectly fine. No one could explain it.

They stood, some speaking, some waiting impatiently. Cecil picked up the menu card to see what they'd be having: Lobster Mayonnaise, Roast Venison, Orange Soufflé. How unimaginative, he thought. Their quietest evening at Stronach Castle wouldn't have seen such lacklustre fare.

It was some moments before the footman returned. He whispered into Hudson's ear and then stepped to the wall. The butler nodded, cleared his throat, and announced to the room that His Lordship had not yet returned from his afternoon of fishing.

The room erupted in disbelief.

'What do you mean he's not back? Hamish is never late!' cried Lady Georgina.

'Why didn't his valet say something? Surely he noticed Father wasn't back,' Angus barked, irritated.

Cecil shook his head slowly. 'No loyalty in servants these days, my dear boy.' He fingered a wine glass and gazed at the footman, hoping the boy would take the hint.

Lady Inverkillen looked slightly confused and drifted towards the window, as if she hoped to spot him on the grounds. Iris wondered what she was humming.

But Fergus charged to the doors. 'This is most unusual. We should organise a search party. Hudson, get some torches.'

'The staff are already searching the grounds sir. Mrs MacBain organised it some minutes ago.'

'Oh, yes well . . . well done.' He sat down slowly, forgetting the odd numbers.

Angus and Bella smirked at one another, delighting in their brother's humiliation. Eva was mortified. *Why must he always try to do things? He isn't good at doing things.* Doing Things is what servants are for, she thought irritably.

'Should we ring the police? What time did he head out? How did his valet not realise he wasn't back?' Fergus sputtered.

Hudson assured him it all was well in hand, but he knew very little about His Lordship's movements that afternoon. 'Would you care to wait in the Drawing Room until Lord Inverkillen is located, milady?'

When Lady Inverkillen didn't respond, Elspeth replied, 'Yes, I think we should. Thank you, Hudson.' As she reached the door, she turned to see that no one was following her. 'We'll be more comfortable next door. Come.' They followed her like confused kittens.

The fire had only just been lit and the room was still glacial. Then again, all of the rooms in the Abbey were glacial. Even with a roaring fire, it took so long for the larger rooms to warm up that during the winter months, the ladies ate dinner in their furs. The central heating was only ever turned on for guests. No self-respecting Scot needed heat.

Yes, some of them will be more comfortable, thought Eva bitterly, but I shan't be. Eva was freezing. Her entire time at Loch Down had been marked by inordinate cold. She didn't know how the women managed it. It was all well and good for the men, in their wool, but the ladies were in silk with exposed shoulders. Even her pearls were cold.

She had learned, on her first evening at the Abbey, that proximity to the fire was a matter of rank and importance, much like seating in the Dining Room. She wasn't nearly important enough for a fireside seat, of course, but she was apparently welcome to stand by the fire, which she quickly opted to do. She made a mental note to write to her mother in the morning. If she were going to survive, she'd need warmer clothes – and looking at the gowns of the ladies assembled, she'd better get them from London while she could.

Iris hovered in the window seat, as was her custom, watching more than participating, trying to blend into the background. She was wearing a dress that was slightly too large for her. It was one of two Bella had given her. Neither dress suited her, but tradition dictated evening wear should be worn for dinner, and so she needed a dress. But not a new dress; that would be money wasted. Governesses did not need evening dresses, Bella had argued. Iris tugged a sleeve back onto her shoulder absentmindedly. She was musing about the background on the painting above the fireplace when Bella's husband Hugh drifted over to speak with her.

That Hugh was an author led to much despair in the family, in spite of the fact he'd made a tidy sum writing books about – well, Iris wasn't quite sure what they were about, having never read one. No one in the family had ever read one of his books, although there was a faint idea that Angus had. But Iris was a reader and when she had realised, as a young girl, that he was a famous author, she had combed the Library to find one of his books. The family did not seem to own one, so she went to the public library in the village, but when she had asked about it, the librarian had seemed offended. The staff there had looked at her very queerly for months after, whispering and pointing – actually pointing! – whenever she came in, so Iris stopped going to the library altogether. One afternoon, she had plucked up the courage and asked Hugh if she might borrow a copy.

Hugh had looked spooked. 'Oh, no. I couldn't possibly, my dear,' he had said. 'Not something a girl your age would be interested in, I shouldn't think. No, no. I haven't a copy going spare at the moment, anyway.' And then he had walked across the room to speak with his brother-in-law Angus, both of them staring intently at her for some time, as if they were afraid of her. He had actively avoided her for years after that until he had found her reading *Death in Venice* – she'd mistaken it for *Passage to India* – and thereafter wouldn't leave her alone.

'What are you reading these days, my dear?' He did not wait for an answer and merely blabbered on about some new novel or other that he himself was reading. Simply groundbreaking, genius of the author really. Staggering work. They were always staggering works. Iris kept staring at the painting, wondering if she dared ask Hudson for a cup of tea. It was a bit chilly in the window.

Lady Constance was staring into the fire. As Angus's wife and a future countess, she was accorded a seat nearest the fire. She was the youngest daughter of a prominent banker from Edinburgh and had been enjoying her season out, when her father announced she was to be married to Lord Inverkillen's eldest son. As Countess of Inverkillen, she'd outrank all her sisters. The thrill of marrying an Earl's son quickly faded, though, when she realised the Estate was on Loch Down, deep in the Highlands, and that his entire extended family would be living with them. But she said to herself: Chin up. If it means becoming a countess, make the best of it. That was five years ago.

In those five years, she had learned to embrace the solitude of the Estate. And while she loathed the family, she was still focused on becoming Countess. Once she was the senior member of the family, things would change. The only hiccup was the children. She had none. It would be Bella's children that inherited the Estate if she failed in her marital duty, something Bella mentioned regularly and gleefully. And now Eva was on the scene, looking young and frightfully fertile, and Constance was in a constant state of near panic.

She looked over at her husband, who had just gone over to pull Hugh away from his conversation with Iris. She and Angus had had separate bedrooms for years – all the smart set did – and if she admitted it to herself, she rather preferred it that way. He snored. But with Katherine of Aragon continually in her thoughts, that arrangement would have to change. Maybe a new hairstyle would help. Eva looks so chic in her modern wave, damn her. Yes, a fresh start, she decided. She'd ring the hairdresser in the morning and see if he could fit her into the schedule.

What started as minutes stretched into hours. They tried to keep themselves distracted but as members of the aristocracy, they were unused to waiting. Philippe played two entire chess matches against his son. Fergus admired the young lad; he was getting quite good. Angus and Hugh stood in the bay window discussing something in low voices over cigarettes. Cecil sat happily in an armchair, reading the correspondence and letters of the 15th Earl. The ladies did their best to rake over the gossip from the ball. It wasn't very satisfying and before long, Elspeth and Constance were taking a turn around the room, like heroines in a Regency novel, and peering out the windows. Lady Georgina kept up a constant stream of inane chatter, doing her best to engage both Lady Inverkillen and Bella, both of whom seemed to wish they were elsewhere.

The grandfather clock finally chimed eleven o'clock, and a decision was made to halt the search for the evening.

'It is impossibly dark now,' said Fergus. 'I think we'd best begin again at first light.' The family agreed and quietly shuffled towards their beds.

'But what if he turns up after we've all gone to bed?' Iris asked as they were dispersing. 'The door will be locked. How will he get in?'

'That's a very good point,' said Fergus. 'I'll stand guard by the front door tonight. Hudson can give me the key.' Eva rolled her eyes.

Constance spoke up. 'Shouldn't Angus do that? He's the eldest, you know.'

Angus looked horrified. 'I'm not doing that! Hudson can do it.'

It was Hudson's turn to be horrified.

'He knows the front door is locked,' said Elspeth. 'Surely he'd go to a side door.'

They started squabbling about doors: where His Lordship was most likely to enter, could he wake a servant, which doors should be manned that evening, who should do it. No one wanted to sleep in a chair in the cold, except Fergus apparently, but he could only watch one door, so unless others helped, he might easily miss Lord Inverkillen. Iris wouldn't have minded if she could get her blanket and hot water bottle, but every time she tried to volunteer, someone shouted over her. She never could get a word in when the family was fighting. But it wasn't until Constance complained about Fergus getting all the glory – whatever that meant – that Lady Georgina finally snapped.

'Enough!' While the room was silent, she rose to her feet and gathered her dignity. 'Hudson and the male staff will stand sentry at those doors most likely to be used by His Lordship. I'm sure he'll turn up in the night, but if he isn't back by daybreak, we will phone the local constabulary and mount a larger search. Now, bring the car round. I am exhausted.'

The butler sighed. It was going to be a long night.

★

Inspector Jarvis was not a busy man and he liked it that way. He was in charge of the Loch Down Police Force, which consisted of two constables and a secretary. They mainly dealt with petty issues: children pinching sweets, lost dogs, the odd drunken punch-up at the pub, that sort of thing. It was a small village, and the police were largely regarded as window dressing. At the start of his career, he'd been posted to Inverness and stayed for several years before begging to return to Loch Down. Big city life wasn't for him, he'd realised. He hadn't been back long, but he loved the slower pace of the village. It gave him more time in the pub.

But then Mrs MacBain rang that morning, far too early in his opinion, to report that Lord Inverkillen was missing. He dressed quickly, assembled his force of two and went immediately to the servants' hall. He'd been trained to speak to the staff first. They were invaluable for information these sorts of families refused to give. Also, he really needed a cuppa before he interviewed the family.

He arrived at the forecourt and sorted the men into search teams, sending them off to different parts of the Estate. He then walked round to the servants' hallway, where Mrs MacBain was waiting for him. She showed him into her sitting room and settled a cup of tea on him while they waited for news from the search parties.

'When did he leave the house?' Jarvis asked, biting into a ginger biscuit.

'I'm not sure, Roddie.' She and Jarvis had known each other as children. 'They arrived back from the ball late yesterday morning and that was the last time I saw him. As far as I knew, he was in the Map Room shouting at his sons about the Distillery.'

Jarvis nodded thoughtfully. Everyone knew the Distillery

was failing. With whisky that bad, there was no way the business was going well. 'Where was everyone else?'

'Scattered throughout the house, as usual. Several in baths as soon as they got back from the ball. Naps. Luncheon and tea were sparsely attended, which isn't unusual. Everyone was tired from the trip back.'

'The trip back? From the Macintyre Ball?'

Mrs MacBain nodded.

The Inspector stared at her. 'Don't they hold that at their Estate?' Mrs MacBain nodded again, taking a sip of tea, knowing what would come next. 'But that's only, what, six miles away? How could they be tired? It's a half-hour trip in a car.'

Mrs MacBain shrugged, tactful as ever. No one, especially not Roddy Jarvis, needed to know what she really thought of her employers.

Jarvis's eyebrows shot up. 'Okay, so. Everyone was tired, some took baths, most didn't come to tea. Then what?'

She thought for a second. 'Then we discovered that Nanny Mackenzie had died.'

Jarvis nearly dropped his teacup. 'What? I didn't hear about that. What happened?' Jarvis was astounded. There were few secrets in a small Scottish village – he could not fathom how this one hadn't reached him yet.

Mrs MacBain set her tea down with a sigh. 'Well, it's only just happened. I'm sure word will be out by the end of the day.' She knew Jarvis prided himself on knowing everything that happened in the village. He didn't, of course, but he prided himself anyway. 'The doctor seems to think it was just her time. She was seventy-eight, you know.'

'Yes, I suppose she was,' Jarvis said slowly, struggling to remember the woman.

'To be honest, I'm not convinced,' Mrs MacBain went

on. 'She was a healthy woman; strong and really active. To see her, you'd think she was in her fifties! So, to go from that to dying of old age a day later, it just doesn't sit well with me.'

Jarvis nodded thoughtfully. Was it impolite to ask for another biscuit?

'Plus, one of the footmen is also sick,' Mrs MacBain continued, almost to herself, 'and he's nowhere near seventy-eight.'

His stomach lurched a bit. 'You think it's this sickness in the papers?' His voice was anxious.

'I don't know, but it doesn't comfort me that we're two staff members down in a single day and neither of them showed any warning signs.'

Before Jarvis could process it all, a constable burst into the small room, sweaty and exhausted.

'Sir!' he panted. 'We've just found His Lordship's fishing tackle. It was on the riverbank just behind the Distillery.'

Jarvis grabbed his hat and sprang to his feet. 'The river? Take me there. Focus the entire search downstream from that location. Thanks for the cuppa, Alice.' And with that, he dashed off with the constable.

Mrs MacBain sipped her tea contemplatively. The river behind the Distillery? He must mean the weir. Something in the back of her brain was stirring. The weir. She sat for some moments in deep thought. It wasn't until the maids rushed past her door with the breakfast trays that she snapped out of her reverie. She stood up and shook herself mentally. The house didn't run itself; she needed to get moving.

Hudson had set up tea in the Library instead of the Morning Room, thinking that it would be best if the family waited together for news in a larger room, with a bit more space to move around. Everyone was on edge and tempers had flared at breakfast.

Lady Georgina arrived, looking at the butler with some confusion. 'Why are we in here, Hudson?'

Hudson merely nodded towards the room and Lady Georgina turned to see Bella and Angus sniping at each other over the appropriate blend of tea for the occasion, while Cecil glared at Hugh, who was reading a wrinkled and torn newspaper with a smug smile on his face. Turning back to the butler, she nodded wearily and said no more.

Lady Inverkillen was seated at the desk, looking out the window, but rather than her usual vacant stare, her attention was sharp and focused. She was frowning at something on the lawns. The children, it seemed, were outside. 'Hudson, please have Nanny take the children to the Nursery. This is no time for them to be outside.'

Startled, Hudson's eyes shot to the window, disturbed by the idea of children on the loose. He dispatched the footmen.

'Nanny died, Mama,' said Bella, moving towards the window. 'Remember? Iris is looking after the children for the moment.'

Lady Georgina moved to the window. 'And none too well, it would seem,' she sniffed, catching sight of a small, naked boy disappearing into the hedge at the end of the terrace. She turned back to the room. Lady Inverkillen had drifted back to the sofa and was humming something, staring into the fire. Elspeth was fidgeting with her skirt. They needed distracting, Lady Georgina decided.

Perching elegantly on the sofa, she looked to Elspeth and asked, 'What did you think of that new gown Lady Carrue was wearing? In my day, a woman her age wouldn't have dared to show so much décolletage.'

Elspeth looked up distractedly. 'Lady Carrue? Was she the one in the yellow? I didn't think it was so very much.'

Constance rolled her eyes. 'Clearly, you've been in France too long.'

Elspeth ignored her. 'And I thought the colour suited her marvellously.'

Bella disentangled herself from her skirmish with her brother and sat delicately beside her aunt. 'I thought it was quite a lot of display for very little effect. She needed a larger necklace to distract from her cleavage.' Lady Georgina nodded her approval.

'I do love that little tiara she wears,' Constance remarked. 'It's so delicate. I do think it would be better in dark hair, however.' She involuntarily touched her own dark hair.

'I heard they had a replica made and sold the original.'

'Bella!' Lady Georgina was scandalised. And thrilled. 'Where did you hear that?'

They spent several unenthusiastic minutes dissecting the ball, but all talk faded when the clock struck eleven. They'd been waiting since nine, and the air of unease in the room was palpable. Hudson brought in a tea tray with cakes.

Having munched in silence for some minutes, Lady Georgina could no longer stand it and played her best conversation card: how difficult it was to find suitable candidates for servants. It had been half a day since the advertisement went up in the village for her lady's maid and they had received no letters of interest. She couldn't understand it. Lady Eva again offered to place an ad in *The Lady*.

'I don't think it will come to that,' said Lady Georgina dismissively. 'I'm so looking forward to having Maxwell help out, Victoria. Thank you for sharing her with me. This morning was an absolute disaster. A house maid might do at a pinch, but she's no substitute for a well-trained lady's maid.'

Lady Inverkillen smiled weakly at her mother-in-law and turned back to face the fire, sipping her tea.

Across the Library, Angus and Fergus half-heartedly chatted about the village fête, which took place every June, and if they should continue to allow the men to play rugby. It always ended with injuries and grudges, and no one from last year's winning side would admit to having the trophy. It had belonged to the 16th Earl and was supposed to be kept on display in the pub, but the celebrations had got out of hand, and no one had seen it since that night.

Hugh was still reading the paper, rattling the pages deliberately, it seemed. It annoyed Cecil. He moved to another chair and contented himself with an old copy of *Country Life* from the year Elspeth came out. He flipped to the Debutante page to find her portrait. They had certainly done their best to marry her off well, he thought. Looking across to her husband, Philippe, playing chess in the bay window, Cecil couldn't help but wonder how big their château was.

A hidden door at the back of the room opened and a footman entered. He crossed the room and whispered to Hudson. Hudson blanched. 'That can't be!' he gasped. The room snapped to attention; all eyes were on the butler.

'Hudson,' called Lady Georgina from across the room, 'what is it?'

'They've found Lord Inverkillen, milady. I'm afraid he is dead.'

Jarvis was finally with the doctor, breathing heavily. When the constable's whistle had sounded, everyone involved with the search ran towards it. Jarvis had still been at the weir and had been forced to run downstream through the woods, not realising just how far down river his constable had been. He had just been about to give up when the river turned sharply, the Old Chapel in view, and a clutch of men stood, staring at the ground.

'Death by drowning, I'd wager,' said the doctor. 'He does have a gash to the back of his head but that could have come from the rocks in the river.'

Jarvis put his hands on his hips and leaned over the body, hoping he looked thoughtful, not worn out from the run. 'An accident, then?' he panted. Lord, he was out of shape.

'That's for you to say. From my end, it's a simple drowning. He wasn't a very good sportsman, you know.' He closed his briefcase and looked at his watch. It was nearly time for Elevenses and after such an early start that morning, he was starving. 'I'd wager he went in mid-afternoon yesterday. Let me know if you'd like an autopsy. Good afternoon.' He walked off, leaving Jarvis to decide what to do next.

Well, next he needed to tell the family. He didn't relish this part of the job. No one did. Lord, why couldn't he have just run off with a mistress? Now he had to tell a woman her husband was dead, and that was far more difficult news to deliver. When the good Lord above wants you, he takes you, his mother was fond of saying. Clearly, the good Lord above had wanted Hamish. Clearly? Yes, clearly. Accidents happened – even to the gentry.

Jarvis poked his head into the small office. 'Alice?' he said quietly. 'I need to see the family.'

Mrs MacBain looked up, her face a picture of apprehension. 'It's true then?' Jarvis nodded. How was she always one step ahead of the news, he wondered? 'Right. You'd best follow me. They're in the Library.'

The servants' hall was eerily quiet – news had clearly reached them. Jarvis struggled to keep up with Mrs MacBain and started to breathe heavily again as they walked. He was surprised how far they had to go. He knew the house was large, but this was a bit ridiculous. When they finally reached the green baize door to the Armoury, he took a moment to catch his breath then said to her, 'That's quite a distance. You walk that every day?'

She turned to him, looking surprised and a touch amused. 'Yes, several times, in fact.' Shaking her head, she walked swiftly across the large room and hesitated by a discreet door. She opened it and stood back so he could enter. 'I'll just wait here.'

They were indeed in the Library, some sitting, some pacing, several smoking – all waiting for the arrival of the police and looking none too happy about it. Inspector Jarvis observed them for some moments; no one had looked up when he entered. Hudson was supervising the footmen as they served tea and brandy to the family. When they were finished he sent the footmen below stairs, and then retreated to a corner where he positioned himself discreetly. No one spoke.

Jarvis recognised Cecil and Elspeth from childhood, and their mother Lady Georgina, of course – not that he could claim to know them but growing up in a village, one tended to know, or know of, everyone, and especially the important families. He studied the room for some time, trying to place the rest of them. His eyes landed on Iris. She must be family, he thought, maybe one of Elspeth's girls? But who's the other one? He was musing on Eva when Fergus glanced up and noticed him. Jarvis nodded, cleared his throat and stepped towards the centre of the large room, surveying the dark panelled walls, the chandeliers, the portraits in gilded frames. Not a lot of books for a Library, he thought, but then pushed it aside. Not the time for a tour.

'Good afternoon. I'm Inspector Jarvis. We've located Lord Inverkillen. I'm sorry to say that it isn't good news.'

Lady Georgina stared at him disdainfully. 'You're quite late there, Inspector,' she said. 'Clearly news travels faster than you do. How did it happen?'

Jarvis was slightly thrown by her brisk manner – she was awfully matter of fact for a woman who had just lost her son – and he shifted his focus to Fergus. 'Erm . . . We found his fishing gear by the weir. It appears he fell into the river and drowned.' Jarvis fell silent, awaiting their reaction. But they all just stared blankly at him so he cleared his throat gently and said, 'I'd like to ask a few questions, if I may. I realise the timing isn't ideal—'

'Not ideal?' Bella stood swiftly, snapping at the Inspector. 'When would be the ideal time to question a grieving family, Inspector?' She stalked to the end of the room.

Jarvis felt like an ass, but he had a job to do. 'I realise this has been quite a shock, but I would like to have a better understanding of Lord Inverkillen's movements yesterday. Just to be sure.' Damnit. He shouldn't have added that last bit.

'Just to be sure?' said Lady Georgina, looking at him curiously. 'Sure of what, exactly?'

He couldn't tell if she was confused or angry. He hoped confused. Jarvis looked at his feet for a moment, unsure how to word it correctly.

'This was an accident, surely.' Lady Georgina glanced around the room, an incredulous look on her face. 'You can't possibly think this was . . . what do they call it? "Foul play"? What an absurd idea. Honestly, who would have done such a thing?'

From the talk in the village, Jarvis was pretty sure every single one of them could have done such a thing. But he kept that thought to himself. 'It's just procedure, milady,' he said, trying his best to be reassuring.

Lady Georgina continued tutting; the rest of the family stared at him in disbelief.

'What is it you wish to know, Inspector?' Lady Elspeth looked decidedly neutral. What an odd reaction. A stiff upper lip is one thing, he thought, but this lot . . . blood out of a stone. She was quite a bit younger than her brother, from what he remembered; they might not have been close.

Jarvis looked at his notepad, where he had written a few questions. 'Did anyone go fishing with him?' Nothing. 'Or see what time he left the house?' Nothing.

He was just starting to feel irritated with the lot of them when Fergus finally spoke.

'I left him with Angus in the Map Room around three o'clock, I'd guess,' he said stiffly. 'Angus? Mama? Did he mention he was going fishing?'

Angus looked angry to be addressed. 'What? No. Of course not. Does Father ever tell anyone what he's planning? You know what he's like. Was like.' He fished out a silver cigarette case and went to light his cigarette. After several unsuccessful strikes, Hugh stood and lit it for him.

Lady Inverkillen stared into the fire, placid and calm. Jarvis wasn't sure if she'd even heard the conversation. And was she . . . humming? Her husband had just been found dead, on their own property, and she was humming? What a bizarre family, Jarvis thought.

'Mama. Did Father tell you he was going fishing?' Fergus asked, rather louder than before. Jarvis wondered if she had hearing problems.

Lady Inverkillen turned and stared at Jarvis. Through him,

actually; unfocused and rather hazy. It was a bit unnerving. After some moments she turned away from Jarvis and addressed her son. 'What? No, I was having a bath. I find it does wonders after such a long journey. Rosemary and juniper are especially invigorating. Maxwell suggested I add a touch of orange blossom for my headache. She was right, of course. She's always right. I wonder what she'll suggest for this. Perhaps lavender. Yes, lavender seems right. With some lemon balm; soothing but not showy, a bit understated. I must order more from Hambeldon's.' She stood and drifted towards a set of double doors. 'Hudson, please send a hall boy to my rooms. There should just be time to have it delivered today.' And with that, she was gone. The room turned back to Jarvis, who was speechless.

'You must forgive my daughter-in-law, Inspector,' said Lady Georgina. 'Grief does funny things to us all. I'm sure it's the shock.'

'Yes . . .' he said slowly. He had never met Lady Inverkillen, very few in the village had. Lady Georgina headed all the various committees herself, so there was little left for her daughter-in-law to do.

'Is that all, Inspector?' Fergus asked, forcing Jarvis to focus again.

'Hm? Ah, no. Did he fish alone, or did he meet someone, perhaps? Did he often fish in the afternoon?'

'My father preferred to fish alone, Inspector. I rather got the impression it was his escape from us.' Several people nodded, frowns on their faces. 'But you might check with his valet, Mackay, to see what time he left.'

'Yes, I'll do that, thanks.' He paused. Several people started to move, clearly thinking that he was finished with them, and he went on in a loud voice. 'Did he fish often? Maybe he had a favourite spot? I know I do.'

A collective sigh went up. No one knew. Jarvis could feel the distain and hostility emanating from them and it made him suspicious. What were they all hiding? But the more Jarvis asked about Hamish's habits and routines, the less, apparently, anyone knew. Had he been a stranger, they'd have known more about him, according to that morning's interview. Perhaps they just weren't very observant, he reasoned. But you couldn't live with a person and know so little. Could you? His head was starting to hurt.

'It's just that it's a rather funny place to fish, at the weir. Not many fish hanging around at the base of a waterfall.' He looked around to see them staring at him, uncomprehendingly. 'No food for them there. It's almost as if he wasn't out there to fish at all.'

'Who on earth would go fishing without intending to fish?' snarled Angus, losing patience.

'I really do have things to do, you know,' said Bella irritably. 'Are you quite finished?' Without waiting for a response, she stood and started heading for the double doors.

'Not quite, no.'

Fergus was surprised at how offended he sounded. Bella turned and rolled her eyes. Several of the others shifted in their chairs as the Inspector continued. 'It's a strange time of day for fishing—'

Lady Georgina rose, far quicker than Jarvis would have suspected for a woman of her age. 'Inspector, we can second guess Hamish's preferences and motivations all day, but I dare say we'll never know why he chose that location or that particular time, or indeed which lures he preferred. He was a very private man. Now I really must be getting on with my day. I have many letters to write.' She stood and started towards the double doors. 'Hudson, can you have the car brought round?'

Lady Georgina was out of the room before Jarvis could react. This appeared to signal an acceptable moment for the exodus of the rest of the family. A few of them offered excuses as they left, but several simply left. He could have sworn he heard someone muttering about tennis. At a moment like this? Jarvis shook his head and soon realised he was left standing in the middle of the empty room. He was feeling more confused than ever.

'If you're ready, sir, I'll show you out.' Hudson indicated the double doors and waited patiently. Jarvis followed him, stunned, wondering what on earth had just happened.

The mood downstairs was sombre. No one was quite sure what to say. First Nanny, and now this.

Mrs MacBain had gathered the staff to tell them the news. She thought it best they heard the facts from her, instead of trading in rumours. They had work to do and that morning, a kitchen maid had taken ill. Nanny, Archie and now a kitchen maid. Mrs MacBain didn't have time to worry about it, really – she could only hope no one upstairs caught it because apart from anything else, funerals meant additional work. The family's mourning clothes would need to be found and laundered, and no doubt several new items would need to be ordered. Black armbands would be needed for the staff. A hall boy would have to run to the village to order black-banded stationery with a black Inverkillen crest. A housemaid would have to be dispatched with a footman to locate the mourning table linens from the attics, which they would need for the reception after the funeral. The silver needed to be polished, the everyday crystal needed to be replaced with the Regency wedding crystal. All the flowers would need to be replaced with unscented, white arrangements. The family

mourning book would need to be laid out in the Armoury
for those visitors who dropped by unannounced. A table
would need to be set up in the Library for the cards, letters
and telegrams of condolence, and rearranging furniture was
always contentious with the family. Mrs MacBain knew they
would not allow the tea table to be used – where would the
tea go? – and there would most assuredly be a squabble over
which table would be the most respectable. The last thing
she needed was a staff distracted by rumours and gossip.
She told the servants all this, and they listened quietly. When
she was finished, it was only Daisy, one of the housemaids,
who had questions.

'I thought Lady Georgina was the Dowager Countess. If
Lady Inverkillen is the Dowager now, what does that make
Lady Georgina? And where will Lady Inverkillen live if Lady
Georgina owns Drummond House?'

Daisy was new to service and confused by the idea of
succession, but even Mrs MacBain had wondered about that
very thing. Neither Lady Georgina nor Constance, who as
the new Countess would be taking over the Abbey, shared
well, so she doubted Lady Inverkillen would have much
voice in the matter. Lady Inverkillen would no longer be
mistress of any place. I wonder if she'll even mind, Mrs
MacBain mused.

'Lady Victoria will remain in her rooms until she's out of
mourning, I should think. Then it will be up to Angus – I
mean, His Lordship – where she lives.' She somehow doubted
it would be a smooth transition. It felt strange calling Angus
'His Lordship', but they'd adjust.

'And if Angus – I mean, His Lordship – is now the Earl,
will he keep us on?' Daisy asked, her voice full of anxiety.
Mrs MacBain suppressed a sigh; the girl was full of questions, but to be fair to her they were good ones.

Every one of them knew that Angus hated living there, but as heir, he had been under his father's control and had no choice in the matter. Now that he was Earl, however, he could do as he liked. Ollie, the footman, had more than once reported Angus talking about selling the house when he inherited and moving abroad. It was a sobering thought. There weren't that many jobs in the village for housemaids and footmen.

'It doesn't matter who the head of the family is, that lot up there is not living without servants,' Mrs Burnside, the cook, said from the kitchen door, wiping her hands on her apron. 'Now, get back to work, all of you.'

Mrs MacBain glanced pointedly at the senior members of staff, and as the other staff bustled off to carry out their duties, they headed into her sitting room and sat down heavily.

'What does this mean for us?' asked Mrs Burnside even more anxiously than Daisy. Lockridge, the chauffeur, entered the room quietly, saying he'd just heard the news from Lady Georgina's maid.

'I'm not sure,' said Mrs MacBain. They sat quietly for a moment. 'The timing's tight. I'd feel better if we knew it was all finished.' They all looked at Mackay, Hamish's valet, who nodded silently and left the room.

'Is the Inspector sure it was an accident?' Lockridge asked, looking a bit uncomfortable.

Mrs MacBain sighed. 'Well, he does prefer things to be accidents. In the face of overwhelming evidence to the contrary, he clings to accidents and coincidence like some people cling to miracles.' She looked at Lockridge sharply. 'You're not convinced, are you?'

Lockridge recounted the conversation between Cecil and Lady Georgina, explaining that Cecil had been cut out of his wife's will and was desperate for money. As the only link between the Abbey and the Dower House, Lockridge was an invaluable source of information.

'You mean, he gets absolutely nothing?' gasped Mrs Burnside, exchanging a delighted glance with Mrs MacBain.

'That's right, the whole lot goes to some long lost relative in London,' replied Lockridge. 'So, naturally, I wondered—'

'– if the Major is in His Lordship's will,' finished Mrs Burnside. Lockridge nodded, a grim look on his face.

'The Major might be a bit grasping but I wouldn't have thought him violent.' Mrs MacBain tutted. 'Besides, I doubt he even knows where the weir is.' They all smirked. Cecil hated the outdoors. Mostly, Cecil hated getting dirty, which was odd, given his love of changing clothes. His laundry pile was always the largest.

'What concerns me most, at the moment,' began Mrs MacBain seriously, 'is having two members of staff sick. We've all read about that sickness in the papers. What if Nanny brought it back from the ball with her?'

Everyone looked disturbed at the idea.

'But isn't that just happening in the south?' Mrs Burnside's voice was filled with anxiety. 'We're practically in the middle of nowhere up here!'

'What I know is that Archie has never been sick a day in his life and now he can't get out of bed on his own.' Mrs MacBain looked to the group. 'If this is what we've been reading about, I think we need to move them before anyone else gets sick.'

'Move them?' MacKay asked. 'Move them where?'

Mrs MacBain shook her head. 'I don't know. But I think I'd feel a lot better if they weren't sleeping next to us.' The room drew silent, each in deep thought.

A knock at the door made them all jump, and Lockridge opened the door. The hall boy was surprised to see the entire senior staff in the small room but shook himself back to the present and informed Mrs MacBain that Lady Inverkillen needed her.

'Thank you, Tom.' Turning back to the group she said quietly, 'If you can think of a place to move them, let's discuss it tonight after dinner.'

As the group left the office, Mrs Burnside turned and asked, 'Who's taking charge of the children?'

'Miss Iris, naturally.'

'Oh dear,' said Mrs Burnside. 'Those children are a handful at the best of times, but without Nanny, she doesn't stand a chance. They'll be running wild in the woods without a stitch of clothing before sundown, mark my words.'

'Better her than us,' said Lockridge. They exchanged a grim look.

It was still dark the next morning when the kitchen maid banged manically on Mrs Burnside's door. Mrs Burnside harrumphed as she opened the door. 'What do you think you're doing? You'll wake the dead!'

'I'm sorry, Mrs Burnside,' the maid said, breathless and panicked. 'I didn't know what to do. I can't find Miss Maxwell and Her Ladyship's breakfast tray is still in the kitchen.'

Mrs Burnside shook her head, confused. She hadn't had her morning tea yet and was a bit foggy. 'What?'

'I've searched everywhere. I went to Miss Maxwell's room first, but it was empty. Then I went to the privies, then the Boot Room, I checked the laundry and the servants' hall and the yard, in case she was smoking – not that she smokes, but you never know.' She paused to take a deep breath. 'I can't find her anywhere, Mrs Burnside, and I certainly can't take Her Ladyship's tray to her. What do we do?'

Then it was Mrs Burnside's turn to panic. Trying to conceal her disquiet, she sent the maid back to the kitchen to start on the other breakfast trays and then went to find Mrs MacBain.

'What do you mean, the tray is still in the kitchen?' Mrs MacBain said as she glanced at her watch. 'It's a quarter past six, for heaven's sake. Her Ladyship will be in the bath in another fifteen minutes.'

'I dare say she won't. I'll wager you a fiver she doesn't know how to draw her own bath. What will we do?'

'Right,' said Mrs MacBain, pulling the belt on her dressing gown tighter. 'Refresh the tray while I get dressed. I'll take breakfast to Her Ladyship. You find Maxwell. She's due at Drummond House in forty-five minutes, and I'll not be the one answering to Lady Georgina if she isn't there on time.'

Fifteen minutes later, Mrs MacBain knocked softly and let herself into Lady Inverkillen's dressing room, taking in a nervous breath. Ha! She was drawing her own bath. Mrs Burnside had lost her own bet.

She called out, 'You're late, Maxwell. You're never late, what's happened to you? I'll have to skip breakfast now.' She sounded irritated but not angry. That was good.

Mrs MacBain set the tray down and smoothed her skirt. 'It's me, Your Ladyship. I'm afraid Miss Maxwell is indisposed this morning. My apologies for being late with your tray, but we've only just discovered it.'

Lady Inverkillen walked into the dressing room. Mrs MacBain was shocked to see her wearing a loosely tied silk dressing gown; the woman was so thin she was nearly see-through. Mrs MacBain started fussing with the breakfast tray, to avoid staring.

'Indisposed?' Lady Inverkillen looked confused. 'Why can no one be counted upon in a crisis?' She sighed and her whole body seemed to sag. 'Fine. Just leave the tray there. I'll dress myself.' She turned and went back into her bathroom.

'Yes, milady.' Mrs MacBain curtsied and left the room, breathing a sigh of relief. That hadn't been as bad as she'd feared. Had it been Bella, however . . . She shuddered at the thought. As she approached the servants' stairs, her attention was drawn by the sound of rustling fabric and she turned around to see Miss Maxwell in the corridor, looking ashen.

'And where have you been?' hissed Mrs MacBain furiously. 'I've had to take Her Ladyship's breakfast tray to her. Late, mind you. I told her you were ill so be scarce today and don't make a liar of me. She's drawn her bath and will dress herself this morning but really, Miss Maxwell, I know you aren't under my jurisdiction, but this isn't acceptable.'

Maxwell had the good grace to look chastened. When she finally did speak, just as Mrs MacBain was turning to go, it was barely above a whisper.

'I know, and thank you Mrs MacBain, for covering for me. I appreciate it.'

She looked terrible, thought Mrs MacBain, turning back to her and taking her in properly for the first time. Her hair was wispy, her dress was rumpled. She had clearly slept in it, but Maisie said she was not in her room when she knocked. It was all very odd.

'Are you all right, Flora? Do you feel well?' she asked, genuinely concerned. 'This sickness going round—'

'I'm fine, just a bit shaken. Lord Inverkillen . . . And so soon after Nanny Mackenzie's death. I've never known anyone who died, well, no one close to me, that is. Not that they were, particularly, but you know what I mean. I just . . . I just . . . well, it's all very upsetting.'

Mrs MacBain started at her. 'Very upsetting? Good lord,

woman, pull yourself together and do your job. You put all
of us in a tight spot this morning. If one of my girls had
done this, they'd be out on the street looking for a new job
faster than you can say spit. You're lucky Her Ladyship was
only annoyed. Now, go and freshen up. You're due at the
Dower House in half an hour, and you can't possibly dress
Lady Georgina in this state.'

After she had shuffled away, Mrs MacBain thought about
the exchange. Maxwell was clearly upset – deeply upset, one
might say. But why? Nanny's death was distressing, yes, but
none of them were exactly close to the woman. You would
have thought it was Her Ladyship who had died, the way
she was carrying on. It was all very odd, but she hadn't time
to worry about it. She slipped through the green baize door
and headed down to the kitchens to make sure that nothing
else went wrong this morning.

Having finished her breakfast tray, Bella waited impatiently
for Constance's lady's maid to come and dress her. It always
chafed that she did not have her own lady's maid. What was
the point of belonging to the aristocracy if one didn't have
a maid? Bella had lobbied for years for her own, only to be
refused time and again.

When Constance had joined the family, she had brought
her trusted maid with her and it was grudgingly agreed she
would share her with Bella. So, Bella had had to resign
herself to being second behind her brother's wife. It was
Constance's tray that was delivered first; Constance who
was bathed and dressed first. But then Bella married, and
she presumed she would be given her own lady's maid. A
week after the honeymoon, when no new maid appeared, it
was clear she would have to continue sharing with Constance.

Bella fumed. It was a degradation to have to share, she raged. A married woman should have her own lady's maid. Surely money could be found for that. Servants were cheap, after all.

She and her father had fought for weeks. Hugh, her new husband, had stood limply by. As a second son, he was hardly in the financial position to step into the breach. She had married who they had chosen. She had had the children they had asked for. She had done her duty as had been expected of her, and all she wanted was that which was due her, a lady's maid. It was such a small ask, she felt. When Hamish had issued his final word on the subject, Bella had known the discussion was over, but the resentment smouldered. When Hugh's books had started to sell, and they had money of their own, Bella had started to look for a lady's maid, happy that her husband could pay for it instead of her father. But Hamish soon got word of her search and called her to the Map Room. Nothing good ever came of being called into the Map Room. They had fought over it for most of a week. Hamish absolutely would not allow it. Why, he wouldn't say, but as long as Bella lived at the Abbey, she would continue to share Constance's maid. Bella had raged for nearly a month, and her relationship with her father never recovered.

Then Fergus's wedding had been announced, and Bella had thought of nothing but how to convince Hamish that she needed her own lady's maid. There was no way on earth Bella was going to subject herself to being third in the line behind Eva, loathsome creature. Third, behind a tradesman's daughter? Call her 'Lady Eva' all you wish, but that title had been bought and paid for. No, she would accept this no longer. She would be first in her own home if she had to sell a child for it.

The events of last night, however, put a new spin on things. Now, her father was no longer around to object. Angus would not dare to refuse her. Bella hummed to herself as she moved to her desk and wrote out the advertisement. Her morning bath would have to wait.

The Reverend Malcolm Douglas, Vicar of St Andrew on the Loch, arrived at the house near luncheon. He had come, he said, to offer his condolences and to see if he could be of any help. Hudson showed him into the Library and went to fetch both Angus and Lady Inverkillen, unsure who wanted to be in charge now.

Reverend Douglas was a plump man in his fifties, who enjoyed his food slightly more than he loved the Lord. He was a good vicar, though, and the village respected him. His sermons were short and to the point. He introduced 'Pimm's + Hymns', which they held each summer to raise money for the local orphanage. He was a fierce competitor for the village curling club, five-time County Champions. And he was infamous for calling on people just before luncheon. He always feigned disbelief at the hour and he always accepted their gracious – begrudging – invitation to join them. It was whispered among the congregation that he drew up a monthly rota to eliminate duplicate meals. There was some small truth in it. It was Tuesday, and he was very much looking forward to the Abbey's roast boar with baked apples.

He was in the Library inspecting a particularly beautiful book – it was a treat to hold such rare volumes – when Bella entered. His heart sank. She was difficult to get an invitation from.

'Ah, Reverend Douglas, I'm afraid everyone is occupied just now and you'll have to deal with me. My apologies.

How can I help you?' Bella remained standing and did not offer him a seat.

He reluctantly put the book back. 'I came to offer my condolences, Lady Annabella. What a shock this has been for you all. And Lord Inverkillen was such a good man. To be cut down in the prime of his life is so cruel.'

'Yes, yes,' murmured Bella, 'quite so,' but not really listening as he babbled on. He was quick off the mark, she thought. Worried about his neck, she supposed. His church and vicarage stood on the Estate and Bella knew it was the family's right to keep or dismiss him. The last thing they needed today was a gossipy visitor. She must get rid of him.

'Please let me know how I can help with the arrangements. I am entirely at your disposal.' He bowed slightly as he said this last part.

'We haven't had much time to consider anything as yet, Reverend. I'm sure you understand, given it only happened yesterday. We shall ring for you in due course.' She tried to escort him to the door.

'Ah, vicar, how good of you to come. You will stay for luncheon, won't you? We can discuss the arrangements afterwards.' Lady Georgina had materialised out of nowhere, taken the vicar by the arm and was now leading him towards the dining room.

'I thought perhaps a reading from John, followed by that hymn he always loved . . . What was it called? You know, something-something-trumpet-something . . . And perhaps the yellow roses from our Glasshouse. I know they are an untraditional colour, but it would be a shame not to use them. They are especially beautiful this year! Ah, Hudson, please have a place laid for the Reverend. Unless we're an odd number. If we are, have the girl eat in the Nursery today. Now, Reverend, what do you think about . . .' She rattled on until they disappeared into the Dining Room.

You'd think she was planning a ball, thought Bella.

Seated at luncheon, they spoke on the usual topics: the village fête, the weather, some gossip from the ball. Fergus was at the opposite end of the table with his delightful new fiancée. It was lovely to see Lady Elspeth again. If one didn't know better, thought the vicar, it would appear nothing at all had happened yesterday. It was only Lady Georgina who acknowledged why he was present, issuing a ceaseless stream of ideas and thoughts for the funeral, which made it difficult to concentrate on his salmon mousse.

When she again raised the idea of using the yellow roses, Eva gasped. 'Those are for the wedding. You promised me I could have them.' The entire room ceased conversation. Eva stared at Lady Inverkillen, who was absently looking out the window.

'Eva, hush,' said Fergus in a low voice, placing his hand lightly on hers.

Bella glared at her. 'At a time like this, all you can think about are your wedding flowers. Honestly.' The girl had no sense of decorum. Trade never did.

'Bella,' said Fergus firmly, 'she has a right to be upset. Her wedding is being postponed, and—'

'Postponed!' cried Eva

'That can hardly be a surprise,' snapped Bella. 'We are now a house of mourning. Perhaps you didn't notice, but everyone is dressed in black.'

Reverend Malcom couldn't help but glance at Angus and Hugh, both in their tennis whites.

It won't do to have a family squabble in front of the vicar, thought Constance. He was hardly discreet, and it would be the talk of the village by tea. 'Ladies please, we have a guest.'

Eva threw her napkin on the table with considerable force. It startled Fergus. 'We've ordered the engraved invitations, Bella. It's been in the papers, for god's sake. How is it going to look if it's postponed?' Eva was close to shouting.

'It will look proper and respectful, which is more than I can say for your behaviour at the moment!'

The room gasped. Constance held her hands up and spoke calmly but loudly. 'Ladies please! As the head of this household, I must demand—' but she got no further in her demand. Bella and Eva leapt to their feet.

'How dare you demand anything, Constance,' Bella hissed, outraged. 'You are not mistress of this house.'

'I most certainly am mistress of this house now,' Constance retorted. She drew breath to continue but Eva stormed from the room, slamming the Dining Room door behind her. The room descended into a stunned silence.

All this seemed to shake Lady Inverkillen out of her daydream. 'Shall we have pudding now?' she asked mildly, signalling Hudson for the dishes to be cleared away.

The funeral took place six days later. It was sparsely attended by the village, but several titles showed up, out of respect for the aristocracy more than anything. Everyone remarked how beautiful the roses were.

After the service, as more Lords and Ladies arrived at the door of the Abbey, Mrs MacBain started to wonder if anyone would notice the missing footmen. They were down from eight to five because of this damned sickness, and she'd had to resort to using the housemaids to help serve the guests. If this lot drank less, she thought, we might have coped. It's like being at a party. They barely had enough staff to serve and clear away, let alone wash up. Angus was no help; he was tossing back whisky like his life depended on it. At least Hugh was with him. Hugh was the only one who could keep Angus in check.

The Reverend had established himself near the grandfather clock, just inside the door to the Drawing Room, so he would be first to the food coming from the kitchens. He was holding court at, rather than with, any poor soul that wandered over towards him. His enthusiasm often getting the better of him, he inadvertently showered many a cleavage with crumbs and spittle. The Countess of Dryburgh had come away particularly spattered and Mrs MacBain had had to usher her into the first-floor Powder Room in order to tidy up. She would have felt sorry for her, but the Countess had loudly suggested that Sadie, who was sent in to help the woman, was trying to steal the jewels right off her. Honestly, jewels and cleavage at a funeral.

As she skirted the edges of the Drawing Room, snippets of conversation made their way over to her. Nothing of interest, really, just gossip of the upper classes. New fashions, expensive necklaces and rumours of affairs kept the ladies busy. Whisky, shooting and tales of randy maids kept the men occupied.

When would they leave? she wondered. They had dinner to prepare for on top of all this, but everyone was run ragged managing the funeral.

Lawlis and the doctor were having a very earnest conversation. They were tucked in a corner by the nude study in marble, commissioned by the 12th Earl after his Grand Tour. It was rumoured to be his mistress. The doctor was leaning with his arm across the shoulder of the statue, unaware that his hand was dangerously close to cupping her breast. Mrs

MacBain wondered what they were talking about. It looked serious.

I'll just straighten those curtains behind them, she thought, stepping near the two men.

'I honestly don't know how to break the news, but it has to be done tomorrow,' Lawlis was saying, sipping on a large whisky.

'Absolutely sure? No mistake could have been made?' wondered the doctor, looking equally concerned.

Better fluff those flowers a bit while I'm here.

'No,' sighed Lawlis. 'If there's one thing MacGregor is, he's always certain.'

The doctor nodded, commiserating. 'Can you at least put it off? Give them a bit more time to sort something?'

Goodness, those magazines are untidy. She reached for this month's issue of *Country Life.*

'I am duty bound, thanks to Hamish. He wanted it done this way and I stupidly agreed,' proclaimed the lawyer, then gulped down the over-large dram.

They suddenly turned and discovered her. Mrs MacBain smiled innocently and continued to tidy the table. Spooked, the men scurried away like naughty schoolboys.

What was that all about? But she didn't have a chance to think about it. The Reverend was choking on his sandwich again, and she rushed over to help him. *Would you people ever leave?*

Finding herself bored by the whole affair, Eva wandered into the Billiards Room, glancing at the ceiling as she entered. Was there no room free from the Inverkillen tartan? she wondered. She found Cecil playing alone. He didn't seem to be particularly troubled by the death of his brother. Eva leaned against the door jamb. What was he humming? Gilbert and Sullivan? She couldn't place it.

'Too artificial for you? All those crocodile tears?' he asked, taking a sip of his brandy. 'Do you play?' he gestured to the table.

'Does a Lady ever play?' she asked with a smile. Gliding into the room she picked up a cue and perfectly sank a rather difficult shot.

Cecil gave an impressed whistle. 'Not just a pretty face, then.' He considered the girl for a moment. 'So, you're Zander-Bitterling's daughter? We spend a good deal of time in London, you know. During the season.'

'We?' she asked while lining up her next shot. She sank it expertly.

'Well done. My late wife and I. The Marchioness of Drysdale? Wonderful woman, very ancient family. The house is in St James's. Such a convenient location, don't you think? Perfect for entertaining, but I've never come across your father. I would be surprised if we didn't have friends in common. My late wife and I had a wide circle of friends.'

Eva deliberately missed her next shot and walked towards a high table on the side. She picked up the crystal decanter.

Cecil smiled at her. 'Please, have some. I dare say you've never had anything like it. The Berry Brothers bottle it just for me.'

She sniffed the brandy and then turned to watch Cecil, taking the opportunity to study him as he concentrated on the table. He was firmly from another generation, she thought, one that prized doing things properly. He was an immaculate dresser, something her fiancé wasn't, and he clearly took great pride in his appearance. Had he been her age, she'd have called him a dandy.

'Of course,' he continued, 'the house in London is tiny

compared to our main residence here, Stronach Castle. Have you heard of it? Rumoured to be the trysting place for Lord Darnley.'

He rattled on about the history of Lord Darnley, but Eva wasn't listening closely. She was stuck at 'Castle' and 'Marchioness'. Those weren't words Fergus had used in explaining how Cecil fitted into the family. She wondered why.

At the reception after the funeral, Lady Inverkillen stared out into the grounds. What was there for her to say? Her husband had died, and while it was tragic, life would go on. It had to. She was the picture of dignified widowhood, standing in the bay window in the Blue Drawing Room, smiling faintly and nodding as people offered their condolences. She said as little as possible but enough to avoid being rude to her guests. When she had greeted the last of them, she breathed a sigh of relief and took a seat on the sofa, across from her mother-in-law. Serenely, and a bit vacantly, she sipped a glass of champagne, which raised several eyebrows, and mostly stared out the windows. Once again, it fell to Lady Georgina to take the reins.

Yes, it is a shock. So tragic to lose him so young. Angus will indeed make a fine 20th Earl. Yes, the wedding will have to be postponed but we hope not for too long. Of course, we'll be hosting the village fête this year. Hamish would have wanted it that way.

It was all very exhausting for Lady Inverkillen and she was glad to turn over the duties to Lady Georgina who, by her very nature, was far more suited to the task.

When Lawlis and the doctor came to say their goodbyes, Lady Inverkillen stood without a word and escorted them to the door. She seemed grateful for the excuse to leave, Lawlis thought. He mentioned that he needed to see the family the following day and asked if he should call in at teatime. She nodded vaguely and then walked back into the Armoury.

Lawlis glanced at the doctor hesitantly. Had she even heard him? But luckily, Hudson was standing ready with their hats and he assured Lawlis that the family would expect him tomorrow afternoon. They all watched as Lady Inverkillen paused at the door to the Drawing Room, clearly hesitant about rejoining the reception. When the unmistakeable sounds of the Reverend starting to choke reached them, she turned and walked slowly up the stairs, humming softly, and left Lady Georgina to rule in her absence.

Imogen MacLeod studied Lawlis as he drove. She was his new secretary and he'd asked her to come with him to Loch Down Abbey, to take notes. He was reading Hamish's will today.

Goodness, he's nervous, thought Imogen. I wonder why? He's surely done this before.

And then she recalled the meeting Mr Lawlis had with Mr MacGregor, the accountant. They had been behind closed doors for most of the day, but Imogen could tell from the look on their faces that it was not great news. And then she had been asked to cancel all his appointments and bring in Lord Inverkillen's will. Ah, yes, she thought, that rather makes sense now.

Hudson led them to the Library, where the family were having tea. They seemed surprised to see him, Imogen noticed, and clearly thought it was a social call. Lady Georgina offered him refreshment, while staring at Imogen, unsure who she was. The walnut cake was particularly good that day, they were told.

'Ah no, I'm here on another matter. I am here to read Lord Inverkillen's will.'

No going back now, Imogen thought.

A wave of surprise went around the room and several cups of tea were put down.

'What, now?' sputtered Fergus, looking from Lawlis to Imogen and back again. 'Right now, the day after the funeral? Is that normal?'

'Lord Inverkillen specifically requested it to be today and I am duty bound by my promise to him. Now, I have the will here and there are one or two matters that will need to be discussed,' he said, gesturing at the tea table. Hudson cleared the tray quickly and Lawlis set down his briefcase.

Imogen pulled up a chair and took out her notebook. When she looked up, Fergus was still looking at her. She flushed slightly and then looked down at her lap, ready to minute the event.

Lawlis pulled out a few papers, shuffled and straightened them for a few moments and then cleared his throat.

'Get on with it man! We haven't got all day!' barked Angus, who was clearly not drinking tea. He was shushed by his grandmother.

Lawlis started reading the will.

Iris thought it was very dull. It always seems more exciting in books. She wished she had helped herself to more tea before it began. She looked absently out the window. Were the children on the lawn? Of course they were, no one was watching the Nursery. Oh dear. Should she slip out and fetch them? No, that would be disruptive. Were they carrying a stag's head? Oh lord . . . they were such a handful.

As she looked back to the room, she could see stifled yawns and rather vacant expressions. Clearly, she wasn't the only one bored by the proceedings. Finally, after some minutes, Lawlis paused and pointedly cleared his throat. The family sat up straighter, suddenly alert, realising it was time for the bequests.

It was much as they suspected it would be – in the beginning, at least.

Lady Inverkillen, Victoria, was to have a generous allowance for life, and to keep all the jewels that Hamish had purchased for her. The family jewels would remain, as always, with the Countess of Inverkillen, now Constance, who looked beyond pleased. But Drummond House would remain with Lady Georgina until her death. There was a sharp intake of breath as all eyes fell on Lady Inverkillen. Her husband had effectively rendered her homeless. Either she stayed at the Abbey, with Constance at the helm, or she would have to live under Lady Georgina's rule, if, that is, Lady Georgina deigned to give her rooms. Iris couldn't decide which prospect was worse.

Lawlis continued. Angus inherited the title, naturally, and was given the house and the Estate.

Pretty much everything, thought Fergus with unexpected bitterness. The fate of Second Sons of the Aristocracy. Curse, more like it, he thought, glancing at Hugh. He had always felt for Hugh, having to live here instead of his own home, simply because he, too, had an older brother. Not that it had ever seemed to bother Hugh.

Lawlis paused, taking a deep breath. Imogen could feel her employer's nervousness and thought it odd, but kept her eyes on her shorthand. Lawlis read out the names of three people who were all bequeathed annuities of equal amounts: Fergus, Bella – and Iris.

The room fell deathly silent.

Imogen looked up from her notebook to see everyone in the family staring at Iris, who looked as if she wanted the earth to swallow her whole. The clock in the hall chimed the quarter of the hour and then the shouting started.

At Lawlis. At Iris. At Imogen, as if she had anything to do with it. She'd heard talk in the village about the family's tendency to shout, but goodness . . . they were loud.

Why does she get anything? She's just the ward. How could you have allowed this to happen Lawlis? That can't be right, she's not even family! I'm not sharing my inheritance with her. You won't see a penny of if I have anything to say about it. She clearly exploited him somehow. Yes, he never would have left money to her without being manipulated.

Curiously, the only people not reacting were Lady Georgina and Lady Inverkillen. Lady Georgina was concentrating on the lace handkerchief in her lap, looking slightly uneasy. But Lady Inverkillen was staring at the girl with an odd expression that Imogen could not quite read. Curiosity? No, that wasn't quite right. There was something more there. It was a bit unnerving. It seemed to Imogen that Lady Inverkillen was looking at Iris as if for the first time.

Lawlis tried to shout over the outrage but was unsuccessful. He glanced at Imogen and grimaced. She nodded to the chair next to him. After another few moments, Lawlis pushed the chair over. It sounded a sharp thwack as it hit the timber floor. The room fell silent.

'Please sit down, all of you.' Lawlis righted the chair and resumed his place behind his briefcase. Clearing his throat softly, he went on with the reading. Money was set aside in trust for the grandchildren and some jewellery was settled on Hamish's sister Elspeth, who looked pleased.

Lawlis paused and took a deep breath. Imogen glanced at her employer. Another tricky bit, clearly, she thought.

'Hamish's final bequest,' Lawlis said, 'is a small annuity for Miss Maxwell.'

If Iris's good fortune had caused an explosion, Maxwell's caused the exact opposite. The family looked at the lawyer in confused silence.

Elspeth finally broke it. 'What an odd bequest. Extraordinarily thoughtful, yes, but I never thought of Hamish as especially thoughtful.'

'You're quite right there,' uttered Lady Georgina.

Imogen glanced up at Lady Inverkillen again. She had gone white and was staring at the floor, eyes darting wildly back and forth as her hands gripped the fabric of her skirt. Lady Inverkillen was obviously not happy, but was doing her best to supress it.

'Final bequest?' snapped Cecil. 'That's it? Nothing for me? Not even a mention? My sister gets jewels, the orphan gets cash and I get ignored completely?' His tone had moved from raging animal to wounded, and everyone knows a wounded beast is more dangerous.

Lady Georgina tried to calm him, but he marched over to the decanter and poured out a deep measure of whisky, taking half in one gulp. 'He told me I was in the will. He promised.' Still holding the decanter, he turned back to the room. 'For God's sake, even the maid gets some damn cash. What, was she sleeping with him?'

The room gasped, and all eyes flicked to Lady Inverkillen, who was still staring intently at the floor.

Fergus moved towards his uncle. 'Steady on, man. No need for language like that. Ladies present, you know,' he said as he reached for the decanter, trying to disarm his uncle. But Cecil tugged it back, whisky sloshing out of the narrow neck. He poured another dram and then paused, muttering to himself. Fergus was just about to reach for the decanter again when Cecil smashed it against the wall. Broken glass and whisky rained down on the carpet.

No one had ever seen Cecil behave so roughly, he was always the model gentleman. They froze, staring at him, horrified at his behaviour.

Hudson, however, merely rolled his eyes and issued a quiet sigh. That was going to be a mess to clean.

Lady Inverkillen stood to leave, saying she had a headache and needed to lie down. She looked paler than before, which Imogen would not have thought possible. Lawlis was forced to ask her to remain, saying he had another matter that urgently needed discussion. She took her seat again, composed herself and looked at him blankly. 'If you insist.'

He braced himself for the hardest part of his task.

Lawlis cleared his throat and Imogen could see this was what he'd been dreading all morning.

'I realise this has been a difficult day for you all. A difficult few days, in fact, and I have no wish to upset you further. But I must. There is a pressing matter that we need to discuss that directly affects the bequests.' He looked directly at Fergus.

The family looked to one another, some confused, others disturbed.

'Affects the bequests? What do you mean, Andrew?' asked Lady Georgina.

Lawlis shifted uncomfortably and stared at the floor for a moment. 'None of the bequests can be granted until the death duties are paid in full.'

'Yes, we're well aware of that,' said Lady Georgina patronisingly.

'Yes,' he continued, slightly flushed. 'But what you aren't aware of is the state of the family funds. They are perilously low and while they will cover the death duties, just, there will be very little left afterwards.'

This caused an immediate uproar.

You can't be serious! How much are these death duties? That simply can't be true. We should hire a new solicitor, he's clearly incompetent. How could our fortune have disappeared? Embezzlement? Surely not, Lawlis has been with us for years. You explain it then.

Imogen was insulted on her employer's behalf and scowled at the family. She knew how hard he had worked to help them. She banged her heel on the floor to bring order to the room, glaring at them like a schoolmistress.

Lawlis sighed heavily. 'Lord Inverkillen and I have been working for some months to find a way to raise more funds for the Estate. But the truth is, Loch Down has been losing money for years. And now, with the death duties . . . ' He paused, and his shoulders drooped. 'We have five months to find the funds for that, but the Estate will still be in in financial peril. And that's before any bequests are made good.'

'I thought we were selling off the Distillery. That should cover the duties, surely,' said Angus, lighting a cigarette and inhaling deeply. Hugh stood nearby, watching him anxiously.

'We have sold it. However, the buyer only agreed to purchase the physical Distillery: the building, the equipment, and the water rights, etc. – but not the business. The business, Plaid Whisky, is deeply in debt, you see.'

But apparently, Angus did not see. 'What's the difference? The building is the business, isn't it?'

Fergus, Imogen could see, understood perfectly, though. He had gone as pale as his mother, and his legs buckled.

'Oh God,' he said. 'With the water rights gone, we could lose the salmon. He's ruined us, hasn't he?' He looked at Lawlis, his face pleading to be wrong. 'How bad is it?'

Lawless hesitated. 'You're going to have to sell the Abbey.'

★

'They have to sell the house? Ha! Are you serious?' Mackay exclaimed; the valet was amused by the thought of the Inverkillens in a two-up/two-down on the High Street.

'Sell the Abbey? Are they mad?' spluttered Ollie the footman. 'Where would they go? And who would buy this place?'

Hudson had just finished relating the events to the staff. It had been a dry recitation of events – the man was always spare with his adjectives – but it was an accurate one: Angus was Lord, Lady Inverkillen was homeless, and Maxwell and Iris were in the money – if there was any left over.

'Americans, most likely,' said Mrs Burnside with a look of distaste. 'They're the only ones with any cash these days. But you can bet they don't know the first thing about running a house like this.'

They all paused, thinking about working for a new family, dreading the possibility of foreigners who had never had staff. It was unthinkable.

A plaintive voice from the back went up. 'What if they don't need staff at all?' A collective shudder went around the table. No, that was unthinkable.

Mrs Burnside recovered first and barked, 'Right now, everybody needs to get back to work. We can't know what's going to happen next, but you can be sure we need to have dinner ready tonight.'

'Will they even want dinner tonight, d'ya think?' asked Maisie, walking towards the kitchens.

'No idea,' said Mrs Burnside, 'but we won't be caught empty handed if they do. Go!'

Everyone dispersed, leaving Mrs MacBain and Hudson alone. Worry was etched on both their faces. 'Does Miss Maxwell even know?' asked Mrs MacBain in a hushed voice.

Hudson shook his head. 'I don't know. The question is, will she stay once she learns of it?'

'Would you?' Mrs MacBain said, and Hudson gave a helpless shrug.

Mrs MacBain walked through the kitchens to the back stairs. Mrs Burnside was shouting at her kitchen maids, stirring, chopping, readying a dinner that Mrs MacBain was certain would go uneaten.

True to form, no one came down for dinner. Eva called down for soup to be served in the Morning Room. Philippe and Auguste asked for a cold supper in the Billiards Room. The rest asked for trays in their rooms.

It was just as well, really. Several of the stuffed shooting trophies were missing from the Game Room, including a Canadian moose. It took seven of the servants to wrangle the children back into the house and over an hour to work out how to get the moose back in place. Tidying her hair and smoothing her skirt, Mrs MacBain wondered how seventy-eight-year-old Nanny had managed the little monsters.

The following morning, Mrs MacBain was in the kitchen when Miss Maxwell returned with Her Ladyship's breakfast tray, which was untouched.

Mrs MacBain glanced at the tray, then at the lady's maid. 'Miss Maxwell, what's this?'

Miss Maxwell looked at Mrs MacBain, dazed. Her eyes were red and swollen. 'I've been refused entry.' She turned and shuffled towards the kitchen door.

'Refused entry?' barked Mrs Burnside. 'What does that mean?'

The maid turned and looked at the two women, then slowly down to the floor. She shrugged and her whole body sagged.

Once again, Mrs MacBain wondered if she had slept in

her dress. Her hair, always perfectly in place, rather resembled a bird's nest.

'Are you all right, Miss Maxwell? Shall I ring for the doctor?' she asked, suddenly very worried.

Miss Maxwell looked up from the floor. 'I'm fine, Mrs MacBain. I'm just a bit tired.' She was barely audible over the din of the kitchen. Before anyone could reply, she wandered out of the kitchen and up the servants' staircase.

Mrs MacBain and Mrs Burnside exchanged sceptical looks.

'What was that all about?' asked Mrs MacBain.

'I have no idea,' said the cook, 'but I'd wager you're dressing the Dowager this morning.'

Cecil woke in his room on the guest floor, feeling groggy. He had slept poorly, his brain whirring all night, to find the right way to approach Angus. Knowing how much his nephew hated life at Loch Down, there was an opportunity for Cecil. He just needed to figure out the best way to seize it before Angus had time to think. How much of the family, if any, did he need onside? Lady Georgina would support him, obviously, but would Angus listen to his Grandmama? And what to do with Victoria? Scheming was Cecil's truest skill. Scheming, and dressing well.

He rose and began his daily ablutions. He dearly missed his valet. Dressing oneself was such a bore, tiresome where it had once been a thing he looked forward to. Thinking back to days in Stronach Castle in his dressing room, twice the size of his bedroom here at Loch Down, with all those beautiful choices, laid out for him to decide, that large copper bathtub to languish in each morning. A wistful sigh escaped him.

Focus, Cecil! He quickly finished and went down to break-fast, hoping to catch Angus. He needed to know his mood before he could formulate any actual plans.

In the Dining Room, Angus had assumed his father's place at the breakfast table. Time marches on, thought Cecil wryly. But Angus was wearing his tennis whites. Surely that was a good sign? Cecil helped himself to breakfast from the sideboard – eggs, mushrooms, and black pudding – and wondered if he could sit in Angus's vacated seat, so they could speak. When Hamish had been alive, Cecil had been seated as far away from his brother as Hamish could put him. Cecil was always a bit amazed he hadn't been told to stay in Drummond House.

'Would you mind if I sat here this morning?' he asked the table. 'The light is better for my eyes.' When no one acknowledged his comment, he simply sat down and glanced around. How he loathed family. Necessary, he supposed, but so tedious.

The French corner was deep in French newspapers. Auguste, now fifteen, was fast on his way to being a man, but still had the angry red hair of his youth. Except for Bella, all Inverkillen children had unnaturally red hair in youth, which mercifully grew darker with age. Auguste's, however, still seemed to glow in the dark. Such a horrible legacy, that hair. Cecil was glad when his had started to turn grey. Grey was such a distinguished colour on a man. *Focus, Cecil!*

He glanced around the table, trying to gauge the mood. Fergus and Eva were furiously ignoring each other. They had obviously had a row before breakfast. Cecil started to wonder why, but then realised he simply did not care. He had more important things on his mind.

He turned to Angus, who was reading the paper, muttering

something about cricket. Angus folded the paper and tossed it aside, still muttering. Not the best time for a chat, it would seem.

Picking up the paper, Cecil's eye fell to the main headline: MYSTERIOUS ILLNESS BEFALLS ENGLAND. He scanned the story. 'Goodness, this illness is getting serious.' He looked up expectantly, but Angus was concentrating on feeding the family dogs sausages from his plate. Searching for something else to rouse a discussion, Cecil scanned the front page and announced, 'Well, well, it looks like the Yanks are finally giving up prohibition. I can't believe they've lasted this long without a drink.'

'Like anyone cares about them,' muttered Angus darkly.

'Quite so,' concurred Hugh, sitting to Angus's right. 'But maybe now they'll stop coming here. Mind you, I do like the cocktails they've brought over with them.'

Angus looked to his brother-in-law. 'Ready?' Hugh drained his teacup and the men left without another word. Cecil would have to try again if he were to secure a handout. Maybe tea would be more fruitful.

'Well, what's everyone doing this morning then?' Cecil tried to sound casual but felt like his voice was echoing in a canyon. 'It looks to be a beautiful day. Would anyone care to go for a walk?'

Papers went down, eating was paused, all eyes went to Cecil, but no one spoke. After a tense moment, they all resumed their breakfasts without a word, and Cecil felt his colour rise. He had not thought his brother was beloved enough to command grief, actual sorrow at his passing. From their mother, yes, certainly, but there was little love lost between Hamish and his children. But clearly, he had been mistaken.

★

A week passed in stony silence. Iris wisely stayed in the Nursery, avoiding any further confrontation with the family. She was just as bewildered as they were with Hamish's generosity. She had not expected to be remembered at all, but to be given an equal amount as his children . . . it was just too much to comprehend. Then again, if what Mr Lawlis had said was true, and the family did need to sell the estate, how much or how little didn't really matter. She would still be a governess and that was fine. But she did think it was probably time to start looking for a position. How to do that, she had very little idea. Lady Eva was always going on about that magazine, *The Lady*, so perhaps she should start there.

Iris had been staring out the window, watching it rain while the children did their lessons. She would miss the house. It had been her only real home, and even if the family had not welcomed her as warmly as Sister Margaret had said they would, it was a lot better than growing up in the orphanage, really. Coming from the household of an Earl, instead of an orphanage, she'd have better opportunities to take care of herself when she turned twenty-one in August.

Was that one of the children on the tennis court? She whirled round to see the empty Nursery. How did they do that?

May

Inspector Jarvis crashed through the woods that surrounded the house. Like a city boy, he thought. He had been gone too long, could barely call himself a Highlander anymore.

He'd come to deliver the official verdict on Lord Inverkillen's death but before he did, he wanted to see the weir one last time. Something was nagging him, and he hated being nagged.

He emerged from the woods on the near side of the Distillery, stopping to take in the building. It was a very typical building for the Highlands. Built from local stone that had been whitewashed some years ago, the paint was badly peeling and there was moss growing out of the broken slate tiles. He was on the long side of the building, with the yard to his left. The River Plaid ran behind the building and down to his right. He walked down the hill towards the weir. As he came to the edge of the building, he could see the water wheel, turning slowly. Lord, he thought, if they were still water powered, it was no wonder the thing was never successful. Rumour had it the family was having to sell up. He hoped whoever bought the place could make better whisky than old MacTavish. That stuff was rubbish.

Jarvis made his way down the bank to the weir. When he reached the clearing where Lord Inverkillen's fishing gear had been found, he slowed down. He could just see a woman standing on the bank of the river. He peered closer and found to his astonishment that it was Mrs MacBain. What was the housekeeper doing at the river?

Finally coming out into the clearing, he waved and walked towards her. She was staring out at the weir where Lord Inverkillen had drowned, clearly lost in thought.

'Hello, Alice. What brings you here?' he asked.

Mrs MacBain didn't react to his appearance. She'd heard him in the woods. That man had been in the city too long, she mused; stalking this winter would be wasted on him.

'Hello, Roddie. I just wanted to come and have a look. I don't know why; I haven't been down here in years.' She looked around. 'This is where he was fishing, yes?'

Inspector Jarvis nodded.

She lifted the hem of her dress and he could see she was wearing gumboots. Always prepared. Together they slowly waded out onto the rock weir where Lord Inverkillen had got into trouble. It was a natural weir in the river, a large flat rock, worn over time by the water, and sitting just high enough to create a fall in the river. The water tumbled down to a deep but perfectly clear pool two feet below. It was very slippery – such a strange place to fish. Jarvis wondered why on earth he had chosen to cast here, instead of ten paces down river. It didn't make sense. Lord Inverkillen hadn't been known as a great sportsman, but surely he would have known enough to choose a better spot.

As he was musing, something large flew past his left ear, almost hitting him in the head and making him start violently. He had just made out it was a fish jumping from the pool beneath, when his feet slipped. He crashed backwards into the shallow water on the stone just as three more fish jumped the weir as well. Stunned, Jarvis stared into the water, keen not to be taken by surprise again. When he had got his breath back, he swore and struggled to his feet. As he did so, a thought dawned on him. How easy it would have been for him to careen forward into the pool – just as Lord Inverkillen must have done – and get swept down river.

'I forgot to warn you about the fish. Sorry,' Mrs MacBain said, laughing. 'Here's your hat.'

Jarvis thanked her but did not meet her eye; he felt foolish. 'All right, so Lord Inverkillen had definitely been fishing,' he said aloud. He had really wondered about that. 'And that must be exactly why he went into the river.'

Mrs MacBain considered the idea. 'Yes, but it wasn't his first time, was it? If I knew the salmon leapt from the river, Lord Inverkillen surely would have known about it. Wouldn't he have been prepared for that?'

'Perhaps. But they do leap at random, so maybe it was just bad luck?' They stood in silence for some minutes before Jarvis came to a decision. 'There really is nothing to suggest foul play. I'm here to tell the family that the coroner is ruling it an accident.'

'And the gash in the back of his head?'

Jarvis stared at her, wondering how she had known about that. 'Probably from the river. Look, Alice, it's Death by Misadventure. That's the official ruling.'

Mrs MacBain stared at the pool, nodding slowly.

'What?' He had a bad feeling suddenly.

She started to speak and looked at him. 'Oh nothing. It's silly of me. I must go and find Ross. Do you know your way back to the house? There's a direct path between those two oak trees just there.' She waded back to the bank and headed up toward the Distillery.

Inspector Jarvis took the path she'd recommended and had been walking for about five minutes when he heard the sound of distinct footsteps. He stopped and listened hard. Where was it coming from? He scanned the woods to his left. There! The trees were moving. He stopped and waited to see what appeared. And then he heard humming, a woman's voice, relaxed and happy. He was rewarded for his patience when Lady Elspeth appeared from behind a gnarled tree. What the devil was she doing here?

'Hello, milady.' He'd have tipped his cap if it hadn't been clutched in his hand, dripping water.

She spun around, surprised to see him. 'Oh. It's you, Inspector,' was all she said. She looked annoyed, he thought. She was up to something, that much was obvious. Outwardly, all was calm, but her eyes were darting around restlessly, looking for something . . . or someone?

'Have you fallen in the river?' she finally asked, nodding to his coat.

'Yes. Rather slippery at the weir.'

'Yes. It's why we don't want the children running loose in the grounds. Angus nearly drowned there as a child. Have you seen the children, by the way? They've escaped again. I gather they were using suits of armour to sledge down the guest stair. They can be quite a handful.'

'Ah, no. Haven't seen them.' He continued to watch her, wondering what she was really doing in the woods. Was her lipstick a little smudged?

They continued to stare at each other awkwardly for some moments.

'Well, I must get on,' she said, in a breezy voice. She turned to leave, then looked back to him and said, almost as an afterthought, 'Do you know where you're going? The house is just down that path and to the right.' She pointed to the path she'd just come from.

He nodded and watched her as she went on her way. She

was remarkably agile in the woods, he thought. He would not have expected a Lady to know her way about, let alone with such ability. She would be good on a stalk, he thought admiringly.

He followed the path she had indicated and was just starting to think he had got it wrong when he heard someone else in the woods. It wasn't erratic enough to be the children, so he stopped and waited. A moment later, Ross MacBain came into view. He looked as startled and guilty as Elspeth had been to discover Jarvis.

'Helping to find the children, are you?' asked Jarvis.

'What? Oh, yes. Looking for the children. Dangerous place, the forest. Have you fallen in the river?'

Jarvis nodded, irritated and a bit embarrassed to have to admit it to the very capable gamekeeper. 'Almost got taken out by a fish on the weir.'

Ross nodded, trying to hide a smirk. 'Yes, they're like arrows; you only see them when they've gone past. This time of year isn't too bad but when the salmon run, watch out. Do you know where you're going? The house, it's just down that path.' He pointed in the opposite direction.

Jarvis shook his head as he backtracked past the gamekeeper. He'd missed the path entirely. He walked for some minutes, swearing softly, when the tennis courts finally came into view. Jarvis snorted. Whatever those two are up to, he thought to himself, it isn't looking for the children. He could see Iris chasing them across the tennis court.

The Distillery was empty when Mrs MacBain arrived. Ross generally spent his free time here with MacTavish. Where is everyone? she wondered. Shaking her head, she turned around and was on her way back to the house to prepare for dinner when she caught sight of Lady Elspeth across the river. She smiled and nodded a polite greeting at her. Lady Elspeth looked startled but recovered quickly. She shouted something over to her about the children being on the loose again and then ducked behind a large rhododendron. *Oh dear*, thought Mrs MacBain, *Iris really needs to get a grip on them.*

She was just approaching the oak trees when Ross appeared on the path. She glanced back towards Elspeth and then back at her cousin.

'Really?' she asked him, irritated. Ross merely nodded and grinned. 'After all this time? For heaven's sake, her husband is here.'

'Ah, he never leaves the house. Smells too good to the midges,' he said.

'There aren't midges this time of year, and you know it.'

'Well, if he left the house, he'd know it too, wouldn't he?'

She tried not to smile. 'Look here, I wanted to ask you something. You once told me that you'd saved Hamish from drowning, that he couldn't swim. Was that true?'

'Yes. We capsised that little blue rowing boat. Never seen anyone sink so quickly. I nearly drowned trying to save him. He fought me hard.'

'Did he ever learn to swim, do you think?'

'I don't suppose he did. Unless he learned how at St Andrews. The North Sea is mighty cold, though.'

'I thought as much. So, what on earth was he doing on the weir?' she asked, mostly to herself. She couldn't deny now that she really was bothered by it all.

Ross could see the wheels turning in her mind and it made him nervous. 'It was an accident, Alice. Nothing more.'

'Oh yes, an accident. Roddie Jarvis just told me.' They both rolled their eyes. 'He's not the most inquisitive man for an Inspector.'

'And an accident is less paperwork for him, I know. But Alice, don't stir the pot. You don't know what you'll unearth if you do.' He kissed her on the forehead. 'Make your life easy for once.' And he disappeared into the woods, leaving Mrs MacBain wondering what on earth he had meant.

Fergus paced back and forth in the Library. Over the last few weeks, he had spent considerable time with Lawlis and MacGregor the accountant, trying to find a way to pay the death duties without selling Loch Down Abbey. They had twelve weeks left and Fergus was feeling overwhelmed.

It wasn't unheard of for families like his to burn the house to the ground, or at least part of it, in order to reduce the amount they owed. Their nearest neighbour had resorted to it in 1906, moving into the Norman part of the castle, which was damp and gloomy, but cheap. Fergus very much wanted to avoid that but often found his mind wandering, trying to choose which part of the house would be easiest bit to lose . . .

He and Lawlis were in the Map Room with the accountant, who was suggesting they sell artwork, thinking that some of the canvases might be valuable enough to rescue them.

Bare walls Fergus could live with. 'It would be much better if we could get an expert to come to the house to value the art. I doubt we'd be able to pack it all up and send it off without war breaking out.' An image of Angus and his grandmother with swords and shields sprang to his mind, causing him to smirk.

Lawlis was sceptical. 'Even if the collection is valuable enough, the house still needs an income and Angus, as we know, is dead set against changing anything at all.'

'Let's get the art valued first, then we can deal with my

brother,' said Fergus. 'One problem at a time. When the death duties are paid, we can worry about income.' Lawlis gave in and agreed to send to London for an expert.

Meanwhile, Eva was pacing in the Morning Room and the tartan carpet was starting to give her a headache. For Eva, the news they were in financial trouble was distressing. She had not yet married Fergus, thankfully, and in their last letter, her parents had intimated that they were no longer sure that she should. *But, poppet,* they argued, *what is the point of a title if there is no money?* And Eva had to agree. Yes, Daddy would get his fish, but this was not the life she had agreed to when she had accepted Fergus's proposal.

What to do, she wondered? She could hardly break the engagement while the family was in mourning. The wedding had been announced in *The Times*. People knew about it. Leaving now would definitely tarnish her as a gold-digger, and there was no coming back from such a slur once it had been issued. She would just have to keep putting off the wedding until an opportunity presented itself. At least she'd cancelled the invitations. Having been so annoyed at having to do so initially, she was immeasurably glad of it now. Surely, full mourning would be observed for the patriarch, and that gave her a year, didn't it? What she really needed was to speak with her mother. It took too long to get post this far north.

It was Mrs MacBain's habit to have the senior staff to tea each morning, after the family had had their breakfast. She found it a good way to keep an eye on the details of the house.

But in the month since Nanny died it had become a roll call of how many staff members they had left.

'What do you mean, he ran away?' asked Mackay. Hudson had just announced that one of the few remaining hall boys had run off at dawn.

'He was supposed to have gone to the village for the papers,' the butler said wearily, 'but when he didn't return, I checked his room. All his belongings were gone. It caused no amount of grief this morning, I don't need to tell you.'

They all shook their heads in commiseration.

'What are we going to do?' asked Mrs Burnside dejectedly.

'Perhaps we can stop the staff from reading the papers?' suggested Hudson, reaching for a broken scone. 'All they write about is the damned sickness. It's spooking people, and hysteria is something we don't need.'

'We may be able to stop the papers, but we can't stop the letters, Mr. Hudson. They'll find out one way or another. We just have to hope people start to recover, so we can get back to normal.'

'We had more staff than this during the war,' grumbled Mrs Burnside. She helped herself to a slice of stale cake. 'If we lose any more, I'll be waiting at table.'

Hudson twitched. The very thought of a cook in the Dining Room disturbed him greatly. 'I don't think it will come to that, Mrs Burnside. We'll manage.'

Mrs MacBain looked concerned. 'Yes, but we're now down to five footmen, three kitchen maids and only four housemaids.'

Lockridge had just arrived from Drummond House. He surveyed the tea tray and settled on a slice of dry lemon drizzle cake. 'I think I know where we can move people,' he said, pouring himself some tea.

'Thank the Lord!' cried Mrs. MacBain 'Where?'

'I've been helping the staff at the Dower House clean out the attics and set up camp beds so we can move them there. It's not much, but it will do. And it will be easier for them to check on people during the day.' The chauffeur looked pleased with himself.

Mrs MacBain nodded thoughtfully. It was a good plan. 'Do you think we'd put Lady Georgina at risk by keeping them all in Drummond House?'

Lockridge thought for a moment, and said slowly, 'I doubt it. Her bedroom is a full two storeys below the attics. And it isn't even on the same side of the house. It's practically a separate building.'

'It sounds perfect!' exclaimed Mrs Burnside, eager to move the sickness as far away from her as possible.

'Yes,' said Mrs MacBain slowly, 'but how do we get everyone over there without the family seeing?'

Lockridge grinned. 'Dinner.'

They looked to him in confusion.

'We move them while the family is having dinner. That gives us two hours, which I think is plenty of time.' Lockridge helped himself to more cake. 'It'll be all hands on deck, but with the maids and the extra staff from next door, I think we can manage.'

They looked at one another in silent conference. 'All right,' said Mrs MacBain finally, exhaling deeply, 'let's do it. Tonight, if possible. Mrs Burnside and I will speak to the maids now. You and Mackay speak to the hall boys and see if any of the grounds team can help as well. Lugging sick bodies up and down the staff stairs won't be easy.'

'Aagh!' Angus threw the morning paper down in disgust. 'Why is there nothing in the papers but this damned illness?' Picking up a small knife, he cleanly sliced the top of his boiled egg. 'They've clearly forgotten what real news is.'

Fergus glanced at the newspaper to see the headline:

ALARMING RISE IN HOSPITAL ADMISSIONS. He couldn't remember the last headline that wasn't about the illness.

'I doubt it's even real,' Hugh commented. 'It'll be a publicity stunt by some politician so he can look like a hero.' He handed the dogs a sausage.

Eva looked up from her letter. 'I have had several reports from London who know someone who's had it.'

Fergus put down his letter and looked across the table to Eva. 'Are your parents all right, darling?'

'Yes, of course. But their cook was in hospital last week and they had to eat at Daddy's club every evening, which Mama hates. They make women enter through a separate door off the alleyway.' She tsked and picked up her letter. 'It's been a very trying week for them.'

Fergus stared at his fiancée with his mouth slightly agape. Could she really be so callous? He shook himself out of his surprise and looked to his brother.

'Yes, well London isn't the whole of Britain, is it? There hasn't been a single case in the Highlands,' retorted Angus, 'and I think it's jolly irresponsible of the *Scotsman* to keep harping on about it. They'll only panic people and then where will we be?' He paused and drained the tea in his cup. 'Tennis, Hugh?'

That evening, they managed to move the sick staff members to the Dower House. It went smoothly, thanks to Ross and a few of the gardeners. The family were none the wiser. The children, however, seized the opportunity to slip from the house and were found, after a considerable search, playing a raucous game of tennis.

Returning from installing the children in their beds, Mrs

MacBain found Mackay, Mrs Burnside and Lockridge in the kitchen, speaking in hushed tones.

'At this rate, the family will outnumber the staff in a few days' time, Lord help us, and what will we do then?' asked Mackay.

'We can't afford to lose another housemaid. They'd be sure to notice if Mrs MacBain starts lighting the fires and delivering the breakfast trays,' said Mrs Burnside. 'Pray Sadie doesn't come down with it.'

They looked across to the servants' hall. Sadie was coughing.

Lockridge looked more worried than ever. 'What do we do? I think we need help.'

'Let's see how they settle into Drummond House,' said Mrs MacBain. 'If they aren't better by the end of the week, we'll send for the doctor.' They nodded and murmured assent.

Lockridge thought for a moment, then said, 'Lady Georgina has her hair appointment tomorrow morning in the village. I'll call in at the surgery and ask the doctor what we should do.'

Mrs MacBain breathed a sigh of relief. 'Yes, that would be wonderful if you could. But be very careful about it. We don't want to start any rumours in the village.'

Fergus, Lawlis and the accountant were spending ever more time together, trying to work out the finances. Fergus was once again on his own, battling to be heard. This time, however, he was the irrational voice in the fight, not his father or brother. He wanted to save the Abbey, but try as they may, there seemed to be no scenario where it could be saved.

After one particularly long afternoon, Fergus finally relented and gave Lawlis the go-ahead to contact the local auction house, Cleaverings, and have the Estate valued. It was going to be a rough thing for the family, the lawyer thought, but it would be more difficult for everyone else. The Estate employed a fair number of people in the village, himself included, and there was no way to know if those jobs would be safe with a new owner. Then there was the matter of wages until the Estate changed hands. There really was precious little cash left, even after the money for the Distillery came through. And Mrs MacBain had insisted on paying full wages for the sick staff members. It was the right thing to do, he knew, but the ship was sinking fast.

Imogen rang the Abbey and spoke with Hudson about a date for Cleaverings to come do a valuation. She asked if there was a way to get the family out of the house for the day, so it could be done without distressing them.

'I realise the family is grieving, but people generally find the process upsetting, so I do think it would be better if the family weren't home for it.'

There was a slight chuckle on the line. 'You're not from this part of Scotland, are you Miss MacLeod?'

'Um, no. Tobermory. My father owns a shop on the high street.' She couldn't understand what this had to do with anything.

'Then you would be unaware of the Inverkillens' penchant,' he said, with a rather good French accent.

There was silence on the line. 'Penchant?' Imogen asked at last.

'Yes, penchant. En masse, they rarely leave the house.'

He was maddeningly brief in his explanations. 'What does that mean, "they rarely leave"?'

Hudson sighed softly, but not softly enough to hide it from Imogen, who was just as irritated to be having this discussion as the butler seemed to be.

'The family is well known for never leaving the house.

The only exception one can count upon is the Macintyre Spring Ball, which has just passed. Were you from this area, you would know that.'

'They never leave? Surely, they go into the village, to run errands. Or to visit neighbours?' Hudson chuckled again, irritating Imogen. 'Church, then! Anything will do, really.'

'The Inverkillens do not "run errands" in the village. That is what staff are for. I'll have a word with Mrs MacBain and see what we can arrange.' And with that, he rang off, still amused by the thought of the family running errands.

It was Mrs MacBain who managed to create a reason to leave. She suggested that Lady Georgina could give an engagement party for Fergus and Eva. They'd not had one as yet and it seemed a shame to have Eva's only introduction to the neighbours be a funeral. And since they were a house of mourning, it might be more appropriate if it were to be an afternoon garden party at Drummond House. A bit more respectful, she assured them, given the situation.

Lady Georgina agreed and announced the engagement party at dinner that evening. The news wasn't well received by Eva. Luckily, Fergus joined her in the sentiment. The last thing they needed was the expense of a party. But Lady Georgina was not to be dissuaded.

'Yes, yes, house of mourning, but we must look to the future and introduce Fergus's bride in happier circumstances. Life goes on.' Lady Georgina was not a woman to be trifled with when she had made up her mind. 'It will be tasteful, just a small garden party at Drummond House. Leave it with me, I'll make all the arrangements.' She looked to Eva deliberately. 'All of them. Hudson. Please have Mrs MacBain come see me tomorrow morning.'

When Hudson gave her the message, Mrs MacBain rang Lawlis. If the valuation could wait a week, it would be easy to allow access to the house without bumping into the family members. They could return to value the Dower House when Lady Georgina had her next dress fitting.

Lawlis hung up the phone. How on earth did she manage that, he wondered. That woman was wasted as a housekeeper.

Distressingly, the Abbey staff were still getting sick, despite the inflicted having been moved to Drummond House. Those few that recovered were too weak to come back to work right away, and the upstairs staff kept getting smaller. All too quickly, it was Mrs MacBain who was lighting fires and delivering trays in the morning – a previously unthinkable situation. Maxwell tended to Lady Georgina, but Lady Inverkillen still refused to let anyone in her bedchamber. No one had seen her for weeks.

As a former housemaid, Mrs MacBain easily managed to get the fires lit without waking anyone but delivering the trays was impossible to do without being seen.

'Goodness, you're not who I expected!' exclaimed Bella, as Mrs MacBain set the tray down gently.

'My apologies, milady. Sadie isn't feeling well, and I didn't want her near the family. Especially with the party approaching.' She crossed the room to open the curtains.

'Too right. Is that all the post? Hmm . . .' She poured herself tea and then looked through the letters. No reply for a lady's maid. She wondered how her grandmother was handling sharing a maid. Unlike Constance, Mama rose so early each morning that it might not irritate Grandmama the same way it did Bella. 'Has Grandmama had any response for a lady's maid yet?'

Mrs MacBain was stoking the fire. 'Not that I'm aware of, milady.'

'I can't believe no one's jumped at the chance. Poor Grandmama. She shouldn't be forced to share a maid. It's undignified for a woman of her status.' She opened a new letter and unfolded the soft blue paper. 'Please tell me we've had responses for a nanny, at least? That girl simply isn't up to the task.'

Mrs MacBain knew there had been none. And further, she knew there would be none. The pay was so low that anyone outside of the area would not be interested, and anyone from the village already knew the house was going on the block. There would be no one asking to join the staff until after the sale, when the new owners could be sized up.

'It's this sickness going around, milady; people are being more cautious. The Prime Minister himself has asked people to stay at home as much as possible. I hear the village is practically a ghost town, these days.'

Bella put her teacup down. 'That's preposterous. No one here is ill. Do you see anyone sick? No. Life is continuing as it always has. People are blowing this all out of proportion. I just don't understand why it's so hard to find a new staff.'

Mrs MacBain counted to ten slowly as she fussed with the curtains. When she turned to face Bella, she was calm and composed. 'Will that be all, milady? I need to get on with the day.'

Bella waved her hand absentmindedly as she read the letter, nibbling on her toast.

Mrs MacBain glanced out the window as she left the room and saw the children dragging something across the rose garden. Were those bagpipes? She sighed heavily. And the dogs were in His Lordship's kilts. It was going to be a long day.

★

'What's all this, Ollie?' Mrs MacBain was at her desk when the footman stepped into the room holding a box. It had a fishing pole sticking out of it.

'One of the constables brought it up. It's His Lordship's belongings. You know, from the day—'

'Oh, right. Well, put it down there and I'll see to it. Thank you.' She waited until the footman closed the door behind him then walked over to inspect the box. What should she do with this, she wondered. The fishing rod, a picnic rug, a fishing basket. She frowned. This wasn't His Lordship's fishing basket, was it? There was no Inverkillen crest on it. She opened the lid and looked inside. Pastels, pencils, pens, and a small watercolour paint set. How odd. Surely this isn't His Lordship's? Had Jarvis sent the wrong box to them? Picking up the fishing rod again, she could see the Inverkillen crest on it, so it must be. But it couldn't be. Something wasn't right.

She stowed it in a cupboard and walked through the stone hallways back to the Boot Room. After a few moments of searching, she found it: Hamish's fishing basket, Inverkillen crest on the leather; tackle, lures and silver flask inside. But if this was still here . . . he couldn't have been fishing. But if he hadn't been fishing, why had he been at the weir? She closed her eyes to picture it. Lord Inverkillen standing with his fishing kit at the banks of the river. But the bank there was gentle and rather wide. It was nearly impossible to fall in and get swept away. But if he'd been *on* the weir . . . and fell into the pool . . . Would Lord Inverkillen have walked on to the most dangerous part of the river, knowing he couldn't swim? What would compel him to do that? One of the dogs was in trouble, perhaps, and he went after it? Had the dogs gone with him that afternoon? She couldn't remember. But the dogs were in the river all the time. They were hunting dogs, and strong swimmers. He wouldn't have gone after them. Had it been a person, however . . . Oh! What if, she thought slowly, someone else had been there? What if he'd gone to the weir to meet someone? Could the fishing be a red herring?

But who? And why wouldn't they have said something? And it didn't answer why he'd walk out onto the weir. The dressing gong sounded. Oh, to have ten uninterrupted minutes in this house! She sighed irritably. This would have to wait until after dinner.

The day of the party arrived and for once, the weather cooperated. It wasn't warm, being Scotland in the early spring, but it wasn't raining, and that was a triumph. They could use the garden. Always better for a garden party if it takes place in a garden.

Iris came down the staircase in her best dress, which admittedly was a size too large and not quite right for the occasion, but Iris didn't care. A day without the children was a good day. Yesterday they'd broken into the Chapel and started ringing the bells. She had no idea how they kept escaping. One minute they were there, the next they were setting fire to a hedge. It was exhausting.

She was just putting on her hat when the doorbell rang. She looked about her before remembering that everyone else was at Drummond House preparing for the party, including Hudson. She hesitated a moment. She'd never answered the door before. Did she dare? Did she even know how? *It might be guests for the party,* she thought, *calling on the wrong house.* She glanced at the clock; six hours early, so probably not party guests. She took a deep breath, prayed she was doing the right thing and went to open it. On the other side she was surprised to find Lawlis, his secretary, and two men she didn't recognise. She thought it odd that Mr Lawlis would bring a party to a party.

'Hello, Iris – just who I was hoping to meet. We need your help.' Lawlis stepped past her and into the hall. She closed the door behind them, wondering why they wanted her. Both men openly looked around the Armoury, but the younger man was absolutely enchanted with the ceiling. Iris smiled. It should have been rude, openly inspecting someone's house, but somehow, Iris found it endearing. Lawlis removed his hat and then introduced Mr Alistair Rutherford, from Cleaverings Auction House, and Mr Thomas Kettering, an art historian from London. They had been brought to Loch Down to evaluate the house, the paintings, and other decorative objects. It had all been arranged with Fergus and Mrs MacBain.

'How can I help?' asked Iris, looking from one man to the other, confused. Mr Rutherford had stepped over to a display of broadswords and was inspecting them closely.

'I wondered,' began Lawlis, 'if you would be so kind as to show Mr Kettering and Mr Rutherford around the house. Speed is of the essence, and we don't want the family to come back and find strangers wandering the halls.'

Iris realised she was not going to the party, and her heart sank.

'I understand you're off to a party and I must apologise for asking you to miss it, but I could really use your help,' Mr Kettering said, shyly.

He isn't terribly old, thought Iris – were they sure he was an expert?

He continued, staring at the floor, 'I understand it's rather a large house and having someone who knows the layout would help me greatly.'

He was rather kind, she thought, asking for her help. And she would get to spend the day looking at art instead of making small talk and avoiding the family. That was an even better day than a party, she realised. Smiling, she began to remove her hat.

'I'd be delighted to help. Let's start in the Reading Room. There's an inventory of the works that may help.'

She led the way, chattering excitedly to Kettering. Lawlis relaxed.

It was not until they were standing in front of the portrait of Lady Morag Inverkillen that things started to unravel. Iris had been anxious to ask about the discrepancy between the sketch and the actual painting, but she didn't want to interfere with Mr Kettering's work.

It's only a small question, she reasoned with herself, and he's been so nice to me. She felt sure it would be fine to ask. Which is how they found themselves standing in front of Lady Morag's portrait, discussing the finer points of historic tartans. Mr Kettering looked closely at both the portrait and the inventory and furrowed his brow. He studied it for some minutes and then finally stood back and shook his head.

'I can't be certain, not until we do some testing, but I think the painting may be a forgery. Well, not a forgery perhaps, but certainly not the original.' The others stared at him in confusion. 'It could have been overpainted after that sketch. One would hope they would have noted it, but I have heard that some people display a copy of the painting and keep the original in a vault or storeroom of some sort. In case of theft or fire. Perhaps that's the case here.'

Lawlis was instinctively sceptical. He turned to Iris to ask if she knew of any vaults in the house. She did not. The only vaults they had were the wine vaults, which were damp, and she thought there might be one in Lord Inverkillen's private study, but she had never been in the room so could not tell them how large it would be, or if it even existed.

'But this isn't a particularly valuable painting, is it?' asked Iris. 'Why would they have this one copied but not the Rubens in the Map Room?' They looked at her and, in unison, turned to look into the empty Map Room. 'It's far more valuable, isn't it? And smaller. It could easily be stolen, whereas this one . . .'

'Let's have a look at it, shall we?' suggested Mr Kettering.

Iris led them over to the reading snug. A rather beautiful reclining nude hung above the sofa, upon which the family dogs could be found snoring. Iris shooed them away so Mr Kettering could get a closer look.

After mere seconds, he shook his head and turned around. 'It's a copy. And not a very good one. Enough to convince casual viewers, I suppose, but not an expert. It's very strange. I don't see deception in these. Whoever painted them wasn't trying to create a forgery. They feel like hasty replacements. It's very curious.'

Iris moved to the desk and placed the art inventory on it, leafing through until she found the Rubens painting.

'"Portrait of a Girl", by Peter Paul Rubens, painted in the late 1630s, believed to be a portrait of his wife. No signature, authenticated in 1915 by Christies London. Oh yes, here's the certificate.'

'That is most assuredly not Rubens' wife.' Kettering crossed over to the desk to look at the book. 'What are these notes in pencil?' he asked, pointing to the margins.

'Oh!' Iris blushed furiously. 'Those are my notes. They're nothing, really. Just questions or observations I had. I can erase them.'

'"Arm and pillow different." Hmmm . . . Yes, I see what you mean.' He studied the sketch in the book closely and then looked back towards the painting. After a moment, he flipped through a few pages. 'You've made quite a study of these. Very detailed observations, too. I'm rather impressed.'

Iris blushed again. She was nearly purple, and Imogen worried she'd burst into tears, or worse, swoon. *Better rescue her before that,* she thought.

'Iris,' she began, 'is there another piece that you've really struggled to reconcile with the inventory? Or is it just these two?'

Iris thought for a moment and then slowly nodded. Yes, there was one that troubled her greatly. It was a hunting scene, but there was a dog missing in the one on the wall. They'd have to be quick. It was over the fireplace in Angus's rooms.

By half past six, they had finished the tour. Mr Kettering was in possession of the art inventory and a small portrait by Gainsborough that he wanted to have analysed. It was from one of the guest bedrooms and Iris knew it would not be missed. 'I'll have this back as quickly as I can. Here's my card, should you need to get in touch with me.' As he handed her the ivory calling card, their hands touched lightly. Iris felt herself blushing. Mr Kettering stuttered. 'You know, in case . . . in case, um . . . the family notices. I'd hate to get you into trouble.' He bowed and walked through the front door quickly. Imogen couldn't help but smile.

Lawlis said he would be in touch soon. When she closed the door behind them, Iris could still feel the warmth of Mr Kettering's hand. It was oddly thrilling.

'Ah, Mrs MacBain, there you are.' Elspeth came into the room and perched on the ottoman. 'I've been looking for you.'

Mrs MacBain leaned back on her heels. She was in the Library, building the fire for dinner. 'How was the party, milady?'

'The party? Oh, yes. Fine. Like all engagement parties, really; a lot of chatter about dresses and flowers. Quite boring, actually. I wanted a word with you before the family came in.'

'Yes, milady?'

'This Inspector – Jervy, Jarvey, was it?'

'Jarvis, ma'am. Roddy Jarvis.'

'Jarvis, yes. What kind of man is he?'

'What kind of man? I'm not sure what you mean, milady.'

'I rather got the impression he isn't the sharpest tool in the shed.'

Mrs MacBain couldn't help but smile slightly. 'No. That he is not.'

'It's just that I wondered if I should have told him about the fight between Hamish and Fergus. I didn't want him to get the wrong impression and so I said nothing. But now I wonder if I've done the right thing.' She was staring at Mrs MacBain with a slight frown.

'The argument in the Map Room? He knows about that, milady.'

'No, not that; the fight they had in the service yard later that afternoon.'

'What? I didn't know about that.' Why didn't I know about that? she wondered. Ah, I was dealing with Nanny just then. Poor Nanny.

'Tea finished early and I was in the Boot Room getting dressed when I heard shouting; something about a business plan. I looked out the door and saw Hamish and Fergus toe to toe. Fergus stormed off and I slipped out the kitchen door and didn't think anything of it. But when I was coming back, I heard shouting in the woods. I just presumed they were still at it. And I didn't say anything to the Inspector, because I wasn't near the weir, you see, so I'm not entirely certain that's where the sound was coming from.'

'Could you tell what was being said?'

'No, I was too far away for that. Do you think I should have told him? He just doesn't inspire confidence, does he? And I'd hate for him to get it wrong.'

'What is it you think the Inspector would get wrong?'

Elspeth started playing fretfully with her bracelet, avoiding Mrs MacBain's gaze. 'I can't say for certain where the shouting came from, or even who it was. It might have been Hamish, but it could just as easily have been the forestry team, or the gardeners. I just know I heard shouting, from somewhere in the woods. But if the Inspector put that together with the fight in the Map Room and the fight in the service yard . . . well, it could quickly go against Fergus.'

The women looked at one another seriously.

'But Fergus couldn't hurt a fly.' Elspeth looked anxious. 'He's too gentle a soul. Do you know, when he shot his first stag, he cried for days? Angus taunted him mercilessly. He was only eleven at the time, poor lamb. But he refused to stalk again for years afterwards. Hamish lost all respect for the boy, rather unfairly, I thought.' She paused and looked around the empty room. 'No, I can't see Fergus doing something like this and then casually carrying on as he's done.' She seemed to have reached a decision and stood up. 'I was right in not bringing it to the Inspector's attention. He would have muddled it together and got to the wrong conclusion. Thank you, Mrs MacBain, I appreciate your advice.'

Mrs MacBain watched her leave and turned back to the half-built fire, staring at it for several minutes. So, she was right: Hamish hadn't been alone at the weir. And he had rejected Fergus's plan, which had clearly upset the boy. That must be what they'd fought about in the Map Room. But then to have a fight in front of the staff . . . Fergus must have been more than angry. Where did he go after that row in the service yard? And how, she wondered, could she find out?

The doctor finally came the following day. He managed to get into and out of Drummond House and then over to Mrs MacBain's sitting room without anyone seeing him. It was not much of a feat, to be fair, given the family's general lack of interest in anything not related to themselves.

What he had found at Drummond House concerned him greatly. Eleven members of staff with the same fever, one after another, crammed together on camp beds in the attic. Of course none of them were recovering fully! It was cold and damp up there, and in no way suitable. You should have come when Lockridge told you about it, he chastised himself. He had chalked it up to hysteria. But now that he was examining them, it was painfully obvious that it was indeed that illness in the papers that they had all caught. But how? No one ever left the Abbey. Except for the ball when Nanny had come home sick. Damnit! How had he missed it? And how had those squawking hens in the village spotted it before he had. Nanny hadn't died of old age. His pride had blinded him.

Thankfully, Mrs MacBain never missed a trick. She'd had the foresight to isolate the infected people to the Dower House, but it was unsafe both for them and for Lady Georgina. The staff needed to be moved to better quarters, and Lady Georgina needed to be moved out of harm's way. No one, however, wanted to explain it to her.

'It's not my job to tell her what you've done!' The doctor

was aghast. There was no way he was going to risk the wrath of Lady Georgina.

'But you can't be sacked for it and we can!' cried Mrs Burnside, wishing she was holding something threatening, like a cleaver. She scowled at him instead. That generally worked on the footmen.

'But I didn't move them. You did. Rightly so, but it was your decision, so it should be yours to tell,' he insisted.

Lockridge stood in the doorway, blocking any escape the doctor might be contemplating. 'We're not even allowed to switch beds without getting permission from the family first. Do you honestly think taking over an entire floor is going to go well for any of us?' Shame he hadn't brought something menacing with him, like a tyre iron.

Mrs MacBain tried to appeal to his vanity. 'They respect you, Doctor. You have an authority we simply don't have. If you tell them, they might be annoyed but, frankly, they're annoyed at most things. They'll listen to you.'

'Be that as it may,' he said, and as he sat up a little straighter, Mrs MacBain could see flattery was the way forward, 'if it had been my decision – which it wasn't – I'd have moved them to the hospital, not the attics. How do I explain that away?'

'I sincerely doubt they'll work that one out,' muttered Mackay.

'Just don't give them a chance to ask questions. Give 'em the news, invent an emergency and bolt.' How hard could it be, wondered Mrs Burnside. The man had no backbone.

In the end, it was agreed that the doctor was to tell them. The staff agreed, at least. Hudson escorted the doctor, who was still protesting, into the Library. The family were surprised to see him but offered him tea.

'No thank you, I'm here in an official capacity,' he said,

shuffling slightly. 'I've just been over at the Dower House.'

'Were you? I must have missed you,' said Lady Georgina, amused at the thought.

'I was called to check back on Archie,' the doctor went on. The family stared at him blankly.

'Your footman. He was taken ill the night Nanny died.' He forged on. 'I'm afraid he's caught Virulent Pernicious Mauvaise.' They stared blankly at him again. 'That's the name of the disease that's been in the papers.'

'Oh my! That's rather a mouthful,' said Constance.

'Indeed. Couldn't they have shortened it?' asked Lady Georgina. 'Spanish Flu practically rolls off the tongue by comparison.' Several members of the family nodded in agreement.

The doctor drew breath to speak and then surrendered to his confusion for a moment. That was her concern? A catchy name? 'Yes, well . . . Your footman was moved to quarters in the attics of the Dower House, so that he couldn't infect the rest of the staff here at the Abbey. But now that other members of the staff have fallen ill, I think it might not have been soon enough.' He paused, and no one spoke. Had Bella just stifled a yawn?

'Now, the good news is, the staff members that do remain in this house are healthy. But this thing needs to run its course before it's safe to have your full staff again.' He gave them a moment for the news to sink in.

'What do you mean, full staff?' said Angus, his brow furrowed in confusion. 'I wasn't aware we were missing anyone.'

The doctor stared at him, incredulous. 'You're missing fifteen members of staff, my Lord. That's nearly half. Most of them are in the attics in the Dower House, but I gather four or five simply scarpered in the night. Had you really not noticed?' He could scarcely believe it.

'Wait a minute, Doctor,' interjected Lady Georgina, alarmed by the idea forming in her head. 'Do you mean to say my house is being used as some sort of convalescent home? With neither my knowledge nor my permission?'

The doctor could sense that they were in dangerous territory. Best cut her off now. 'It was at my request, Lady Georgina. The staff bedrooms and the Nursery in this house are on the same floor and I wanted to keep the infection as far from the children as I could. So, I asked for them to be isolated elsewhere.'

For once, Lady Georgina looked to be speechless, but she swiftly recovered. 'Well, they must be moved at once! Surely we have another house on the estate to put them in?' Lady Georgina looked to Angus first and then to Fergus. Neither spoke. Angus was lighting a cigarette, Fergus trying to absorb what the doctor was saying. 'Or the hospital?'

'I'm afraid we're out of beds, milady,' said the doctor. 'They've been over-run for several days now.'

'Perhaps we should move them back to the servants' quarters in the Abbey and seal off that floor of the house?' suggested Cecil, trying to be reasonable. 'We can move the children to the second floor of the East Wing. Would that do, Doctor?'

'It would be better to have them in their own beds, yes. But I'm quite anxious to separate you from the sick staff altogether.'

'What, you want the family to move to the Dower House?' asked Bella incredulously.

'I know it isn't ideal, but . . .' The doctor paused and held his hands up.

'Not ideal? All of us in the Dower House? We'd never fit,' cried Lady Georgina 'And even if it could be managed –

which it can't be – how would we even call for the servants? Hmmm? The bells don't work between the houses. Are we to telephone every time we need something?'

'If we keep the servants in Drummond House and move Mama here,' said Elspeth, hoping to find a reasonable solution, 'then they only need to walk over in the morning at their usual time.'

'No, you don't understand,' interrupted the doctor, trying hard to mask his growing impatience. 'You cannot be in contact with them at all if you hope to escape this infection. We don't know how it spreads, so the safest course of action is to isolate them in the Dower House until it's run its course.'

'What, and run the house with no servants!' Angus was appalled.

'Well, yes,' said the doctor reluctantly. 'If need be.'

It caused an uproar, as he had known it would.

The Ogilvy-Sinclairs do not live without servants. It is an affront to decency and the King himself. How would that even work? Am I to make my own breakfast tray each morning and then carry it to my bedroom? Do I look like the sort of woman who carries breakfast trays? What's the point of belonging to the aristocracy if one has no servants? I don't even know where the kitchens are. Do you?

It was a sickening cacophony of privilege. But he let them rage for a while – mentally escaping to his garden, deciding to plant golden beets that year – then finally raised his hands to quieten them down.

'Please, everyone, calm down. You will still have Mrs Burnside and I can assure you, she's quite healthy.' No one reacted, and he rolled his eyes. 'Mrs Burnside is your cook.'

'Oh, well that's something then,' said Lady Georgina. 'Who else can we keep?'

In the end, it was agreed that those the doctor deemed to be healthy would stay but they would wear masks and gloves while on the family floors. He would send some up from the surgery that afternoon. At the first sign of illness, they were to be removed to the Dower House.

There was only one more thing.

'Due to the nature of this illness, I must ask you not to leave the house and to strictly limit the people who visit. The fewer the better.' He braced himself for another onslaught.

None came.

What a strange family, he thought.

'So, we're to wait on all of them, nineteen of them with just the two of us?' asked Ollie, the last remaining footman. 'Crikey! How does that even work?'

'It doesn't work!' shouted Mrs Burnside. She was in a full-blown panic. 'I have no kitchen maids left and there is no way I can handle four meals a day for twenty people, plus the children's meals and the staff meals, without help. I'm only one person for goodness sake! And I can't even reach the top shelves in my pantry! That's what Maisie was for!'

'No one is happy about this,' said Hudson. 'We're all going to have to do a variety of strange jobs for now. Mr Lockridge, can you please help Mrs Burnside in the kitchen? I know you're a chauffeur, but with the Dowager here, you won't be driving her back and forth for some time and I dare say you can reach the top shelf.'

'I'd be happy to Mr Hudson.' Lockridge nodded quickly. 'I spent a fair amount of my childhood in my mother's kitchen.' Mrs Burnside looked unconvinced.

Mrs MacBain was pacing in the kitchen, trying to find a solution. She was quite unsure, muttering to herself. 'One footman and a butler are not enough to run things smoothly upstairs. Ollie and Maxwell will have to help lighting the morning fires. Oh! Maxwell, thank the Lord above. And we have Mackay going spare as well. This is starting to look possible.'

Maxwell and Mrs MacBain would have to dress the ladies after their breakfast trays. It would be busy, but they could do it. Luncheon and tea were never an issue since it was always just Hudson and a single footman. But dinner. Dinner presented a problem. Not to mention the laundry. And making up the beds. And, oh goodness, who would light the evening fires? Especially in the bedrooms? Mrs Burnside might have to appear upstairs, after all.

Bella took immediate exception to the masks and gloves the doctor sent to the house the following morning.

'What on earth are you wearing? You look like a nurse in a pantomime play.'

'It's what the doctor sent us, milady.' Mrs MacBain set down the breakfast tray and proceeded to open and dress the curtains as usual. The gloves were not difficult to get used to – she had worn them in service when she was a maid – but the mask was a bit claustrophobic. Still though, better safe than Nanny.

When she turned around to face the bed, Bella looked up from her letter and grimaced. 'No, that will never do. If you must wear it, at least make it look like part of the livery. And have it done for this evening. I simply won't be waited on at table by plague doctors.' She turned back to her letter, munching on her toast.

Mrs MacBain took a deep breath, made all the more difficult by the mask. Part of the livery? As if their jobs were not hard enough as it was. How on earth could they make it part of the livery? But she said that she would see what could be sorted. That was the upside to the masks, she realised; no one could see her jaw drop.

But Mackay was not daunted by the task; as a valet, he was used to sewing. He simply went to work harvesting material from the footmen's uniforms. Lord knows they had plenty going spare these days. He was a deft hand with a needle, thought Mrs MacBain, watching him as he worked. As much as she hated their livery – everyone did, so much tartan – it made excellent mask material. At the end of the day, he had fashioned everyone a dress mask to cover the surgery masks. He had even used the silver braid from the coats. It was a triumph. A viciously coloured triumph of Inverkillen tartan.

That night at dinner, Hudson, Ollie and Mackay appeared in the tartan masks. Bella merely nodded her approval, but Lady Georgina was quite complimentary.

'Oh, Hudson, how wonderful. I was concerned about the masks, I'll admit, but you've made them fit so well with the livery. I can't think why we haven't done this before. Well done,' and she raised her glass to the butler.

'Milady,' was all he said.

Fergus still weighed heavily on Mrs MacBain's mind. She couldn't work out how to ask him about his fight with Lord Inverkillen. No one in the staff remembered seeing him that afternoon, so as far as she knew he was without an alibi. Lady Elspeth was right about one thing: he was a gentle soul. But he had worked long and hard on that business proposal of his and she knew His Lordship well enough to know there would have been no sugar coating in his rejection of it.

And he'd lied to Jarvis, hadn't he? He told the Inspector he'd left Hamish in the Map Room with Angus and didn't know anything about the fishing. That didn't look good, she had to admit.

She turned devil's advocate on herself. Let's say, she thought, Fergus did go to the weir to continue the fight. Hamish sets his things down on the bank. Fergus arrives, they argue, Hamish ends up in the water. But it's too shallow to be swept away, so Fergus drags his father into the deeper water and then goes back to the house. But his clothes would have been soaked and no one mentioned that.

What if Hamish had been out on the weir when Fergus arrived? He falls in, and Fergus does what? Watched him drown? No, Fergus would have done something. He'd have tried to rescue him and, failing that, he'd have gone for help. But again, no one saw him in wet clothing.

Maybe it hadn't been Fergus at the weir at all; Lady Elspeth only presumed it was Fergus, she had no proof. It could have been anyone, she had said. But who? She needed to know where everyone was that afternoon.

Mrs MacBain went to find Hudson. He was in his pantry, muttering softly as he polished something silver. She knocked faintly at the door and stepped into the small room, closing the door behind her.

'Can I help you, Mrs MacBain?' the butler asked formally.

'Yes, Mr Hudson.' She hesitated, then asked lightly, 'When the family came back from the ball, who was at tea that afternoon?'

Mr Hudson stopped his polishing and looked to the house-keeper, perplexed. 'At tea? May I ask why?'

She groaned inwardly. She'd been hoping he wouldn't

ask. What could she say? I suspect one of the family murdered
His Lordship? Not exactly subtle.

'Something's been bothering me since that afternoon and
I just want to get it straight in my head. I don't know why,
but it's all I can think about it.' That sounded neutral enough.
She hoped.

Hudson slowly set the silver he was polishing down and
looked at Mrs MacBain intently. After the longest pause in
history, he spoke slowly.

'And because you think someone pushed His Lordship
in the river.'

They stared at one another for a moment. Either he was
shrewder than she'd given him credit for, or she was more
obvious than she'd have liked. But they were at this moment
now, so better an ally than an enemy.

'Yes,' she said quietly, sitting down.

'Is there someone in particular you feel we should be
watching?'

Mrs MacBain flushed slightly and looked down, point-
lessly straightening her skirt. 'No, I just wanted to know who
was there.' The butler was silent. 'And don't give me that
look!'

'What look?'

'The look you give the footmen when they've messed up.'
She paused. 'I just want to know where everyone was that
afternoon, for my own peace of mind.'

'All right, then.' He brought his fingers together under
his chin, as he tended to do when thinking. 'Bella, Angus,
Hugh and Lady Inverkillen arrived promptly. Then Iris
arrived, and Lady Georgina came late.'

'Did she come with Cecil?'

'No, but I gather he had a bath drawn for him.'

'He doesn't draw his own bath?' She was surprised.

Hudson gave her a look. She shook her head. 'No, of course he doesn't. Right. What about Fergus and Lady Elspeth? And Constance.'

'Ah, yes. Lady Elspeth was there. She came in with Lady Inverkillen, as I remember it. But neither Fergus nor Constance attended.'

'And the rest? Phillipe, Eva?'

'You can't think they'd have anything to do with this?' He was scandalised. 'Lady Eva hardly knew His Lordship.'

She forced a smile. 'No, of course not. But it helps to know where everyone was. Like chess pieces.' She stood and opened the door. 'Thank you, Mr Hudson.'

'Always a pleasure, Mrs MacBain.'

She walked slowly back to her room, lost in thought, tossing the family members around in her head. She didn't really believe that Hugh, Phillipe or Eva had been arguing with Hamish. Heavens above, Eva had only been here four or five days before it happened. No, it had to be a member of the family. But Fergus? She shuddered.

Then a thought occurred to her. How long did it take to get down to the weir and back, she wondered? Between tea and dressing for dinner, could someone else have slipped down and back? Glancing at her watch, she decided there might just be time to check, and went to put on her gumboots.

Later that day, the entire staff was summoned to move Lady Georgina from Drummond House. Finding rooms for her had proved tricky. Acceptable rooms, that is. The Abbey had been her home for nearly fifty years, and as the Countess she had always had the Stuart Suite. But she would not dream of displacing Lady Inverkillen while in mourning. Not that anyone had asked Lady Inverkillen about it; she had not yet re-emerged from her rooms.

Lady Georgina inspected all the rooms on the family floor and found none to be suitable. The idea of going to the second floor was simply out of the question, though. In the end, Fergus gave up his room, after a particularly loud shouting match between Bella and Constance. Bella refused to give up her bath and Constance refused to move to a lesser suite of rooms – she was the new Countess, for god's sake! If she moved rooms, it would be to the Stuart Suite. Once it was settled, Lady Georgina immediately started to remove the masculine furniture from the room. Lockridge and Ollie were tasked with bringing hers from Drummond House.

Fergus's dressing room was cleared, and she ordered both her dressing table and her jewellery box to be brought over. The jewellery box was a tall cabinet with forty shallow drawers, each marked with an engraved plate to identify the piece inside. Why she needed her entire jewellery collection, no one was quite sure. But it was installed nonetheless, and Lady Georgina demanded Maxwell be the one to pack and unpack this particular piece, insisting that only a lady's maid understood how to do it properly. But no one could find her, and Mrs MacBain had to step in and do it. On top of all this, Lady Georgina was starting to insist on having her own bed brought over.

Horrified, Mrs MacBain immediately set about changing her mind. She pointed out that Lady Georgina's bed had been built inside the bedchamber and was too large to remove without cutting it into pieces. After much discussion, Lady Georgina grudgingly accepted that Fergus's bed would have to do, but demanded that the tapestries be changed to something more feminine. Mrs MacBain nodded, happy with the compromise. Anything to avoid chopping up furniture.

But then Lady Georgina said she needed a study, and she insisted that nothing short of the Music Room would do. It was large enough for her to receive her visitors but not so grand that she would feel foolish. The fact that Lady Inverkillen used the Music Room in the afternoons was dismissed breezily by Lady Georgina: Women in mourning do not play the piano. And so, the Music Room was re-arranged to make room for her writing desk, a rather large and ornately carved piece she had inherited from her father. It looked ridiculous once installed in the airy, delicate room. They had to remove a sofa so the French doors could open. Lockridge had worried she would ask for the piano to be removed, but thankfully it didn't seem to occur to her.

Once it was all finally settled, Lady Georgina was surprised to find she was delighted to be back in the house. True, she was in a lesser suite of rooms, but she had re-assumed control of the household. Lady Inverkillen had never been much for schedules and Constance was barely able to arrange a napkin, let alone a grand household. It was Mrs MacBain who really ran the house these days. No, she thought, Loch Down needs a firm, aristocratic hand at the helm again. Angus needed discipline if he was to be successful. Seeing no choice in the matter, Lady Georgina seized control and re-instated the routine of her days as Countess, which was a relief to Mrs MacBain, who loved a good schedule.

Lady Georgina held court in the Music Room, promptly at nine o'clock each morning. On Tuesdays, she met with Mrs MacBain to discuss the menu for the week and other household matters. She met with the gamekeeper and the agent on Wednesdays to discuss plans for the Estate. On Thursdays she had her dress fitting and hair appointment. Fridays she met with Hudson. She used to reserve Saturday for touring her roses with her gardener, but now that she was back in the Abbey, she wondered that she'd be able to find the time. What a pity, she tutted. They were showing such promise this year and she could see the silver cup that was usually presented at the county show slipping out of her grasp. But needs must, and the Abbey needed her. The regime she had reinstated was one the staff knew well, and they defaulted to it without an objection. Not that Lady Georgina would have countenanced an objection from the servants, of course. But, in the staff's eyes, the regularity of Lady Georgina's ways made their jobs easier. Mrs MacBain was starting to understand how the house could be run efficiently with far fewer people, and it was somewhat of a revelation to her.

But Mrs Burnside was struggling. It was not just the volume of food she was expected to produce with only Lockridge to help, but she was also having difficulties getting hold of the food to begin with. Stock was being delivered sporadically and the greengrocer was always running short of items; potatoes and sugar one week, flour and butter the following week. They never knew what would be missing from the deliveries. The staff dinners were easy enough to cobble together but the elaborate menus the family expected were becoming tricky. Short of churning her own butter, Mrs Burnside said, they would run out in two weeks' time. What then? Did they expect her to start milling flour?

Mrs MacBain broached the issue gently with Lady Georgina, who reacted rather more reasonably than she had expected.

'Tell Cook to take out the cookbooks from the rationing days. I daresay we still have them. She can figure something out from there. We had so little during the war, but you wouldn't have known it. Standards must be upheld. This house has lived through rebellions, famine and invasion. We survived the English, for heaven's sake. We will not give in to this.' She tutted. 'Tell Cook to make whatever adjustments she deems necessary based on availability. The foods might have to change but we still expect things to be done properly.'

Mrs MacBain was speechless. Mrs Burnside was speechless when it was recounted to her in the kitchen moments later. It was an eminently sensible thing to do, letting Mrs Burnside set the menus based on foods she could buy. Sensible, but somehow radical.

With all the commotion of the previous few days, Mrs MacBain had quite forgotten the fishing basket with the drawing supplies. As she opened the cupboard in the search for something else entirely, the basket full of pencils spilled out. She studied it as she put it back together. Someone in the house had been at the weir with Hamish. Of that, she was convinced. But who? Her trip to the weir and back had proved that any one of them could have slipped out after tea and been back in time for dinner. But it was such an unlikely bunch to begin with, and really, only Lady Elspeth and Lady Inverkillen ever walked out after tea.

Mrs MacBain wondered if anyone in the family knew about Lady Elspeth and Ross. The Ogilvy-Sinclairs weren't the most observant of individuals, true, but those children looked nothing like Philippe. Supposing Hamish knew. Why say something to Elspeth now? Maybe he had just found out? How, though? And why meet at the weir? Surely, he'd have gone to confront Ross at his cottage. And Elspeth – well, there were any number of rooms in the house to have that discussion in private. Could her story about hearing shouting at the weir have been a cover-up? She needed to speak to Mrs Burnside about it. Elspeth had said she'd gone through the kitchen door. If she had, Mrs Burnside, or someone on the kitchen staff would have also heard the fight in the service yard.

She found Mrs Burnside in the cold pantry, checking in the grocery delivery. 'When you finish, can we have a private word?'

'Of course. Give me ten minutes to finish this.' Mrs Burnside pointed at the crates on the floor of the Pantry. 'The dogs will get it otherwise.'

'I'll be in my office.' But Mrs MacBain walked to the kitchen door instead. She stepped out into the drive and walked around the grocery van. A path into the woods was opposite the door. Mrs MacBain turned right and walked to the edge of the house and into the service yard. It was such a public place to have a row. She continued to the door to the Boot Room and stood on the threshold, trying to visualise the scene Lady Elspeth had painted for her. There simply wasn't a way to leave the Boot Room and get into the woods without being seen in the yard. And she knew from long experience that any noise in the yard could be heard in the kitchen. If there had been a fight that day, Mrs Burnside would know. She turned and walked back to her office to wait with a mounting sense of anticipation.

Mrs Burnside came carrying a tray. 'Thought we'd have some tea while we chat. They put in some new biscuits from a bakery out of Glasgow, Tunnocks. Wants to know what we think of 'em.' She set the tray on the desk as Mrs MacBain closed the door.

'Oh, that's too kind. Thank them for me.'

They settled into the chairs, tea in hand, biscuits between them.

'So, what's on your mind?' asked the cook.

'It's just something I heard the other day and wondered if you knew anything about it. Apparently, Fergus and Hamish had quite a row in the service yard the day His Lordship died. Did you hear anything?'

The question clearly surprised the cook. 'Who didn't? The way they were carrying on, the village most likely heard it.'

Mrs MacBain felt her pulse quicken. 'What happened?'

'Well, from what I gather, Fergus was angry about the Distillery being sold and Hamish was tired of hearing about it. Something about his plan being ruined and the Estate losing money. I didn't like to listen, but you know how it echoes in the yard.' Mrs MacBain nodded. 'Luckily, it was just me and Sadie in the kitchens.'

'How did the fight end?'

'Oh, like they always do: name-calling and someone storming off in a huff.'

'Who stormed off?'

The question seemed to throw the cook. 'Um, not sure. Lady Elspeth would know. She came through the kitchen just then, dressed for her evening walk. What's this all about?'

Mrs MacBain didn't answer. She was staring into the fire, worried concentration etched across her face.

'Oh, you're wondering if Fergus went and pushed his father into the river,' said Mrs Burnside casually. Mrs MacBain looked up, startled. 'Thought so. You can stop worrying. He came through the kitchen door about ten minutes later and I fed him a cup of tea and a sausage roll. He apologised all over himself for the commotion.'

Mrs MacBain breathed in sharply. 'Did he say where he'd been?'

'I gather he was doing some angry wood-chopping. Ollie said the woodshed was a mess, shards everywhere.'

A shaky sigh of relief escaped Mrs MacBain's lips. 'Angry wood-chopping. Thank the Lord above for that.' She smiled and helped herself to a biscuit. 'Not that we'd ever order in cakes . . .'

Chewing thoughtfully, Mrs Burnside said, 'My mother would have described these as moreish.'

'Yes, they're quite good, aren't they?' They munched in silence for some moments.

Mrs Burnside eyed the housekeeper carefully. 'Do you really believe someone shoved him in the river?'

Mrs MacBain shook her head slowly. 'I really don't know. I just know that something isn't right about the whole situation. And we can't exactly rely on Roddy Jarvis to sort it out.' The women grimaced. 'Forget I said anything. I should let sleeping dogs lie.'

When she was alone again, Mrs MacBain contemplated the cook's question: did she really believe someone in the house killed His Lordship? Accident or intentional, someone had been at the river with him; of that she was convinced. But who that person was, she wasn't sure.

Angus? The Distillery was part of his inheritance and Lord Inverkillen had sold it without telling the boys. Not that Angus seemed to care much for the Estate. The title, she felt, was important to him, and the money, but the responsibility of the Estate, the house, the businesses . . . They could barely get him out of the Tennis Pavilion for the few responsibilities he already had. No, Angus wouldn't have rushed into that. Lady Constance, however; that was another story. She desperately wanted to be the Countess and to run her own household. She easily could have gone down to the weir and been back before dinner. Not that Mrs MacBain had ever seen Lady Constance out of doors.

Her mind drifted to Lady Inverkillen. She walked out

frequently and could easily have been down to the river and back before Maxwell drew her bath. But why would she kill her husband? What did she have to gain by his death? Nothing that Mrs MacBain could see. Lady Inverkillen would be dependent on Angus to house her, in the Abbey or somewhere on the Estate, and he would control her allowance. No one would be in a hurry for that life. But why now? Why not last year, or six months ago? What could have changed that would spur her to action? Mrs MacBain wondered if something had happened at the ball that no one had mentioned. It was certainly possible.

A loud crash from the kitchen brought her back to reality. Oh, whatever now? she thought irritably, and headed into the kitchen.

The following week, Mrs MacBain met with Lady Georgina to check that the meals had been acceptable. Mrs Burnside had had a much easier week, being allowed to change the menus as needed. Lady Georgina was delighted, and Mrs MacBain breathed a sigh of relief. At least one thing is going well, she thought.

She was on her way back to the staff stairs when she noticed the door to the Map Room was ajar. She was just reaching for the handle to close it when Cecil stepped through, nearly knocking her over with the door. He roughly apologised and strode off, one hand on his forehead. She glanced in, expecting to see Fergus, who generally worked there in the afternoons, but to her surprise, it was empty.

What was Cecil doing in the Map Room, she wondered? That man rummaged around the house a lot, but she'd never run across him in the Map Room before. She stepped across the threshold and surveyed the room. The dogs were snoring on the sofa. The main desk looked tidy, as always. She glanced at the sofa in the snug; the throw cushions were in total disarray. She'd fluffed and tidied them herself about an hour ago. Tutting, she went to straighten them. When she'd finished, she noticed a smudged handprint on one of the shelves. He must have been fussing with the books. Mrs MacBain growled softly. There was no reason for that amount of dust. She shook her head, trying to recall which maid was last assigned this room. Unable to remember, she resolved to speak to all of them. When they recovered, that was. A sudden sadness ran through her.

Shaking free of sentiment, she fished in her pockets for her handkerchief, thinking it best she dealt with the dust now, before anyone in the family saw it. Stepping behind the end table to reach the corner of the shelf, she noticed a piece of writing paper behind the sofa. So that's what Cecil had been doing. He'd been reaching for the letter.

She reached for it and banged her head painfully on the bookshelf, and swore softly. She crouched down, carefully this time, and reached in with her arm. The sofa really needed to move just an inch to the left. She walked to the other side, moved the end table slightly, and pulled on the sofa. Her back objected loudly. How can a sofa be this heavy? she wondered. Restoring the table, and noting the dust on the floor, she moved to the right and tried to shove the sofa. It didn't budge. No wonder Cecil had left in such a mood. Looking around the room, she seized upon the fire poker and retrieved it. The dogs woke, looking hopeful for a treat or a walk, and followed Mrs MacBain back to the sofa. Poker in hand, she fished out the letter. She was about to read it when Fergus burst in the room. She instinctively shoved the letter in her pocket and hid the poker in her skirts.

'Oh, Mrs MacBain!' Fergus had started and had his hand over his heart. 'I didn't realise you were in here.'

'My apologies, sir. I was just coming in to tidy up a bit.'

Fergus continued reading the letter in his hand as he walked to the desk. He made no reaction when he reached it, so clearly Cecil hadn't disturbed anything there. Mrs MacBain walked to the fireplace. She reached up and nosily straightened a photo on the mantle as she carefully replaced the poker. 'I'll come back later, sir.' He absentmindedly waved a hand.

As she closed the door behind her, Mrs MacBain took a deep breath and looked up at Lady Morag's portrait. 'That was close,' she whispered. Lady Morag seemed to smile back.

Safely back in her office, with the door firmly shut behind her, Mrs MacBain looked at the letter. There was no date, and it was unaddressed, but it was unmistakably Lord Inverkillen's writing. She sat in her desk chair and read the black script.

I know about the affair, and it must end.

Mrs MacBain's heart nearly stopped.

I do not know when it began, or why, nor do I care. But it must stop. A dalliance, I could accept. But an out-and-out love affair is intolerable, most especially between a Lady and a servant. I am unsure whose betrayal hurts more, yours or his, but I will put it away to insure against scandal and humiliation for the family. You will end it immediately and he is never to set foot in Loch Down again.

Mrs MacBain dropped her hand heavily into her lap, the letter falling softly to the floor. *Oh lord, Ross, what have you done?*

With the family firmly seated at dinner, Mrs MacBain walked slowly through the woods to the gamekeeper's cottage. She needed to speak to Ross about the letter but wasn't quite sure yet what to say. She'd spent all afternoon replaying the day of His Lordship's death in her head, trying to remember where both Ross and Lady Elspeth had been. She simply hadn't seen her cousin that day, which wasn't unusual. But it did mean he could have met His Lordship, which pained her. She struggled to reconcile Ross and murder. He just wasn't that sort of person.

And what do you know of murderers, Alice MacBain? Only what she read in novels.

But Lady Elspeth didn't seem the right sort either. Yes, she walked in the woods each evening so muddy clothing wouldn't have raised any questions. But what about her story that she heard voices at the weir? If it was true, it could have been Ross arguing with him. If it was a lie, it could have been Elspeth. Or both of them. There was no way to know.

She replayed the scene in her mind, first with Elspeth, and then with Ross. An argument, a struggle, and then a splash. All that was perfectly logical. But leaving him to drown? That was where her disbelief was rooted. Someone had done exactly that, though. And with this letter, that someone might have been her cousin.

This damn letter! She would never have suspected Ross until this letter. It was the only thing that put him in the firing line. If it didn't exist there would be no motive. She could destroy it and no one would be the wiser. But then Cecil popped back into her mind. She groaned inwardly. Had he read the letter? If he had, did he understand? Cecil could have dropped it before he'd had a chance to read it. But could she risk it? How many people know about Ross and Lady Elspeth, she wondered? She needed to clear Ross.

The cottage came into view and she could see Ross chopping wood. She still had no idea what she was going to say. It wasn't normal to ask your cousin if he'd killed someone. Taking a deep breath, Mrs MacBain stepped into the clearing and called to him.

Ross turned, mid-swing, and lowered the axe. 'Alice. What are you doing here?' He was surprised to see her. It was quite a long walk from the house and she rarely had the time to spare. But here she was in the twilight, looking worried.

'I wanted a word. Are you busy?'

Ross set the axe on the ground, leaning against the wood store. 'Nah, this can wait till tomorrow.' He grabbed his shirt and put it on as he walked to the front door. 'I'll put the kettle on.'

Ross's cottage was more of a bothy than an actual cottage. It was a low stone building with only two windows, one each side of the timber door. She hadn't been here in years and was amazed how small it was; just a front room with a fireplace and make-shift kitchen and a bunkroom to the left with a timber door that she presumed led to a privy or bathroom of some sort. It wasn't much, but Ross never seemed to need much. He settled her into a chair near the fire and put the kettle on. When the tea was ready, they sat facing one another.

'Now, what's happened to bring you all the way out here?' Ross tried to keep his tone light, but the look on his cousin's face told him this was a very serious matter.

She took a deep breath and fished the letter out of her pocket. 'I need you to tell me the truth, Ross.'

'Why would I lie to you?' Ross asked, taken aback by her grave tone.

'I found this in the house this afternoon and it needs explaining.' She handed it to him but held on to it for a moment when he reached out. He read it quickly, no reaction on his face. Looking back up to her, he cocked his head to one side and asked, 'Where did you find this?' He now looked guarded.

'It was in the Map Room, behind one of the sofas.' She looked at her cousin closely. 'It's from Hamish, isn't it? Did you know about it?'

Ross hesitated and then nodded once, sharply.

'How long had he known? The letter isn't dated.'

Ross stared at his cousin for some moments and then read the letter again. When he finished, he stood and leaned against the mantle, staring down into the fire. What was he thinking, she wondered?

'Ross, if Jarvis had got his hands on this letter—'

'But he didn't.'

'But he could have.'

'But he didn't, Alice.'

'Only because I came along when I did. Otherwise, it would be in Cecil's hands.' Ross stared at her, clearly disturbed by the idea. 'I don't know if he read it or not before it fell out of reach. I do know he tried to retrieve it, so he knows it exists.'

'He can't do anything about it. It's not dated, and it doesn't have names on it.'

'He could blackmail you. Or hand it over to Jarvis. Lord knows, if Jarvis got his hands on this letter, he'd jump to the easiest conclusion.'

'And what is the easiest conclusion?' he asked, smirking slightly.

Leave it to Ross to not take this seriously. 'That you and/ or Lady Elspeth shoved Lord Inverkillen into the river!'

'You can't think either of us would do something like that! Seriously, you can't think that. You found a letter behind a sofa. It means nothing.'

'It means motive, Ross. This letter gives you, and Lady Elspeth, a powerful motive for murder. Even if his death was an accident, it won't matter much, because this letter paints you in a terrible light.'

'Except that letter isn't about me.' He said it quietly, but it was enough to take the wind out of her sails. Mrs MacBain opened her mouth several times to speak but nothing came out. 'I can't believe we're having this conversation. Alice, I told you to leave it alone. This is a can of worms, but not the worms you think.'

'Then explain it to me. Because, at the moment—'

'At the moment you have an undated letter with no names on it and you've jumped to the easy conclusion! God, you're just as bad as Jarvis.' Ross paced the room, clearly irritated. 'Do you honestly believe I'd hurt him? He was my best mate. I loved him like a brother.' He stalked into to the kitchen, grabbed two glasses and a bottle of whisky, slamming the cupboard door behind him.

It was only then that she realised he was angry. *What did you expect, Alice?* You've just accused him of murder, she chastised herself and watched him carefully as he returned.

He set the glasses and whisky down on the tea tray, poured himself a large dram and leaned one arm across the mantle, kicking a log on the fire in brooding silence. At long last he said, 'This never leaves the room, you understand me?' He looked at her sternly until she at last nodded. 'The letter isn't about me because Hamish has always known about us.'

'What?' Mrs MacBain was shocked. 'What do you mean "always"? How did he find out?' Her questions came out like bullets.

Ross cut her off in the middle of her questions. 'Take a breath, Alice, and stop interrupting.' He stoked the fire a moment or two, waiting for her to settle. 'He's always known. You don't carry on with your best mate's sister behind his back. It's just not done.' He took a slow sip and continued. 'I didn't want Elspeth sneaking around and lying to her brother, so I went to Hamish and asked his permission, which he gave.'

'When was this?'

'She was nineteen and just back from her year in Paris.'

Mrs MacBain was stunned. 'He's known from the very beginning?'

Ross nodded and kicked the fire again.

Mrs MacBain was confused and took a moment to think. 'Then what's this letter to Lady Elspeth?'

'Hamish wasn't writing to Elspeth.' Ross took a deep breath and slowly exhaled. 'He was writing to Lady Inverkillen.'

Cecil suggested bridge after dinner. With the family in one room, he could easily slip out when he was dummy and get into the Map Room. He wanted to see that letter. All he had seen, before it dropped from him hands, was his brother's writing. And if Cecil was going to find a copy of an earlier will, he needed to find it sooner rather than later. He'd been searching for weeks.

Letting himself into the Map Room, Cecil went quickly to the sofa and switched on the lamp. The family dogs raised their heads and then immediately went back to sleep, knowing from long experience that Cecil never meant walks or treats. Peering behind the sofa, he found nothing. Damnit! Mrs MacBain must have found it. The woman is too efficient for her own good. He was running out of places to look. His brother had been fickle in his tendencies and Cecil had no doubts, but equally no proof, that a previous will existed. Somewhere. He just needed to find it, change the date, and draw on the dubious but considerable skill he had for forging his brother's signature. Of course, he still needed to locate Hamish's seal, but one step at a time. He moved to the desk and started to search the drawers.

Nothing. Nothing. Nothing. Hello! That was a pretty letter opener. He turned it over and saw the smith's hallmark. Silver, quite nice; Georgian, Cecil supposed. Slipping it into his jacket pocket, he closed the drawer and looked up. The painting over the sofa caught his eye. Instinctively, he moved towards it. Cecil was just reaching for the frame when the door opened, and a startled footman stared at Cecil.

'My apologies, Major. I saw the light on and presumed it was a mistake.' He bowed and hurried from the room. Cecil slumped onto the arm of the sofa and breathed a heavy sigh of relief. The pointer raised his head and stared reproachfully at Cecil.

'Yes all right! I'll go,' he said to the dog. 'But I'll be back, you little fleabags.'

Walking back to the Drawing Room all Cecil could think of was the painting. There had to be something on the back of it. It was the last place he could think of.

Mrs MacBain was beyond speechless. She gaped at her cousin, who poured her a dram and held it out to her. She reached for it, but he kept hold of it. 'Remember, it doesn't leave this room.' After some moments, she nodded, and he let go of the glass. She took a long sip and waited to hear what her cousin had to say.

'It all happened long before you arrived at Loch Down. Hamish and Victoria were strangers when they married. And when they did meet, they didn't really get on well. I never understood it; she was a lot of fun in the beginning.' He noted the surprise on Mrs MacBain's face. 'Really. She was lively and chatty, always laughing. Hamish just never took to her. But they did their duty, produced the heirs and then, basically lived separate lives. Except, she didn't have much of a life here. Her set back in England, well, they were very social. They rode and hunted, went to balls and had house parties. She expected that same life here.' He paused and poured more whisky. 'Didn't get it, obviously. Lady Georgina refused to surrender the house to her, and Hamish – well, Hamish spent all his time in his study, or on the Estate with me. So Victoria had nothing to do, which is how she met Garvey.'

'Wait,' Mrs MacBain said, shaking her head, 'Old Garvey? Who tends Lady Georgina's roses?' She couldn't believe that; the man looked like a gnome.

'His brother, actually. Not as gnarled. After they shipped Angus and Fergus off to boarding school, Victoria decided she wanted to cultivate exotic flowers, and someone recommended Garvey to build the Glasshouse for her. They spent a lot of time together; she was unhappy and lonely. In hindsight, it was inevitable. Eventually, Hamish found out about the affair; he was surprised but not bothered.' A confused look swept across Mrs MacBain's face. Ross noticed it. 'I think he assumed it would fizzle out when the Glasshouse was finished. It was only supposed to take a few months, but then Victoria announced Garvey was staying on permanently, so Hamish knew it wasn't just a fling. He never expected love from Victoria, but a full-blown love affair, with a servant, that sent him over the edge.'

Mrs MacBain started to object. 'But you and Lady Elspeth . . .'

Ross held up a finger. 'Ah, but Elspeth wasn't married, so it was different. That letter,' he gestured to her hand, 'was an early draft. There were several. When Victoria got the final letter, it changed her, overnight. Two days later, Garvey left and was replaced by his brother, and Victoria became a hollow shell of herself. I've never seen anything like it. It just emptied her.'

He set his glass on the mantle and went to fetch more logs for the fire, leaving Mrs MacBain to digest all that she'd been told. Lady Inverkillen had been lively and chatty. Would wonders never cease? She'd only ever known Lady Inverkillen as a vacant, almost ghost-like creature. She took a big gulp of her whisky and stared into the fire, relieved that any motive for Ross had disappeared. But oh, poor Lady Inverkillen!

Ross entered the tiny house and threw the log on the fire and poked it into the perfect location. Sitting down, he looked at his cousin for a moment and then asked, 'Any other ghosts you'd like to raise this evening? Or maybe you'd like to accuse me of something else? I seem to be lacking in all sorts of moral fibre in your eyes.'

Mrs MacBain sighed and shook her head mournfully. 'Oh, Ross! I'm so sorry. I read the letter and was so worried for you, I just . . . I just . . . failed to think. Can you ever forgive me?'

Ross plucked the letter from her hands and tossed it on the fire. 'Finish your whisky. I'll walk you back up to the house. I don't fancy your chances in the dark with those skirts.' He nodded to her uniform. Thankfully for her, Ross was a man who refused to hold a grudge.

June

Mrs. MacBain couldn't get the story of Lady Inverkillen out of her mind. It was a tragedy, in a way. Lady Inverkillen sitting in the Glasshouse her lover had built her, cultivating flowers and watching life pass her by. Like Miss Havisham. She had no duties to keep her occupied; no entertaining, no people to stay. She didn't head any committees or charities because Lady Georgina was already head of them. She didn't run the household because Lady Georgina constantly interfered and changed things. She couldn't even set the weekly menus because Lady Georgina would then send changes from Drummond House. Thinking about it, it was something of a wonder Lady Georgina hadn't been pushed into the river.

But why would Lady Inverkillen choose now to act? The timing of it all didn't sit right with her. Why now and not last year, or ten years ago? What could have angered her so much that she pushed her husband into the river? Short of bursting into Lady Inverkillen's rooms and demanding answers – a sure way to lose her position – she was at a dead end.

Which was how she found herself in the Distillery having a dram with Old MacTavish one evening. If something happened in the woods, he always knew about it. But maddeningly, he was refusing to answer her questions. She'd had three drams of his whisky already; her mouth tasted of wet dog and her head was starting to swim.

Had he seen His Lordship at the weir? 'Ay, seen him lots

of times. Boy was a terrible fisherman, too impatient, always used the wrong lures.' That had been a ten-minute lecture on lures.

Had he been alone that day? 'Never good to be at the river alone, the current is swift, especially this year. The runoff from the hills is particularly fierce.' Then another fifteen minutes on how the water levels were falling each year and impacting the taste of the peat for the whisky.

She was getting nowhere but drunk.

'Mr MacTavish, with respect; I know he was with someone at the river that day. I don't know who, or why they've never come forward, but you clearly do.' She sighed. 'If it was an accident, then there is nothing to fear.'

He stared at her for some time. 'It's not my story to tell. It's late. You should be getting back.' He helped her to her feet and escorted her to the door. 'The poor creature's been through enough. Let her grieve in peace.' He shut the door quietly.

Let who grieve in peace? she wondered as she wove her way back to the Abbey. Well, at least one thing was clear: he hadn't been alone.

As often happens when there is ample whisky in the evening, the next morning is chaos. Miss Maxwell was late with the breakfast trays, again. The dogs got loose and ate an entire batch of sausages. Ollie tripped going up the stairs and sent scrambled eggs flying everywhere. It took some effort to quell the mayhem and Mrs MacBain's head was having none of it. When relative calm was restored, she retreated to her office for a moment of quiet.

Whisky with Old MacTavish. What a mistake! She wished she'd said no to the last dram. Actually, saying no to the first dram would have been wiser. The taste wouldn't leave her mouth.

Let her grieve in peace, he had said, but who was she? Lady Georgina? Lady Inverkillen? Constance? Bella? Eva? Lady Elspeth? Iris? There was no shortage of women in the family, that much was certain. But really, Lady Georgina at the weir, pushing her son into the water? It was laughable. And she gained nothing by his death. Although she would be in charge of the Estate. Angus wouldn't stand in her way. But did she want that power badly enough to kill her son?

She sighed, and it hurt her head. Hudson walked by her open door. Maybe the butler did it, she thought wryly. Didn't they always do it in novels? She rooted through her desk drawer until she found a packet of Beecham's headache power. She poured herself a glass of water, stirred it in and then crossed to shut the door. Settling into her armchair, she sipped the bitter water and mulled over the women in the family.

Iris was a laughable suspect, as was Eva. But after learning about Lady Inverkillen, she again wondered if something had happened at the ball to spur her into taking action. Had her resentment lingered all these years? Spending all day, every day in the Glasshouse your lover built for you; yes, perhaps. Replaying the day in her mind, she hadn't really noticed Lady Inverkillen acting any differently. If she'd been upset, upset enough to kill her husband, she had hidden it well.

Then there was Bella. She and her father didn't get on well, everyone knew that. But to kill your father because he won't give you a maid? Even for Bella, that was a stretch. Although, with Eva on the scene, she would be further down in the pecking order and her contempt for Eva was plainly obvious. Bella had never been able to win against her father; but she could easily steamroll over Angus to get a maid, and then she could go back to doing . . . whatever it was Bella did all day.

No, it was definitely a race between Lady Inverkillen and Constance. But she wasn't quite sold on either of their motives. Lady Constance wanted to be the Countess and killed her father-in-law for it? Or Lady Inverkillen finally got revenge for having her lover sent away thirty-odd years ago? Could Lady Inverkillen even push His Lordship? He was a large man, very solidly built, and she was, well, she was a feather. But the weir was slippery, and if she'd caught him off his guard . . .

A knock at the door interrupted her thoughts. It was Ollie, the footman. The dogs had chewed one of the pillows in the Map Room and there were feathers everywhere. Oh, and Mrs Burnside needed her in the jam larder.

She nodded and got to her feet wearily. No rest for the wicked.

Lawlis, Imogen and Mr Kettering rang the bell at the front entrance and were disturbed to be greeted by Hudson in his new tartan mask. They politely said nothing but staring couldn't be avoided. As they were putting on the surgery masks and gloves Hudson offered them, Iris entered the Armoury on her way to the Library. She had been studying the Rubens painting again and wanted to see if they had anything else on him, since Mr Kettering had her notes. Seeing him walk into the house again sent a warm chill up her spine, and she was a bit appalled at her delight in seeing him again.

'Ah, Iris, well met,' said Lawlis, crossing past Hudson and gesturing towards the Library. 'I wonder if you might join us as well. If you're free, that is.'

'Join you?' she asked, confused. Mr Kettering moved from behind Imogen and Iris could see he'd brought the book and the painting back. Iris did some quick thinking. Unannounced visits irritated Hudson beyond measure, but he looked perfectly at ease. They had been expected, then. Oh dear, was she in trouble? Has the family noticed the missing items? Her heart pounded.

'Um . . . I'd be delighted,' she finally said, trying to sound far more confident than she felt.

Hudson ushered them into the Library, where Fergus was waiting. Iris tried not to panic but she could feel the blood rushing to her face. The men shook hands.

Fergus looked quizzically at Iris. 'Can you come back a bit later, please, Iris? We're having a meeting just now.'

'I've asked her to be here actually,' Lawlis said politely.

'Oh, how curious. Well then, better have a seat, Iris.' He ushered her to the sofa and then sat down beside her. 'Now, how can I help you, Andrew?'

It feels strange to be sitting on the sofa instead of in the window seat, thought Iris. I've never noticed that bust above the door before. She felt her attention wandering from the conversation and decided to stand in her usual place instead. Less distraction. Her eyes flicked to Mr Kettering.

Lawlis explained they had come to visit the house with Mr Kettering during the engagement party, and that Iris had been an excellent guide. Fergus turned to her, clearly surprised, but he smiled at her.

'Yes, you are perfect for that job, aren't you? Always studying the pictures.' It was only slightly patronising, and Iris managed a faint smile.

Mr Kettering spoke up. 'Iris very kindly loaned me these two items. I wanted to study them a bit more carefully. My apologies for keeping them for some weeks, but I wanted to be absolutely thorough.' He turned to her. 'This book is fascinating and your observations, Iris, were quite helpful.'

Again, Fergus turned to Iris, puzzled but amused. Iris blushed and looked at the floor.

Kettering cleared his throat softly and continued to address her. 'The painting is, as we suspected, a fake. And I dare say many of the paintings you've made comments on are also fakes.' Turning to Fergus, he said, 'Of course, we need to verify that with each canvas, which will take some time, and I gather we don't have that luxury. I wondered if, perhaps, you could tell me where the actual canvases are stored?'

Fergus barely registered the question. He hadn't got past the word fake. 'That can't be right. The Gainsborough has been in the family for generations.' He pointed to the canvas.

'That may be true,' said Kettering carefully, 'but this canvas is not by Gainsborough. I believe it's been done in the last twenty years. We wondered if it had been a replacement and the original canvas stored somewhere in the house?'

Fergus tried to digest the news. If this was fake, and others were fakes, the entire collection would be worthless. If it were worthless, they really would have to sell the Abbey. He let out a stuttering breath.

Taking pity on him, Imogen stepped in. 'There's no need for panic just yet. It might just be this one canvas. And the Rubens in the Map Room.'

'The Rubens?' Fergus gasped.

Imogen thought he might hyperventilate. 'These days, it's rather commonplace to store the original and display a copy. It doesn't mean all is lost,' she said gently, placing a hand on his knee. 'Do you know of anywhere in the house that someone might have stored the canvases?'

Fergus looked from her hand to her face, not really seeing her. He thought for a moment.

'Erm . . . We could check my father's study. I believe there's a rather large safe in there. I've never been in the room, so I can't say for certain. We could ask Mama. How many of the others do you suspect are fakes?'

Before Mr Kettering could respond, the doors burst open and Lady Georgina swept into the room. She sized the group up quickly, taken aback by the masks. With some difficulty, she turned her attention to Iris, who was standing by the desk. 'Oh, there you are, Iris. The children have broken into one of the larders and stolen tonight's pudding. Cook is livid. It shouldn't be difficult to find them; apparently they've left a trail of half empty jam jars all over the gardens.' She looked at her, clearly expecting Iris to leap into action and give chase.

'Actually, Grandmama, I asked her to be in this meeting,' Fergus said, getting to his feet.

'Meeting? How formal.' Lady Georgina considered the group on the sofas, and largely forgot Iris and the children. 'And who might you be?' she asked Kettering, a touch rudely, crossing the room towards them. Imogen had the distinct feeling that Kettering was being sized up as prey.

Mr Kettering got to his feet, bowed his head, and introduced himself.

'Yes. Well,' she said distractedly. Turning to Fergus and Lawlis, she asked, 'And why is he here?'

Imogen looked at her closely. Lady Georgina was clearly not happy, and she was struggling to conceal it. We're in dangerous territory, Imogen thought, but why? Surely Fergus was allowed to meet people in his own home? But looking to Lady Georgina again, she realised it wasn't Fergus's home at all – not in the Dowager's eyes, at any rate.

Lawlis and Fergus looked at each other, each unsure who would be best placed to explain. Fergus finally decided to speak. Blunt truth would be the best course of action, he felt. Grandmama was looking a bit angry.

'I asked Lawlis to have the artworks appraised and he sent

Mr Kettering to us. I was hoping we might have enough value in the collection to pay the death duties, rather than put the house or the Estate on the block.'

Lady Georgina looked decidedly uneasy. 'You really should have come to me first, Fergus.'

'It was the accountant's idea, a jolly good one, I thought. Quite frankly, I'd rather live with bare walls than no walls. It couldn't hurt to have an expert opinion on the collection.'

'And were you going to sell it – lock, stock, and barrel – without consulting me?'

'No! Of course not.' Fergus wilted slightly under her gaze, but forged on. 'But we needed to know if the collection was valuable enough to be a real financial option. Mr Kettering came to view the works the afternoon of the engagement party and took this little painting back with him for analysis.'

'Analysis?' She looked at Kettering, alarmed. Turning back to her grandson, she said, 'What does that mean?'

Mr Kettering shifted on the sofa and spoke firmly. 'We ran some simple tests. Nothing that would damage it or change the value, of course.' They paused to look at the canvas. 'Unfortunately . . .'

'Unfortunately, what?' she asked sharply.

'There's no good way to say it, Grandmama: it's a forgery.' Fergus braced himself for her reaction.

There was a long pause and Lady Georgina blinked. 'Yes, I wondered when this conversation would come around. Although I had rather thought it would be with Angus.' She moved to a chair and sat delicately on the edge, looking at Fergus.

'You knew?' he asked incredulously.

'Yes. How do you think we paid for the tennis courts?' She looked nearly amused. 'If we'd sold it a month later, we'd have been able to build the boules court and pavilion as well.' She looked at Imogen. 'The art market is so unpredictable.' She tutted and straightened her skirt.

Imogen shook her head in disbelief. This was not where she thought the afternoon would go.

'And the Rubens in the Map Room?' demanded Fergus.

'Roof over the east wing,' she replied. 'We put it off as long as we could, but of course it started to cave in, and we had to act rather quickly, so a few pieces went off to Bonham's in London.' She shifted on her chair slightly and continued, looking at Fergus. 'It was a bit difficult, I'll admit; I've always liked that little Rubens. But, needs must.'

Fergus didn't know what to think. 'Who's we?' he asked. 'Who else knows about this?'

'Just your father. Although I suspect Elspeth knows. That Gainsborough hung over her bed for years. Surely she could tell it wasn't the original.'

Iris's head was spinning. All this time she had been asking about paintings, wondering about the differences, constantly talking about them at dinner, and never once had Lady Georgina slipped. Iris had to hand it to her; that woman could keep a secret.

'How many of the paintings are copies, Countess?' asked Kettering delicately.

'Oh, goodness me. Several. I'm not sure how many. We are not the first generation to sell a painting in secret, you know.' She looked at Imogen again and said in a tone of explanation, 'It happens all the time in families like ours, but one doesn't advertise such things.'

'No, I suppose not,' Kettering agreed hesitantly. 'Countess, were you intending to pass these off as genuine for the auction?'

Lady Georgina looked scandalised. 'Certainly not! You're confusing me as part of this hairbrained scheme.' She pointed to Fergus and Lawlis. 'Had you come to me, I'd have told you there was nothing in the idea. He might have been rather good with a brush, but Hamish was no Rubens.'

'Hamish!' the entire room erupted at the same moment.

'Yes. He studied art when he was at St Andrew's. Surely you knew that. No? Oh. Well, now you do. He started with economics but switched to art after his first year.' She looked to Lawlis. 'He wasn't much for finance, as you know.' Lawlis nodded and tried not to roll his eyes.

'Let me get this straight,' said Fergus, struggling to keep his composure. 'My father secretly sold off the family's priceless art to raise money for building projects. And then painted copies – bad ones – to replace them, and no one noticed? For what, twenty years?'

'Yes, I was always amazed by that,' said Lady Georgina placidly.

'I never even knew he liked art,' said Fergus, sitting down heavily on the sofa.

It would be a comic opera if it weren't real, thought Imogen.

'So, what were you intending to do when the house went up for auction?' Kettering asked, tentatively.

'If you'd left things to me, there'd have been no auction! I'd have continued to sell paintings and objects until we had the money. Bonham's have been after that landscape in the Billiards Room for years. But now that Hamish is gone, I'm not sure what to do about finishing the copy.'

Fergus's head was spinning. His father had been an art forger. His grandmother had been selling off priceless art to pay for tennis courts. What next? 'Where was he painting all these canvases without being seen?'

'In his private study, just off his dressing room. Why do you think we keep that huge vase of flowers at the end of the first-floor hallway? It masks the smell.'

Iris had to admit, she had always thought it a strange place for flowers. But she also had to admit that she had never smelled anything but flowers there. The afternoon was becoming a masterclass in deception.

Lady Georgina started to rise off the sofa. Looking to Lawlis, she asked, 'Is there really no way to avoid selling the house?'

'If the art collection is mostly copies, I'm afraid not.'

'Well then, I suppose he'd better make a thorough study of the entire collection while he's here. Paintings and objects.' She crossed to the fireplace and rang for Hudson. 'I honestly have no idea how many of them are originals.' She glanced pointedly at Imogen's shorthand notebook. 'It isn't something one writes down. Ah, Hudson, can you please ready a room for Mr Kettering here? He'll be staying with us for a few days to make a study of the art.'

Hudson bowed, issued forth a 'very good, milady' and left the room.

'Now, is there anything else? Or can I get back to my meeting with the gardener? No? Excellent. Fergus, Mr Kettering is in your charge while he's here. See that he understands our schedule and does not disrupt the household. Iris, you have children to capture.'

And with that, she swept from the room, leaving a stunned silence behind her.

Things needed to change.

The staff had managed reasonably well as their numbers steadily dwindled, but they had reached a point where it could no longer be denied: they were struggling. Mrs MacBain once again steeled herself for a meeting with Lady Georgina. The family hated changing anything, but Lady Georgina had been quite reasonable about the dinner menus, so there was hope that she might be reasonable now, too. But somehow, this issue felt stickier.

'Right, is there anything else we need to discuss?' Lady Georgina said, shuffling papers and reaching for her favourite pen.

'Actually, there is one thing I think we need to consider.' Mrs MacBain took a deep breath. 'It's about the tea cakes.'

'The tea cakes? Goodness, from your demeanour I was expecting something more consequential.' She chuckled.

'It would help us greatly to reduce the number of tea cakes set out each day. Instead of six, perhaps three would do?'

Lady Georgina regarded her stonily. '"Help you greatly"? I was unaware the family were required to change habits to suit the servants. Last time I checked, we still paid them.' She paused and Mrs MacBain squirmed in her seat. 'What's behind this, Mrs MacBain?'

Mrs MacBain hesitated. 'In truth, it's this sickness, milady.'

'Oh, not that again. I struggle to see why that should make a difference to tea.'

'Aside from the fact that we're down to a skeleton staff, Cook is still struggling to purchase the items we need.'

'I seem to remember we discussed this already.'

'We did, milady, but the situation has only got worse since then. I gather from the grocer that people have begun to stockpile supplies and certain items have been bought out completely. Sugar and flour are the main ones.'

'Stockpiling? People have lost their minds. But surely we have quite a store. Cook buys supplies every week. Are you telling me she doesn't have a little stockpile of her own? May I remind you that we should be first priority in the village? Does the grocer remember that?'

'Well yes, but the main issue is that he can't get flour at all. It seems to be a countrywide phenomenon. Everyone's stuck at home and so everyone is baking far more than they would usually. It makes it difficult for those of us that function this way normally. I gather yeast is now in short supply.'

'Yeast?'

'For bread, milady.'

'Bread?'

'Yes.'

'Why am I suddenly thinking of Marie Antoinette?' She shifted in her chair and looked out of the window for a moment. 'And what do you suggest?'

'If Cook made fewer cakes for tea, that would be a good start.'

'Start? What else?' Lady Georgina was irritated now. This part was going to be tricky.

'Serving three new cakes each day is somewhat taxing on the supplies. I'd like to serve slices instead. It creates less waste.'

'What, and eat the same cake, day after day, as it grows stale? It's like the war again!'

'It would help us stretch our supplies, Your Ladyship. I'd rather keep you in cake longer, but with slightly fewer choices than stop serving it altogether.'

Lady Georgina was silent. Her face was turned from Mrs MacBain slightly, but not enough hide her obvious irritation. She took a deep breath and sighed slowly.

'We must have a fruit cake. Victoria sponge is non-negotiable. And if we can keep the walnut, Angus won't notice.'

'Yes, milady. We can handle that. And thank you.'

Lady Georgina waved her away and turned back to her writing paper. Mrs MacBain was just at the Music Room doors when Lady Georgina spoke again.

'You said flour and sugar were the main shortages. Are we to expect anything else?'

She hesitated. She had never dreamt she would be discussing

such things with a Lady, and she felt herself blushing faintly. 'Bathroom tissues, milady.'

Lady Georgina looked faintly amused. 'Well, let's hope it doesn't come to that.'

Cecil was more unsure than ever what to do. After he'd been cut off for a third time in his life – the indignity of it all – Cecil was forced to take stock of his situation. It wasn't pretty. He was homeless, fortuneless, title-less, and now could not even come back to live with the family because the family house was going on the block. What to do, what to do? There simply had to be a way. He could not, would not, be forced to live in a ruin on Orkney, penniless and friendless. There had to be a solution, he just needed to find it.

He spent ever more time in the Cards Room, just off the Drawing Room. No one used it in the daytime, so he was perfectly alone. It gave him space to think. He shuffled and dealt cards to invisible players as he sorted through scheme after scheme. He was in particularly deep thought when Eva entered. They startled each other.

'Goodness!' she said. 'I didn't know anyone was here. My apologies for interrupting.' She turned to go and slightly bashed the into door frame.

Cecil, for his part, lost control mid-shuffle and sent cards flying through the air. There was something rather comic about him, Eva thought. Ridiculous, but somehow incredibly serious. It was a strange combination.

Together, they quickly and awkwardly gathered the cards and Eva handed her pile to him. He stuttered a thank you, looking a bit sheepish – was that a blush? But after a moment, he regained his composure, settling back into his chair, automatically sorting the cards.

'How can I help you, my dear?'

'Oh, I was, um, looking for my gloves. They've gone missing and I wondered if I left them here after the funeral.' She gave a cursory glance around the room. It was not an overly large space, and other than the card table and the fireplace mantel, there was really no place to have set them down. Cecil wondered what she was really doing there.

'Gloves? No –' he looked around the room – 'I can't say I've seen any. Are you going somewhere?' It had been ages since the funeral; how was she just now missing them? He wondered again what she was really doing there.

'Hm? Going somewhere?'

'For which you need your gloves? I presume you don't wear them indoors, like the servants. Maybe it's a fashionable new London craze that hasn't made it to the Highlands yet.' She could see he was trying to tease her. It was . . . well, it was.

'Oh, no. I thought I might walk into the village, do some shopping. Nosing about, really. I'm feeling a bit cooped up, need something new to read.'

'Cooped up? We have a hundred and twenty-five rooms, a Library, and five thousand acres of land. My, my, how do you survive in a London townhouse?'

'One hundred and twenty-five rooms?'

'Yes, didn't you know? That doesn't include the servants' quarters of course; one never counts those. You really should know more about the family and the Abbey if you're going to reside here.'

'I hadn't really thought about it that way. Since it's going to be sold.'

'Oh, my dear, it won't be sold. Houses like ours are not simply sold. No, no, no. Some small parcel of land will be sold, maybe a cottage on the estate, something that will cover the death duties, and then life will continue. Our family has resided in Loch Down Abbey for nearly six hundred years. Rest assured; we shall carry on.'

Eva watched him speak, smoothly and confidently, as he slowly shuffled the deck of cards in his hands. Did he really feel that way, she wondered? Or was it a brave face? He was hard to read.

'Perhaps I should accompany you? I have one or two telegrams to send. Shall we risk scandalising the old women and go without your gloves?'

Eva weighed up her options. She really had not wanted to go into the damn village and yet here she was, not only going, but with an escort. Now what? In reality, she had been looking for a private place to make a telephone call to her mother, to discuss what to do. The lack of family fortune in her intended could hardly be discussed out in the open air of the Armoury, and that was the only telephone she could find. She'd been looking for days but the servants kept interrupting her. But a trip to the village, and to shop of all things, was the last thing she wanted. Besides, there was nothing to be had but a few out-of-date magazines and some very sad hats at the milliners. Well, only one way to get out of it now, and it might just help her in the long run.

'Perhaps you can show me around the house instead? You seem to know so much of the family's history, it would be wonderful to see it through your eyes. If you have the time, of course.' What better way to search? she thought.

Cecil appraised her quickly and found an idea forming somewhere in the back reaches of his mind. *What better way to search?* he thought. 'I should be honoured. Shall we begin in the Armoury?'

*

Lawlis and Imogen were in the Armoury when Cecil and Eva appeared at the far end of the room. Imogen strained to listen to Cecil, who was telling Eva about a suit of armour. She'd have loved to hear more about it, but she and Lawlis had an appointment with the family to discuss dates for the sale. Cleaverings was a busy firm and they were lucky to have two cancellations in their calendar. Lawlis wanted to confirm one of them. Otherwise, they would have to work with a less prestigious auction house or wait another fourteen months for Cleaverings and Lawlis knew they could not wait that long. They only had three months before the death duties were due.

Fergus settled them into the Map Room with an apologetic smile. Angus could not be found. No surprise there, thought Lawlis. Fergus went to find Lady Georgina and left them to wait.

They looked around curiously. The Map Room was a double-height space with a cast-iron catwalk around three sides of the room, which gave access to the shelves further up the walls. This is more a library than the Library, thought Imogen. But the furniture in the main part of the room had been crafted specifically with maps in mind. The drawers were shallow but wide and there were several places where the sheets hung vertically. She pulled out a rail marked 'Loch Down Estate 1654' to inspect it, but then remembered they had no evidence the maps had been forged, so pushed the rail back gently. She made a mental note to ask Kettering if he knew a maps expert and crossed over to look at the little faux Rubens again.

It was a pretty canvas, no matter who the artist had been, but it was clearly not a Rubens. How had that escaped everyone's notice? In a large room, it is rather small, she thought, but it also hangs in a place of pride just above the sofa. She looked down and watched the family dogs snoring lightly; why would anyone sit here when the dogs so obviously own the sofa? She returned her gaze to the painting. No, it wasn't a Rubens, but Lord Inverkillen had definitely found the right type of model to sit for him, sensual and curvy. She was quite a beautiful woman, as well. Positively radiant. Was she, no . . . Was she?

When Fergus returned with Lady Georgina some moments later, Imogen barely heard them; she was so absorbed in thought. It was only when Fergus was standing beside her that she finally came out of her reverie.

'It is such a pretty little painting, isn't it?' he remarked softly. 'I don't know how I missed that it wasn't the real thing. It's quite obvious, really.'

It left her lips before she had a chance to think it over. 'Is she pregnant? I think she is.'

Fergus stared at Imogen for a moment, then looked back at the painting. 'What? No, of course not. Rubens always painted women in a quite voluptuous way. His nudes are always fleshy and round, soft; like a ripe peach.' He slowed his speech as he neared the end, looking quite seriously at the painting now.

Lady Georgina called across the room, 'If you two are finished gawping, can we please get on with this? I have things to do, you know.'

'Right.' Fergus turned and went to sit down. It took Imogen another moment or two. She'd have to speak with Kettering.

She was late to dress Bella that morning but there was nothing Mrs MacBain could do about it. The whole morning got off to a bad start. The milk and papers had arrived late, and Ollie had had to set them out without ironing them, which of course set off Angus. Luckily, Fergus had been able to smooth things over before Ollie got the sack. They really couldn't afford to lose him. But the late delivery also meant the breakfast trays went up late, which meant dressing the ladies was pushed back, which meant making up the beds was pushed back. She'd had an earful from both Bella and Constance. It was only ten o'clock and already the day was a mess. She was on her way now to speak with Lady Georgina about the matter. Something had to change.

'What can I do for you, Mrs MacBain?' Lady Georgina was reading a letter, tutting and shaking her head. Mrs MacBain waited until she set it down.

'Oh, this looks serious,' she said, upon seeing Mrs MacBain's face.

'It is, milady. We ran behind schedule this morning, which upset both Lady Annabella and Lady Constance. I'm not here to make excuses for it, but I can see that this is going to be an ongoing issue.'

'Ongoing?'

'Yes, milady. With the full staff, we can work around a hiccup like this morning and still run to schedule. But with so few of us left because of the sickness – well, there just isn't anyone to help pick things up when they go wrong, and that puts the whole day out of kilter.'

Lady Georgina sighed wearily. She was so tired of hearing about this wretched illness. 'And what do you recommend?'

'I'd like to stop the breakfast trays.' Mrs MacBain held her breath. It took a moment for Lady Georgina to process the statement, and Mrs MacBain could see the flicker of anger. 'Except for yours, milady,' she rushed to say, and Lady Georgina settled back in her chair, mollified. 'And Lady Inverkillen's, naturally.'

'Naturally. But how would that help, exactly?'

Mrs MacBain explained the number of trips back and forth to the bedrooms required each morning: light the fire, bring in the tray, take the trays away, dress the ladies, then finally make up the beds and clean the rooms. Quite frankly, it was getting in the way of far more important duties, like laundry.

'Normally, that work is done by six maids and two footmen, but with just Maxwell and me – well, when one thing goes late, the whole day gets pushed back. But if the ladies were to dress themselves and breakfast in the dining room, it would give us more time to get to all the rooms. And it would help Cook as well. She's on her own in the kitchen now, and we've had to draft Lockridge to help out.'

'Lockridge? The chauffer is cooking? What has the world come to?'

Mrs MacBain couldn't help but smile.

'And now, married women having breakfast in the dining room. It is all highly unorthodox, Mrs MacBain.' She looked out of the window for a moment. 'I think I'd better be the one to break it to them, don't you?'

Immeasurably relieved, Mrs MacBain curtsied and left the room.

Lady Georgina summoned the married ladies to the Music Room before luncheon. Bella stood at the French doors, looking bored, while Constance, on the sofa, mentally re-arranged the furniture. Only Elspeth looked curious as to why they were all there.

When Lady Georgina had explained the situation, she was surprised to find that it was Constance who led the opposition. She would have bet her second-best tiara on Bella.

'I should not have to forgo my breakfast tray. I am the senior member of the family now and I have earned the right to have a breakfast tray in my own home.' Constance was actually pouting.

'You are merely the custodian of this house, my dear, not the owner. You'd do well to remember it that way.' Lady Georgina had never liked Constance. She was one tall step above Eva, certainly, being the daughter of a banker instead of a fishmonger; but still, it appeared in this day and age, one could no longer choose one's family.

'And why wasn't I consulted on this matter?' Constance whinged. 'Given that I am now the mistress of this house, I should have been involved in the decision.'

Lady Georgina slowly exhaled while mentally counting to ten.

'I don't mind at all, Mama.' Lady Elspeth was very sanguine about the entire idea. She had been calm and attentive throughout Lady Georgina's explanation of the new morning routine.

'Thank you, Elspeth.'

'Well, I mind very much.' Bella felt every bit as insulted as Constance. 'It's bad enough I have to share a lady's maid but now you want me to forego one altogether. To help the servants. Funny, I was under the impression the servants were here to help us, not the other way around. No, I'm sorry, I refuse.'

They could be so stubborn, thought Lady Georgina. 'Stay in bed, by all means, but know this: your morning post will be delivered to the Dining Room.' She smiled tightly and swept from the room.

Two hours into the tour of the house, Eva's eyes were starting to glaze over. For the most part, the tour had been of some interest, but mostly it had been over-informative. Cecil had an intimate and zealous knowledge of the history of every single object, artist and maker in each of the twenty or so rooms they had visited thus far. He'd spent nearly thirty minutes in the Chinese Room alone, showing her every single compartment in a pair of apothecary cabinets. He was not a subtle man and was clearly searching for something – not that she cared, but there hadn't been one damn telephone in any of those rooms. Eva was starting to despair. She didn't know how much longer she could feign interest. They were now in the Hall of Miniatures and Cecil was droning on while examining the back of each small painting.

'Of course, many of the early miniatures were painted by the Robertson brothers but this one is very special – '

Eva had to drag her thoughts away from the telephone to listen. It wasn't enough to just give her the history, he was also quizzing her occasionally.

' – being one of the few to be painted on ivory.'

A clock somewhere in the house reminded her it was nearly time for luncheon. She suggested to Cecil they make their way back to the main part of the house, so she could freshen up before they ate. They were just entering the Armoury when Eva spotted Fergus chatting with a woman in a mask. Her hand was on his arm, and they were laughing together. Eva stopped to observe them. Were they flirting? It was such an intimate gesture. And who was the woman, anyway? She wasn't a servant, but she looked vaguely familiar. Was he blushing? Eva scowled in spite of herself.

'This looks cosy,' she said in a steely voice as she neared them. The woman's hand slid quickly back to her side and Fergus, Eva could see, straightened his posture. They had been flirting! But who was she? Eva gave her the once over. Dreadfully cheap shoes and hat.

'Oh hello, darling,' said Fergus. 'We've just finished our meeting and we're waiting for Lawlis. You remember Miss MacLeod?'

Both Eva and Cecil looked at Imogen, who could tell they did not remember her. Eva looked faintly hostile, but both gave her a strained smile and small nod before turning back to Fergus.

'Have you two been together?' he asked, gesturing to Cecil.

'Yes, I've been showing your Beloved the house. I'm surprised you haven't done it. She needs a thorough grounding of the house and family history before she joins us. She's quite a quick study, I must say. Very bright.'

Eva feigned a blush and threaded her arm through Fergus's. 'I was just going to freshen up before luncheon. Is there still time, darling?'

Fergus extracted his arm to look at his watch.

'Yes, about ten minutes. Jolly shame you can't join us before heading off,' he said to Imogen. 'Rather a long drive to Inverness without lunch, isn't it?'

Lawlis rejoined them at that moment. 'Yes, it is,' he said, 'but we have an appointment and just enough time to arrive punctually, barring any catastrophe on the roads.'

Fergus walked them to the front door and said his goodbyes. Did he walk everyone to the front door, Eva wondered? She turned to mount the stairs, but Cecil was clearly waiting to speak with Fergus. He looked, she wasn't sure, slightly upset perhaps. Eva walked as slowly as she dared up the two flights to her room.

'So, Nephew, what were you meeting with Lawlis about?' he asked calmly, fingering one of battleaxes on the wall.

'We've settled on a date for the sale. Seems Cleaverings is quite a busy firm and we were lucky to get a choice of dates before the deadline.'

'And how is any of that your place?' Cecil snapped. His tone shocked Eva, and from Fergus's expression she could tell it had shocked him, too. 'I seem to remember that Angus is now Lord Inverkillen. Surely he should be making these decisions.'

'Yes, well, if Angus would only come out of hiding, he could make these decisions. But as it stands, I seem to be the only adult on deck. Even Grandmama is burying her head in the sand.' Eva could taste Fergus's bitterness from the half-landing.

'My dear boy, you don't really intend to go through with the sale, do you? It's a humiliation we don't need to face. Surely we can sell some land before the whole family reputation goes up in smoke?'

'It's not that simple, Uncle Cecil. I've been going through the accounts with Lawlis for weeks now and there really is no other option. The estate hasn't been supporting itself for several decades and we've reached a point of no return. There is no more money.' He said this last as though hoping to wound. 'The sale of the Distillery was just enough to cover Lawlis's fees. The salmon sales will give Mama enough to live on, but only the barest essentials – and that's only if the new distillery owners let us keep fishing the river.'

'But surely we can dispose of one or two of the more valuable pieces? I know people in London who could help us find the right audience.'

Eva saw Fergus run his hands through his hair in what was clearly frustration. 'You don't get it. We are in debt. And the death duties have only put us farther into debt. Debt that will be repaid by bailiffs seizing and auctioning off the house and the contents to the lowest bidder if we do nothing!' He was shouting now. Eva spotted Ollie, the footman, quietly slipping into a recess to avoid being seen. 'I am trying to keep us from that particular humiliation by finding a private seller first, and all you can think about is if it's "my place" and "can't we just sell a vase?" This family, honestly. Lawlis is heading to Inverness this afternoon to speak to someone who might be open to a private sale, a quiet sale. For a better price than a public auction.' He shook his head sadly. 'Grandfather may have crippled us, but Father and Angus ruined us by not dealing with it. Had they listened to me sooner, we'd be in a different boat. Hell, had they listened to Lawlis sooner, we'd be in a different boat. But no, they knew best and now we're mired in debt and on the brink of bankruptcy and ruin. If we lose – no, *when* we lose the house, where is everyone going to live? How would everyone live? And where is Angus when all of this is happening? Where? Hiding in the Tennis Pavilion watching Hugh write another sodding novel! So, knowing all that, Uncle Cecil, do you really think I should wait for "Lord Inverkillen" to take charge of his Estate? Do you? No. I didn't think so.' Fergus turned and stormed out the front door, slamming it behind him. It echoed through the Armoury like a war cannon, leaving Eva with an icy dread in the pit of her stomach.

Downstairs, luncheon was a quiet affair. Everyone had heard the argument. Everyone had heard the door slam. It was no longer a secret. Quite frankly, it was all the staff talked about.

Though they had all heard the argument, Ollie had given them a full, first accounting of it, and the gathered group listened breathlessly. When he'd finished the tale, he simply helped himself to stew and bread. 'Oooh, onion bread, excellent.' He munched the bread for a moment and then asked, 'Do you suppose we'll be included in the sale? If it goes private, that is. Or will we be out looking for new jobs?'

'I don't know, Ollie,' Mrs MacBain replied. No one knew. 'A private sale. And you're sure that Mr Lawlis is heading to Inverness now to meet a buyer?'

Ollie thought for a second and then shook his head. 'Said it was someone who might be interested in purchasing it.'

'It's not a done deal, then,' Mackay said quietly.

'No, no it's not. I wonder how we can find out,' Mrs MacBain replied. A look passed between them and then she shook herself back into the present, to find Ollie looking between them curiously. 'Ollie, you'd better get a move on. They'll be heading to the Dining Room shortly. And don't forget your mask.'

'Yes, Mrs MacBain.' He slurped down the last of his stew, careful not to get any of it on his livery, and then bolted from the servants' hall. MacBain and Mr Mackay were alone.

'I'm on it,' was all he said, and he stood to leave.

Lady Georgina herded Fergus and Cecil into the Library as everyone gathered for luncheon. Cecil had not seen her this angry since he was a teenager, when she had caught him sword fighting with Hamish on the stairs. By God, the woman had a temper.

It had been quite some time since Lady Georgina had been the one to dress down a child, but she clearly hadn't lost her skills. She was absolutely livid and while she was ruthless in her words, she never raised her voice above a loud whisper.

'I will not have the servants gossiping and telling tales to the village,' she said, glaring at both men. 'And I certainly will not have that man from London presuming we are a pack of wild dogs. I do not care how bad things are looking, airing one's dirty laundry in so public a way is beneath all of us. Fergus, you will, in future, refrain from discussing the family's business in front of the servants. And Cecil, well, Cecil do try to remember that being married to a Marchioness implies some dignity and gravitas. Actually, both of you should remember that we belong to the aristocracy, and the aristocracy. Docs. Not. Shout.' She glared at them for a full, uncomfortable minute and then exhaled sharply. 'Now, if you can be civil and speak in acceptable tones, can someone please escort me into luncheon.'

It was silent in the Dining Room. No one knew what topic to introduce. It seemed ridiculous to discuss the weather, or the newest crop of debutantes, given they were so near financial ruin. If, that is, what Fergus had said was true. Finally, Elspeth asked if anyone had seen Lady Inverkillen that morning, and apparently no one had.

Constance gave a disgusted sigh. 'She can't hide in there forever.'

Lady Georgina glared at her and signalled for the next course.

But Constance was not going to be distracted by food. 'It's been two months. Surely she should at least be appearing every now and then?'

Where is she going with this? wondered Lady Georgina. 'My dear, you've never buried a husband. You cannot put a timescale on grief.'

'But surely sitting in her rooms only serves to remind her that he's gone.' Constance had adopted a conciliatory tone. 'Wouldn't it be much better – for her emotional well-being – to be in another set of rooms?'

Ah yes, thought Lady Georgina, the Laird's rooms. Constance had been less and less subtle in her lobbying to move Victoria out of her rooms, the finest and largest suite in the Abbey. The Earl and Countess were always housed in these rooms and Constance, it seemed, was in a terrible rush to occupy them.

'Not this again!' Bella was absolutely exasperated and threw her napkin on the table. 'Angus, do something about your wife.'

Angus looked up, startled to be involved.

'And what is that supposed to mean? Angus doesn't control me.' Constance was nearly shouting.

'No, because if he did, you'd have learned how to be a proper countess instead of a grubby little social climber,' shouted Bella, making Lady Georgina wince.

'Bella!' several of them shouted, shocked. The ladies had never quite got along but relations between them had never been this openly hostile.

'How dare you?' Constance jumped to her feet and shouted across the table at Bella. Bella too stood abruptly, knocking over her chair, and shouted back at Constance. Others tried to get them to sit down, to no avail. Lady Georgina put her head in her hands. Had she known the breakfast trays would cause such a fuss, she'd have waited until after dinner to tell them.

Fergus and Angus managed to get the ladies seated and quiet again after some minutes. Hesitantly, Hudson and Ollie began serving the main course.

Trying to change the subject entirely, Lady Elspeth looked at Hugh.

'I understand you're writing another book, Hugh. Is that right? What's this one about?'

Hugh looked at Elspeth, rather like a startled deer, then at Angus, and then Bella, as if waiting for someone to answer for him. Hugh never spoke about his writing to the family and that was quite as he, and they, wanted it.

'Um, yes. I am, in fact. About halfway through at the

moment. It's been slower than normal, given everything that's been happening.' The whole table nodded. He hoped that would be the end of the discussion.

'What's it about?' asked Elspeth. Angus glared at his aunt. 'I must confess, I've never read any of your books. They don't seem to have distribution in France.'

'No. The, um . . . wordplay doesn't translate well into French.' He took a sip of wine, hoping the subject would move on.

'And what is this book about?' Elspeth's interest, sincere as it was, discomforted him greatly. He had no wish to discuss his writing with the family.

'About? Oh, um . . . it's a work of fiction. It's not really fully formed yet.' He turned to help himself to vegetables, thinking wildly about something, anything he could introduce to change the subject. But his mind was blank.

Elspeth was helping herself to potatoes and simply considered this a pause in the conversation. She finished and looked at Hugh again, expectantly. There was no way out now.

'Yes, well, it's, erm, a romantic adventure tale, of sorts. About a young man in the 1700s. A handsome Naval officer, who has been kidnapped by pirates and must find a way to pay for his freedom. Lots of swashbuckling, cannons firing, that sort of thing.'

'Sounds thrilling. What's his name?' asked Elspeth.

'He doesn't want to talk about it,' Angus snapped. Elspeth and Fergus looked at him in surprise.

'His name? Oh, erm . . . I haven't quite decided yet. These things take time. Need something suitably, um, heroic.'

'It sounds to me like there should be a romance. With the Admiral's daughter, maybe?' Constance joined in. She'd never read Hugh's work either. 'Being rescued from pirates, how thrilling.'

'No, no. No women on board, you know; bad luck, super-stition and all that. Men only.'

Constance looked confused. 'But if there are no women, who is the hero going to fall in love with? You can hardly have a romantic adventure story with only men.'

Ollie snorted behind his mask. Hudson glared at him.

'Enough!' Angus banged his fist on the table, upsetting his wine glass. 'Clean this up and serve the food,' he barked at Ollie. He glared at Constance, who looked both confused and mortified. Curious glances went around the table, but no one spoke. The rest of luncheon was silent and brief.

'It would be good to get into his studio, don't you think?'

Iris looked up from the art inventory and was for a moment, startled. She thought Mr Kettering was speaking of the Duke of Wellington, whose portrait he was studying. They were in the Wallace Room, dedicated to military prints. Many of Wellington's generals had been Scots and so the family held a begrudging respect for the man and had purchased a portrait of him. Tempera though, not oils. It took her a moment to realise he was talking about Hamish's studio, which made a lot more sense.

Iris did think it would be good, but gaining permission would be a tricky matter. Lady Inverkillen still hadn't left her rooms and Iris hated to disturb her. But she really wanted to please Mr Kettering by showing him the space. Plus, she had to admit, she was very curious about it all.

'I'm not sure how to ask her. I mean, how much does she even know of all of this? Does she know he paints? If not, then what reason are we going to give for going into his private study? There isn't anything listed in the inventory about his rooms, and I'm a terrible liar. I really don't want to upset her.'

Mr Kettering nodded. He'd been mulling the issue for some time and couldn't come up with a way to gain access without a whole lot of explanation. And he wanted to speak to as few of them as possible.

'What would Lady Georgina do in this situation?' he asked her.

Iris thought for a minute. 'She'd stride in waving her hand and saying she wouldn't be but a minute. But she has authority. I need permission. Ah! Here is it! I knew it.' She held out the book triumphantly.

She was wonderful. Not for the first time, he felt she was utterly wasted here.

Eva pestered Cecil about the same thing on their next tour of the house, which she orchestrated for that very purpose. He had mentioned several times that Hamish's private study had never been seen by anyone in the family and each time it made her more curious. What was he hiding? And why was he hiding it? She knew he conducted his daily affairs from the Map Room, so having a second study was just indulgent, really. Well, in London it certainly would be. Clearly something was happening in the room and Eva wanted to know what.

They were in a particularly boring room in the west wing, staring at a display of ancient wax seals or something equally dull, when Cecil finally agreed. They sneaked to the first floor and stood in front of the vase of flowers. Like all illicit plans, neither had considered what to do when they arrived, so they stood for a moment – Cecil uncomfortable, Eva wildly excited – and wondered about a plan of action.

Cecil was mentally reviewing the layout of the suite of rooms. The children had seldom been allowed in, but Elspeth had sneaked in several times, having been dared to by her brothers, and reported back. Cecil had tried only once and been caught at the door of his mother's bedchamber.

The door opened into the sitting room connecting the two halves of the apartment. Victoria's rooms were to the right, Hamish's to the left. If they entered the main door, they could not avoid being seen. They might be able to gain access to Hamish's dressing room through the valet's entrance, but he wasn't sure where that was. It would be a discreet door, as he knew from his own at Stronach Castle, but the hall was so dark it was impossible to see clearly. He tried feeling the wall panelling, hoping to find something to indicate the door, and rejoiced when he felt the gaps between two panels. But how to open it? There was no knob and pushing on it did nothing. Was it locked from inside? It was definitely a door, though, so they were in the right place.

Younger eyes found the solution. Eva put her hand on the moulding and lifted it, and the door opened. She turned back to Cecil with a conspirator's smile, and they stepped across the threshold.

Once inside the dressing room, Cecil stepped quickly to the open door leading to the sitting room and closed it quietly. A hush fell over the room. Eva looked around. Hamish's dressing room was a rather thin room with wardrobes lining the long walls. It was the epitome of Edwardian masculinity: serene, tailored, restrained. Quite at odds with the gruff man Eva had known for only a few days. She wondered if he had liked it. Then again, when one inherited an estate, one's own preference had little to do with it, she supposed. There was, at the far end of the room, a raised step in the bay window, which overlooked the garden. This must be where he stood to be dressed, she thought, as she stepped onto the platform. *I would have.* It was a wonderful view of the rose garden. She turned to face the room again and saw she was facing a framed mirror that covered a large portion of the wall on her right. It had been hidden by the wardrobes as she walked by. Stepping forward, she immediately saw a keyhole. It was a door!

'We need the key,' she whispered excitedly.

'Key?' Cecil turned to look at her, hastily fastening the cufflinks he had just taken from his brother's drawer. Looking back to the mirror, his eyes settled on a discreet keyhole. 'Of course. He was absurdly private about this room. No one could enter. Literally, I see.'

'Where would he have put the key?'

'Oh, he most assuredly would have kept the key upon his person. He could be quite paranoid about this room. I never understood it. Well, luckily for us, I have a few skills from my time in the military that aren't, shall we say, above board.' Cecil took several jewelled tiepins from the open cufflink drawer and knelt in front of the mirror. Using the dullest of them – a simple gold and pearl thing he'd always thought rather cheap – he fiddled with the lock, and after some moments, the door popped open. 'Useful skill, lockpicking. Not altogether honourable, but very useful.' Eva beamed at him. Cecil stood in front of the mirror, taking a moment to place a sapphire tiepin in his cravat. He fluffed the cravat, looking pleased with himself, and pocketed the rest. 'That's better. Now, shall we?' he opened the door and Eva stepped in.

They stood at the threshold in silence for some minutes. It both was and wasn't what they had expected to see. Not that either had thought about what they would encounter – but this, this was nearly shocking.

The room was quite large, the walls lined in the same timber panelling as the dressing room but painted white. Light flooded in from the ceiling and a bank of high windows on one wall. There must have been hundreds of canvases, stacked against the walls of the room. And standing in the centre of it all was the most enormous four-poster bed Eva had ever seen. It was messy and had an easel standing in front of it.

'Isn't that the painting in the Billiards Room?' she asked, moving to the unfinished canvas near the windows.

Cecil nodded, looking confused.

She moved to the easel in front of the bed. 'And this is the Rubens from the Map Room. Cecil, I don't understand.'

Cecil was staring at a nude study that was standing on the floor. It was a woman by a river. *Our river,* he thought. She looked vaguely familiar. Who was she? Cecil shook his head and started to look through the stacked canvases. 'They're all of her. Every painting is of her. Oh my!' He quickly slammed the stack back in place. 'You needn't see that one, my dear.'

'I didn't know your brother was an artist. Fergus never mentioned it,' Eva said, turning the pages in a sketchbook. It was all the same woman. Hundreds of pages of her, spanning years. 'Do you think they were lovers? Oh! Do you think Victoria knows?' Eva's mind was reeling with all the possibilities. This was not where she thought the afternoon would go. It was turning out to be quite an adventure.

She turned from the book to see Cecil standing in the middle of the room, staring at her, thunderstruck. 'I've no idea. I didn't even know he painted. I'm starting to wonder if I knew anything about him at all.'

The dressing gong sounded, making them jump. They looked at one another and then quickly scurried for the valet's door. They needed to move swiftly before the rest of the family came up the stairs. There was no hiding in the hallway once that happened. As Eva mounted the stairs to the guest floor, she marvelled about having a secret room in the house.

And who was the woman he so obsessively painted? She was so familiar . . .

Lawlis and Imogen arrived the following afternoon and asked to see Fergus and Lady Georgina. Hudson was delighted to see they brought their own masks and gloves. Less laundry to do.

Fergus was just stepping through the Armoury and went to greet them both. He was delighted to see her. Them!

'Hello! Were we expecting you? Hudson, can you have tea brought to the Music Room for us? I'll take them to Grandmama.' Hudson bowed his head and slipped through a hidden door behind the columns.

As they made their way to the Music Room, Imogen listened vaguely to the conversation the men were having. The Music Room was further into the house than she had ever been before, and she found herself distracted. They had moved from the Armoury into a long hallway, a passageway really, and they were hurtling forward in time, from the Tudor period to the Restoration. It was a remarkable house. *Shame they have to sell it,* she thought. *It would make the most fascinating museum.*

They turned left into another corridor, which was lined with benches and floor-standing glass candelabra. Mirrors lined one wall, and there were French doors to the garden on the other. At the opposite end was a pair of enormous doors with pale green silk panels. This was a house? It was unbelievable. Imogen knew her mouth was open, but luckily it was behind her mask.

Fergus stopped and smiled at her; clearly her mask wasn't hiding all of her amazement. 'It's something, isn't it? I believe it was done after the 13th Earl visited Versailles. Our own Hall of Mirrors.'

'It's very, erm, effective,' said Lawlis, staring up at the painted ceiling.

'It's just . . . I mean it's . . . I just feel so underdressed!' Imogen stuttered, blushing.

'Yes,' laughed Fergus, 'I know exactly what you mean! And here we have the Music Room, which Grandmama is using as her study at the moment.' He knocked at the door and then pushed both doors open with a grand flourish. 'Subtle, isn't it?'

Lawlis and Imogen entered the room. It was more of the mirror, green silk and painted ceilings from the hallway. There were pretty chairs dotted around, a few French sofas. Was that a pianoforte in the corner? My word, how enormous. And in the middle of it all sat Lady Georgina at her desk, an ugly, dark carved timber object so totally at odds with the room, it positively offended Imogen.

'It was my father's desk,' said Lady Georgina by way of greeting, noticing Imogen was staring at it. She waved her hand towards the sofas and perched on a chair. 'It needs a more commanding room, I grant you. Ah, Hudson, perfect timing. Thank you. We'll pour ourselves; you may leave.' Hudson hesitated and then bowed, leaving the room with a soft 'yes, milady'.

'Now,' she said, turning to Lawlis and Imogen, 'how do you propose to drink anything with those ridiculous masks?'

'There are still quite a few people ill in the village, milady, so we'd prefer to keep them on. Better safe than sorry,' Lawlis answered smoothly.

'No one here is ill, Andrew. You're perfectly safe,' replied Lady Georgina, exasperated by the very idea. 'Servants in masks are one thing but honestly, this has gone on far too long.'

'We've been to Inverness twice, milady. We don't know

what we may have been in contact with there. I'd rather we were cautious.'

'Twice? Does that spell good news for us, then?' Fergus looked hopefully between the two of them. When Imogen looked away, he knew the sale hadn't gone through, and his heart sank. 'What happened?'

'We had agreed a deal with a local landowner, from some-where near Wick; quite respectable, very wealthy. Did some-thing with fishing, extremely interested in the salmon here, I gather. We were waiting on the paperwork to arrive, but his solicitor's just rung and rather sadly, the man has died.'

'What? How?' Fergus gasped.

'Apparently, he caught this illness that's going around.' Lawlis didn't trust himself to look at Lady Georgina as he said it.

'And he died? How can that be?' Lady Georgina looked affronted by the very idea. 'We've had several cases of it here, and no one's died.'

Lawlis, Imogen and Fergus looked at one another uncom-fortably. No one wanted to remind her of Nanny.

'We'll keep trying, Lady Georgina. We did have a second offer, but there simply wasn't enough money on the table.' Both Fergus and Lady Georgina started to interrupt, but Lawlis held up his hand to silence them. 'It wasn't quite enough to have paid the death duties, so we'd have had to use the Distillery funds to make up the shortfall and then there would have been nothing left for anyone to live on.' He looked pointedly at Lady Georgina. 'And my concern is you, milady. Everyone else can fend for themselves if need be, but you need an income and a home.'

Lady Georgina seemed startled by the fact, but it had been the subject of numerous discussions between Lawlis and Imogen. He was genuinely concerned about her future. She'd spent her entire life in grand houses, he had explained, cossetted by staff, never even thinking about money, let alone worrying about it. She knew nothing of the real world or how to engage with it; and she certainly didn't know how to earn a living from it. The others were able bodied, and while they would struggle, they would survive. But Lady Georgina was from another world entirely, he argued. It would be like turning a kitten loose in the forest.

Fergus had never seen his grandmother speechless before. It was worrying. 'I will take care of Grandmama, don't worry about that. She'll hardly be wandering the streets.'

'I'm still looking for private sales and we have eight weeks yet. But I would like to widen our search. I know we agreed to keep things discreet, but I do think it would benefit us to be a bit louder. There are a tremendous number of Americans paying ridiculous sums and—'

'No!' Lady Georgina came back to life with a vengeance. 'We may lose the Estate, but it will not be to foreigners. Scotland has lost enough to outsiders and I will not be the family that loses this house to yet another invasion.'

The room was silent, but her words rang in their ears. Fergus knew it would be a battle to get her to agree. And he wondered again if she had any say in the matter. Technically, the house and estate belonged to Angus, so it was Angus who had the burden of the death duties to pay, not Mama and not Grandmama. Angus, who was absent as always. Leaving everything for others to deal with while he plays tennis, or whatever it was he did all day. His anger once again boiled to the surface. It was no coincidence the family motto was *Nous Commandons, D'Sutres Servent* – We Command, Others Serve. But at the moment, he needed to find a way to allow the sale to be open to Americans. Or a nice Canadian. They were rich, too.

The trio tried to talk her round, but she gave no way. It was long and tense and, in the end, Lawlis was given a fortnight to find another private, domestic, sale. After that, they would have to announce the auction.

Fergus walked Lawlis and Imogen out, asking Lawlis if his grandmother had any legal right to stand in the way.

'Well, no, but you don't have any legal right either,' he pointed out. 'It's Angus's house.'

Fergus sighed heavily. 'So, if I poke that bear, I disqualify myself as well and we're left waiting for Angus to engage. Right. Well, that's motivation, then. I'll find a way to bring her around. You look for a buyer anywhere you can get one. Anywhere. Have you had Kettering's report on the value of the art and objects yet? I've asked him to include pretty much anything of value in the house, not just the paintings. If the tablecloths are valuable, he's including them.'

'We'll be in touch with any news. But at this point, I think we need to announce the sale dates, just in case. I'll tell Kettering to get his assessment done as quickly as possible. It might yet prove crucial.'

They said subdued goodbyes and Fergus wandered back to the Map Room. Though he felt like Atlas, with the world on his shoulders, he had a slight spring in his step. There was something to be said for those masks. They really showed off her eyes.

'What do you mean, you can't order any?' Mrs MacBain wasn't sure she understood what Mrs Burnside had just said. It was such a ridiculous idea; it couldn't possibly be true.

'That's what he said. Apparently, the entire country is buying it up like free passes for the Pearly Gates. He's had to ration the village to two per household.'

'We're hardly a typical household—'

'I tried that; he wasn't having it. I've been given our ration for the week, and that's that.'

Mrs MacBain shook her head in utter disbelief. 'How many do you normally order per week?'

'Twenty-four. They're changed out on Tuesdays when the grocery order is delivered, and the partial rolls go to the staff.'

Mrs MacBain took a deep breath. 'Right. Whatever next? I'll have a word. Thank you for letting me know.' She went straight off to find Lady Georgina. Mrs Burnside didn't envy her this conversation.

Mrs MacBain recounted her conversation regarding the rationing of bathroom tissue, keeping her eyes averted from Lady Georgina's all the while.

'Surely we have a store set by?' Lady Georgina was aghast.

'No, milady. We don't keep it in stock, because it takes up so much space, and it does tend to mould in the damp of the cellars.'

The women stared at one another for a long, silent moment.

'Well, surely we can't be expected to share with the servants. They'll just have to go back to . . . whatever it was they used before tissue.'

Mrs MacBain couldn't suppress a small grimace. 'Newspaper, milady. Even if we did that, it wouldn't quite solve the issue, I'm afraid.'

'Why ever not?'

'Well, for a start, we take the *Scotsman* and *The Times*, and they aren't quite suitable for the purpose.'

Lady Georgina sat up as tall as she could and said with an expression of outrage, 'I'll not give up the *Scotsman*.'

'No, of course not. But perhaps we can take the *Daily Mail* instead of *The Times*?'

'Why the *Mail*?'

'*The Times* is rather crisp, and it creases. The *Daily Mail* is larger, to begin with, but also softer; it folds.'

'I see. I do hate to support the *Mail*. They weren't nearly hard enough on Lloyd George and that Buchanan fellow.' Mrs MacBain smirked behind her mask. 'Fine. Make the change. I've always said it was a rag. Problem solved?'

Mrs MacBain hesitated.

'There can't possibly be more to this issue.' Lady Georgina's temper was wearing. This would be tricky.

'In order that no one in the family gets into any, um . . . distress . . .'

'We wouldn't want that.'

'No, milady. But in order to keep an eye on the levels, it would be best if we limited that, um . . . activity to pre-selected rooms.'

Lady Georgina's expression was thunderous, and she spoke tersely. 'In other words, because the entire village is panicking, I must go back to sharing . . . facilities with the entire household.' She stood and walked to the French doors, her back to Mrs MacBain. 'No, I won't do it. It's positively indecent!'

That's a bit rich, thought Mrs MacBain. Lady Georgina had been the strongest opposition to the family's bathing rooms being added in the first place. 'I don't understand what's wrong with the water closets. They were perfectly suitable for my parents,' she had said. It had taken them weeks to talk her round. She could be so stubborn.

Mrs MacBain waited patiently, staring at her employer's back. After a few moments Lady Georgina's shoulders slumped forward.

'What are we being reduced to? Every day brings another indignity.' She sighed loudly. 'Which rooms? I'll not have people traipsing through my boudoir to relieve themselves. That can't be good for my silk gowns.'

'I had thought we could use the first-floor water closets again. We've not used them since the bathing rooms were added to the family's bedrooms, but they still function perfectly.'

There was a long pause. Mrs MacBain was acutely aware of the clock in the hall ticking. Had it always been that loud?

'We'll need one on the ground floor as well. I can't be expected to go up and down those stairs all day.'

'Of course not, milady. I thought perhaps the Powder Room off the Armoury? It's generally kept for guests.'

'What about the one just down the hall? It's far closer.'

There was a small water closet near the Music Room – Mrs MacBain hadn't thought of it. But it was quite out of the way and would require a special trip each day, and the less time she spent walking in front of Lady Georgina's study, the better.

'My only fear is,' began Mrs MacBain slowly, formulating her argument as she spoke – not her favourite way to proceed – 'that the increase in foot traffic might disturb you as you work. People might be tempted to pop in, say hello . . .'

Mrs MacBain let the implications dawn on Lady Georgina. Thankfully, the idea of Lady Eva stopping in to discuss the wedding was enough for Lady Georgina to readily agree to the Powder Room.

'Well, that's settled then. Thank you, milady.'

'There's just one last thing, Mrs MacBain.'

'Yes, milady?'

Lady Georgina fixed her with a steely glare. 'This time, you get to tell the family.'

They took it better than she'd expected. Not well, but it only took forty-five minutes. Bella put up the initial fuss, but as long as she could keep her bath, she'd abide by Mrs MacBain's ridiculous wishes. Constance, however, stormed out of the Library shouting about being overlooked as mistress of the house, again. The men took it all in stride, except Cecil. He'd hated those water closets as a child. Hamish and Elspeth used to lock him in just before tea. Nanny would berate him for being late then he'd not get any cakes. The memory of it still enraged him. But he would do as he was asked. It was the only home he had – for the moment.

Mr Kettering had been with the house for some time now, and while they all accepted he was there to make a study of the art, something about it didn't sit right with Mrs MacBain. He and Iris were snooping around the house even more than Cecil usually did. She presumed they were assessing which pieces should be sold to pay the death duties but she couldn't understand what was taking him so long to decide. Of course, she knew that some of the paintings had been replaced over the years. The maids had quite an intimate knowledge of the frames, after spending so much time dusting them regularly. They would report to Mrs MacBain if something had been disturbed – an occurrence that increased in regularity when Cecil was in residence. But surely, someone in the family kept a record of which ones had been replaced. Wasn't that what the art inventory was for?

It wasn't until she'd seen not just Mr Kettering and Iris, but also Fergus, then Eva, and finally Cecil staring at the painting in the Map Room that Mrs MacBain's attention was aroused. What was suddenly so interesting about this one, she wondered?

She crossed into the Map Room, checking it was empty first, and went to stand in front of the sofa. The dogs were missing. She'd have to check on the children after this.

Why, she wondered, did women always have to be unclothed? What was wrong with a girl in a nice frock? She'd never understand art. In spite of that, it was a pretty painting, but nothing exceptional, from what she could see. What were they all looking at? She heard the dogs scampering across the room and turned to look as they leapt onto the sofa.

'Are you clean and dry, you little mongrels? Or have you created more work for us? Let's have a look, then.' She leaned down to pet the dogs, who immediately rolled over for belly rubs.

Straightening up, her gaze went to the painting once more and she gasped involuntarily. That's why they were staring at it. How had she missed it? All these years, hiding in plain sight and no one saw it. Mrs MacBain searched her memory. No, she'd never seen her in here. But if she had seen it, and understood it, well, it would be all she needed. Mrs MacBain turned and walked swiftly from the room. There was no time to waste.

Mrs MacBain knocked on the bedroom door. It was quite far from the others, at the end of a long corridor off the main stairs. It was the only bedroom in this part of the attic and Mrs MacBain had always wondered why Maxwell had been assigned it. There were a few storage rooms but mostly it was left open for smaller bits of furniture from the Nursery. She could see a changing table and the Inverkillen cradles. A sheet was half covering the children's rocking horse. No one but Maxwell ever came down this far. Mrs MacBain found it a bit creepy. She knocked again. No one answered.

'Miss Maxwell, are you in there? I'd like a word.' Mrs

MacBain put her ear to the door and listened. She couldn't hear any movement.

Staff doors were required to stand open during the day unless the occupant was in residence, but as Mrs MacBain tried the door, she realised she was only able to open the door a fraction. There seemed to be something in front of the door, blocking it. She pushed as hard as she could, her face screwed up with the effort, and managed to get it fully open, overturning a table in the process. She staggered into the room.

'What on earth was that doing in front of the door, Miss Maxwell?' she panted, righting the table.

But Maxwell didn't answer. Mrs MacBain looked around the room. It was empty.

How can this be? she wondered. Mrs MacBain peeked out into the long corridor, saw she was quite alone and shut the door quietly. Where was Maxwell and how could that table have been placed in front of the door if she weren't in there? It was like a riddle.

Mrs MacBain scanned the little room. It was spare and there was no place to hide. The bed sat against the wall to her left, with a night table and lamp. A dressing screen stood next to a tiny window on the far side of the room, and a chest of drawers on the right-hand wall, with a mirror above and a little timber chair next to it. Mrs MacBain went to examine the dressing screen. Why was there a dressing screen in a servant's room? Especially when the servant in question didn't share with anyone? Something wasn't right.

She crossed the room and shifted the screen out of the way, and gasped as she saw what was hidden behind it. A door. A hidden door behind the screen. She pushed it open and saw not the wardrobe she'd expected, but a set of stairs. What on earth was this? Peeking in, she could see they led down, but it was dark, and she couldn't tell how far. Did she dare go look for a torch? What if Maxwell came back and realised someone had been in her room?

Get a hold of yourself, Alice, she told herself. *You are in charge of this house. If there is something funny going on, it is your duty to know about it.*

She stepped onto the landing and let her eyes adjust to the dimness. She felt the wall to her left; it was rough stone. Must be the outer wall of the house, she thought. As her eyes adjusted, she saw what looked like a candle just two steps down. She took out a box of matches – she always had one with her – lit one, cursed the blinding brightness and then saw she was correct.

This might be do-able, she thought. Lighting the stubby taper, she proceeded down the stairs, feeling like she was in a cheap detective novel. As she neared the bottom, she could see the outline of light spilling in around the edges of what was clearly a door. Stopping to listen, she extinguished her candle, said a quick prayer, and turned the knob.

She was in a room she'd never seen before. It was blindingly white, and it took a moment before her eyes adjusted enough to register Maxwell sitting on a sofa on the far side of the room.

'Mrs MacBain!' Maxwell jumped to her feet, her eyes wide and chest heaving.

Mrs MacBain looked around the room, then shut the door behind her.

'I think you had best explain where we are – and why your face is on all these canvases.'

Maxwell sat back down, and Mrs MacBain walked slowly towards the lady's maid, taking stock of the room, unsure where they were. She'd never been in this room before. Her eyes fell on an unfinished canvas near the bed. Looking back at Maxwell, she could see the woman was terrified. She sat down beside her and smiled encouragingly. It took a few moments for Maxwell to begin speaking and when she did, her voice was calm, but hollow.

'We met when I was nineteen, at St Andrews. I was a life model for the art classes he was taking. We went for tea one day after class, just the two of us, and that was the start of it. We couldn't marry, we both knew that; my family isn't exactly part of the right set in Glasgow. But Hamish didn't care about all that. He said he loved me and when he was Earl, he could do as he wished. And what he wished was for me to be his wife.' She paused and Mrs MacBain looked around the room again. Years of their lives, and lies, were scattered all around them.

'Then his father died, and Lady Georgina sent a car and said she expected him to leave straight away. It happened so suddenly that we didn't have a chance to talk about anything. A footman started packing up his rooms and they were gone within a few hours. It all happened so quickly! I waited for him for months. We wrote to each other, but he couldn't come back, he said. The timing wasn't right yet. They were in full mourning. He asked me to wait a bit longer.'

'That must have been very difficult for you, Flora.'

Maxwell smiled faintly at her. 'It was. But it would all be worth it in the end – at least, I thought it would be. Hamish was now Lord Inverkillen; we just needed the right time to go public. But neither of us counted on Lady Georgina.' Her voice had turned bitter.

'Lady Georgina? She knew about you?' asked Mrs MacBain, aghast.

Maxwell gave a small shrug. 'I don't know, to be honest. But before Hamish and I could make our relationship known, she had arranged his engagement without even consulting him. Victoria came from a wealthy family with a good name, and that was all that mattered to her. It was announced in the papers before he had a chance to break it off, and then it was too late. He had to go through with it. Marriage isn't about love for these people, you know. It's a business transaction.'

Mrs MacBain knew it well. None of them, it seemed, were happy in their marriages.

'But how did you end up becoming her lady's maid? And why would you?' asked Mrs MacBain.

'Hamish arranged it. I don't know how he convinced her to take me. I had no experience, and she knew it. I didn't know anyone who grew up this way – ' she waved her arm around the room – 'I had no idea what I was even supposed to do. Those first few months were hell. She was so short tempered and nothing I did was right. And seeing Hamish in her bed . . . well, it nearly killed me. I almost went back to Glasgow, but Hamish talked me into staying. He loved me and it was the only way we could be together. He could be very persuasive.'

'Did Lady Inverkillen know?' Mrs MacBain said in a hushed voice, trying not to sound as scandalised as she felt.

'No! Well, not until the will was read. Then she worked it out fairly quickly.'

'Yes, I'd say she did.' Mrs MacBain rolled her eyes. The man had really put her into the fire, poor thing. 'So, the morning after, the breakfast tray . . .'

Maxwell put her face in her hands. 'It was horrible. She confronted me. Ordered me out of the house. Called me every name in the book. I didn't know ladies knew those words. But I don't have any place to go, Alice, I just tried to stay out of her way. It's a big house. You can go months without seeing anyone if you try.'

'Yes, but you've been taking breakfast trays to her each morning, lighting the fires . . . How do you do that without her seeing you?'

Maxwell gave a small, humourless laugh. 'You wouldn't know her morning routine, not being her maid. Her Ladyship doesn't eat breakfast. Never has.'

'What?' Mrs MacBain breathed, confused beyond measure. 'But her trays always come back empty.'

Maxwell blushed and shifted on the sofa a little. 'That's because I eat them. Don't be angry. I deliver the tray to her dressing room and then go and draw her bath. She doesn't like trays on the bed. She says they ruin the linens. Each morning she takes two sips of tea – only two – and then takes her bath. She has never eaten breakfast. But she insists on ordering one. It drove me mad when I first arrived. I'm from Glasgow, I know families that would kill for that food. I couldn't let it go to waste, and I couldn't talk her out of ordering it. So, after she leaves, I eat the breakfast. For the last twenty years.'

'Which is why you never have breakfast with us.'

Maxwell nodded.

Mrs MacBain's mind was reeling. The day was getting stranger and stranger. But something was still amiss. 'And what about the luncheon and dinner trays? Surely she's seen you then?'

'Actually, Iris has been doing that for me.'

'What?' Mrs MacBain was scandalised, again. There seemed to be no end to it.

'She'd been struggling to get the children's trays all the way up to the Nursery – she's not very strong, you know – and one day she nearly dropped them. Luckily, Ollie caught her just in time. But I suggested we switch. So, she takes Lady Inverkillen's tray and I take the children's tray.'

'Dear lord, what is happening to this house?' Mrs MacBain shook her head and stood, pacing a few steps about the room. 'The breakfast order changed recently. Mrs Burnside commented on it. It's always been scrambled eggs with toast and tea, and now suddenly, it's sausages and milk.'

Miss Maxwell looked uncomfortable. 'Yes. That would be the children.'

'The children?' Mrs MacBain sighed. 'I rue the day Nanny died. What have they done now?'

'Horrible creatures. I caught them in here one afternoon.'

'In here?' Mrs MacBain was shocked, and a little offended. If she hadn't known about this room, how did the children? 'Where are we and how did they get in?'

'We're in Hamish's private study. That door leads to his dressing room.' She pointed to a door to their right. 'The children were loose one afternoon and say they found the door wide open. How, I don't know. Hamish had the only key. But here they were, jumping on the bed, shrieking and shouting. How Lady Inverkillen didn't hear them, I don't know. So, I closed the door and took them up to my room as quick as I could.'

Mrs MacBain's jaw dropped. 'Did they have any idea of the significance of this?' she swept her arm around the room.

'No, they just know they found a secret. I don't think they care what it's about. Although, Elspeth's eldest girl might understand. My French isn't very strong, but I swear she said the word "mistress" to her brother.'

'Well, they are French. It's sort of a birthright there, isn't it?' The women smiled weakly at each other. 'But what does that have to do with the breakfast trays, Flora?'

Maxwell rolled her eyes and groaned softly. 'Blackmail.'

It took a moment for the word to sink in. 'They're holding you to ransom? For sausages?'

'I thought it a small price to pay.' She shrugged and blushed slightly.

Mrs MacBain didn't know if she would laugh or cry. It came out as a loud snort instead.

'I'm sorry, I am, but that is the funniest thing I've heard in days.' She burst into laughter, and Maxwell grinned reluctantly. 'Heavens above. We really do need to find a new Nanny.' It took a few moments for her to regain her composure. She wiped a tear from her eye. 'So, what's your plan, Flora? You can't keep hiding in here, and I can't keep you on the payroll if she sacked you weeks ago.'

Maxwell met her eyes, looking miserable again. 'I don't really have a plan. I have nowhere else to go and Her Ladyship won't exactly be giving me a good reference.'

'No, that much is true. But perhaps we can sort something.' Mrs MacBain looked around the room once again. It was a remarkable secret to have kept, and for so many years. No wonder the woman was a wreck. It hadn't been about Nanny at all.

The dressing gong sounded. 'Right, we need to get out of here. Look, why don't you keep dressing Lady Georgina and Lady Constance; I can do the others, and maybe, just maybe, we can keep you on for a while longer. You need a plan though, Flora. I can't hide you forever. But Lord knows we need every pair of hands we can get just now.'

★

It was some hours before Mrs MacBain had a chance to think about the Rubens in the Map Room. Now that she had seen it, she marvelled that she hadn't noticed for so long: it was clearly a portrait of a younger Maxwell. If Lady

Inverkillen had seen it, there would be no hiding the affair; and that certainly gave Lady Inverkillen a motive for killing her husband. But Maxwell said she hadn't known until the will had been read. Mrs MacBain thought long and hard about Lady Inverkillen's movements in the days just before the ball. Had she been in the Map Room for any reason at all? It would be unusual. She spent her time in the Music Room, and that was in a different wing altogether. Who would know? Archie. Archie was usually the footman assigned to His Lordship's study. Could she ask him? She'd been told he was quite weak, they'd nearly lost him, and his recovery was slow. Would he even remember? Another dead end, she thought bitterly. Unless someone just happened to be standing in the hall to see her Ladyship . . . standing in the hall . . .

Mrs MacBain flew to the second floor and stood in an alcove, waiting for Iris to return from dinner. Finally, at half past ten, she arrived at her bedroom door. Mrs MacBain waited until she was firmly in her room and then knocked on the door quietly. It took Iris a few moments to answer the door, and when she did, she opened it only a few inches.

'Oh, Mrs MacBain. It's you.' She was in her dressing gown, clutching her hot water bottle.

'I wondered if we might have a quick word, Iris. I know it's late, but it can't wait. Do you mind if I come in for a moment?'

The girl let her in and then perched on the edge of her bed. A small fire crackled in the grate. It wouldn't make a blind bit of difference in this room, she thought.

'I know it's small,' she said, watching the housekeeper. 'I don't really do it for the heat. I just like the sound of it when I sleep.'

Mrs MacBain turned to look at the girl. She was quite

scrawny, and Mrs MacBain could see how the trays would have overpowered her. 'Iris, just before the ball, did you by any chance happen to see Lady Inverkillen in the Map Room?'

Iris looked surprised. 'Yes. How did you know?' Mrs MacBain said nothing, but nodded, encouraging the girl to continue. 'I was looking for the portrait of the Tenth Countess and the art inventory lists it being hung by the Wedgewood Room. But it wasn't there, so I was on my way back to the Reading Room, to check I'd got that right, and just as I got to the Map Room, Lady Inverkillen came rushing out and knocked me over.' She put a hand to her left shoulder. 'She didn't even apologise. But that's when I spotted Lady Morag, on the wall opposite. It was kind of lucky, actually. I'd been looking for weeks.'

'Iris,' Mrs MacBain tried to keep her voice steady, 'was she alone in the Map Room?'

Iris thought for a moment. 'I don't remember anyone else being there. Well, no one else came out after her. But then I went for a plaster . . . I cut my arm on that marble table when I fell. Thankfully, it didn't bruise. That would have looked terrible at the ball.'

'Thank you, Iris. That's exactly what I needed to know.' Her brain was whirring as she walked to the door. 'Good night.'

'Erm, good night, Mrs MacBain.' Iris was very confused.

Mrs MacBain walked slowly down the servants' stairs, her mind fully occupied with Iris's tale. Thank the lord for that girl! Where was Mackay? If something happened at the ball, he'd know. She glanced at her watch. He'd be laying out Angus's bedclothes and then waiting in the servants' hall for the family to go up to bed. Best to speak with him below stairs, she thought, and continued to the basement.

MacKay arrived some twenty minutes later and was

ushered straight into Mrs MacBain's rooms, looking utterly perplexed when she asked the question. 'Yes, actually. How did you know?'

Mrs MacBain held her tongue and shrugged.

'Yes, they had words, very sharp ones, before the ball. I'd just finished dressing him when Lady Inverkillen came into the room and asked for privacy. She was angry, that much I could see. I waited in the corridor and could hear shouting.'

'Could you tell what it was about?'

'No. It was fairly muffled.'

'How long were they in there?'

'About ten minutes, I'd wager. He came out into the hall first, angry but trying to compose himself. She came out several minutes later, very quiet, and wouldn't take his arm. They went down to the ball; I tidied up.'

'And after the ball?'

'He went to bed later than usual. Didn't really say much. But from his mood the next morning, I'd say they hadn't kissed and made up.' He stared at the housekeeper for a moment, trying to read her thoughts. 'What's all this about, Mrs MacBain?'

She was lost in thought. 'Hm? Oh, probably nothing. Thank you, Mr Mackay. I appreciate your candour.'

The valet stood and bowed his head slightly. 'Happy to be of service.'

When she was alone, Mrs MacBain stood and paced her office for some time, wondering what on earth she was going to do next.

July

It was Tuesday morning and Mrs MacBain was approaching her weekly meeting with Lady Georgina with some trepidation. The staff were badly behind with their tasks. The last of the housemaids had succumbed to the sickness a week ago, and with just the six of them left, and no downstairs staff but for Mrs Burnside, she didn't see how they could go on without significant change.

Last night at dinner, Ollie the footman had confessed to Hudson that he wasn't cleaning the shoes nightly. He'd stopped doing it some weeks ago, in fact. Hudson had been livid.

'But, Mr Hudson, they never go outside. The shoes don't have a chance to get dirty.'

He had a point, and it had set Mrs MacBain thinking. There were an awful lot of tasks they simply didn't need to do on a daily basis. She wished they could shutter some of the unused rooms, or at least agree which set of rooms they would use and only clean and light the fires in those.

'How many fires are you lighting at the moment?' asked Lady Georgina, when the subject came around.

'Forty-two including the bedrooms. Twice a day.'

Lady Georgina's eyebrows rose. 'That is substantial. What do you propose?'

'I had hoped we could light fires only in the rooms the

family tends to use heavily: the Blue Drawing Room, the Dining Room, the Library, this room, the Map Room and the Billiards Room.'

'There are one hundred and twenty-five rooms in this house, and we only use six?'

'Other than the bedrooms, yes.'

'What about the Conservatory?'

'It only gets use in the autumn.'

'The Smoking Room?'

'Just on Christmas Eve. And I can't recall seeing anyone in the Green Sitting Room for years.'

Lady Georgina was struggling to even remember the Green Sitting Room.

'I take your point. Then keep the fires in the rooms you mentioned. And the bedrooms, of course.'

There was a pause.

'Surely, you don't mean to deprive us of fires in the bedrooms?' Lady Georgina said, outraged yet again.

'No, not at all. I'd never suggest such a thing. But there are sixteen fires in the family bedrooms, built and lit twice a day. If the family could build and light the morning fires themselves . . .' She could see that Lady Georgina was about to object when Fergus knocked on the door and walked into the room without waiting to be invited.

Lady Georgina grimaced at him. 'Mrs MacBain is proposing more cuts. Have a seat,' she barked.

Fergus remained standing, looking amused. 'Cuts? What do you mean?'

'She expects me to light my own fire in the morning.'

'That doesn't sound unreasonable to me.' On the contrary, Fergus looked rather excited at the prospect. 'How difficult can it be to strike a match? I'm happy to do that.'

'Am I to make my own breakfast tray as well now?' Lady

Georgina cried. 'I suppose next you'll be asking us to make up our own beds.'

Mrs MacBain left a significant silence, and Lady Georgina's mouth dropped open in astonishment.

'I am not making up my own bed! I think that is the least I can expect as a member of the aristocracy. This is becoming too much. I can't take any more.' Fergus could see she was building up a head of steam, and he needed to move quickly to cut her off.

'Grandmama, Andrew Lawlis is here, and he'd like to speak to us.' He extended his hand to help her rise. 'Shall we?'

Lady Georgina stalked out of the room, muttering about indignities. Fergus looked to Mrs MacBain, smiled reassuringly, and said, 'Let's you and I speak later about all this.'

Mrs MacBain nodded mutely, and let out a deep, unsteady breath.

Lawlis and Imogen were once again back to the Abbey, masks and gloves at the ready, pleased to be bearing good news for once. Hudson escorted them to the Library and was surprised to see Cecil looking through the desk. 'My apologies, sir. I was unaware the room was occupied.' He turned and ushered Lawlis and Imogen towards the Armoury.

'No, no! Please, come in. I was just looking for . . . erm . . . some ink. I've run out. Please, have a seat.' He waved a gracious arm towards the sofas.

Hudson's eyes flicked to the desk and then stared back at Cecil. 'I'll have some ink sent to your rooms, sir.' Hudson waved his own gracious arms towards the doors to the Armoury.

'What? Oh. Yes. Please do that.' Cecil scurried from the

room and Imogen detected a slight smile on the Butler's face as he closed the doors behind him.

They waited for Fergus and Lady Georgina for several minutes. Lawlis was sitting on the sofa, sorting his papers. Imogen wandered to the windows. She'd heard about the Inverkillen roses in the village and wanted a glimpse for herself. As Fergus entered, he saw her staring out into the garden, confusion written on her face.

'Miss MacLeod? What's the mat—'

Fergus didn't get farther in his question before Imogen started banging on the window with her fists, shouting, 'Oh! Oh! Child with crossbow! Child with crossbow!' Fergus and Lawlis rushed to the window and then immediately turned and ran from the room. Lady Georgina crossed over and looked out to see a line of bronzed cherubs with apples on their heads and the children some paces away, arguing, presumably, over who got the first shot. Ollie got to them just in time.

'Oh! Oh, thank goodness. We really must get a new nanny. They are quite a handful. Shall we sit down?' Lady Georgina moved to the sofa and settled in, as if nothing had happened. Imogen could only shake her head. Had that been her nephews . . .

When the men had returned and all were settled, Lawlis announced, with an air of ceremony, that they had finally received an offer for the Abbey. Quite a good one as well, and they should accept it. Lady Georgina was to be given the proceeds from the salmon sales, all the family debts would be paid, and the buyers would purchase houses in the village for any family members that wanted to remain in Loch Down. There was only one peculiar request, but Lawlis wasn't sure if it could be honoured. He had sent a letter to the College of Arms to ask.

'The College of Arms?' asked Fergus. 'I don't understand. What have they asked for?'

'They want to quarter your coat of arms.'

'Who does?' asked Lady Georgina. It was as near to a growl as she had ever come.

'I believe you know Lord Eltenbrae? He said he was an old friend of the family.' Lawlis looked quite pleased with himself.

'Oh, no. No, no, no. That will never do,' said Lady Georgina. They all turned to stare at her. 'Tell him no.'

Fergus didn't want to ask but it had to be done. 'Why not, Grandmama?'

'That family has been trying to get their hands on Loch Down for generations! The current Lord has made several plays for the Estate through the years, none of them above board.' She shifted and straightened her skirt, ending the discussion.

Again, Fergus didn't want to ask but it had to be done. 'What are you talking about, Grandmama?'

She glared at him, and they were unsure she would speak. But she did.

'His first attempt, he schemed with others to win the Estate in a cards game against Cecil. Luckily, Hamish heard about the plan and stormed in just in time.' She could see they were less than scandalised. 'Then there was the time he kidnapped Elspeth.'

'What!' They were all startled by this bombshell, and she felt a swoop of satisfaction.

'He was nearly at Gretna Green with her before we caught up with them. She was only fourteen at the time. We should have rung the authorities, but we couldn't risk Elspeth's reputation. And don't get me started on his father!' She shifted with indignation. 'We spent years dealing with that man's plotting and scheming. Do you know, he once loosed a pack of wild boars on this estate, and then gleefully informed everyone that it was our fault. Said we were refusing to do anything about it. Which simply wasn't true. We had our hands full, hunting them down before anyone was hurt.' She looked to Imogen and explained patronisingly. 'Wild boar can be quite dangerous, you see.'

Fergus shook his head and looked to Lawlis, who could only shrug and pour more tea.

'Oh, it caused such a scandal,' Lady Georgina continued, 'It was in the papers for months. Lord Eltenbrae even called for your grandfather to be stripped of his Earldom. Luckily for us, the man who supplied the animals came to the Abbey. It seems Lord Eltenbrae hadn't paid him, and he came to us for the compensation, so it all came out then. No,' she sighed, 'that family must never be allowed to have the Estate.'

Imogen knew that it would be hard to argue against a grudge that deep. She wondered what had started it.

Fergus went over to the tea service and noisily made himself a cup of tea, trying to think how to mount this argument.

'Why do they want the Estate so badly?' asked Imogen.

Lady Georgina huffed for a moment or two and then sighed. 'I think it was the Twelfth, no the Thirteenth Countess who spurned Lord Eltenbrae's proposal. She chose to marry into this family instead, and he didn't take it well. We have endured that family's wrath ever since.'

Fergus spun around, at the end of his tether. 'Grandmama, in less than six weeks, we are facing homelessness and ruin. We might not get another offer that takes care of you.'

'I will not be dependent upon that family for anything!' she said stoutly. 'I'd rather lose the house at auction.'

'But he could easily bid for it at auction and get it for far less,' Lawlis said quietly. 'At least this way, all the debts are paid, and the family can start fresh.'

Lady Georgina walked to the bay window that overlooked the rose garden, her back to them, and Fergus could see it was a lost cause. For today, at least. He ushered Lawlis and Imogen out and promised to try to bring her round.

Clan feuding, thought Imogen. Who knew it still existed?

Fergus had had no idea how much work the servants actually did. Nor had he realised how many servants they'd lost and he was rather ashamed of himself for not noticing. Things had to change, that much was obvious.

He and Mrs MacBain had spoken at length about the daily routine of the household. Fergus wanted a clear understanding of how the house ran, so they had created a list of which tasks could be eliminated or changed and which the family could do for themselves. The very idea of the family doing for themselves made Mrs MacBain uncomfortable, but at least it was Fergus who would discuss it with them. She was happy to hide behind him on this one.

That afternoon at tea, he broached the subject. It didn't go well, unsurprisingly. They had managed to sneak the reduction in tea cakes past everyone, and the while the ladies had felt hard done by, they had eventually given up their breakfast trays with something resembling grace. But waking to a cold room and lighting their own morning fires was, it seemed, the last straw.

'Why on earth should we have to change anything? First the breakfast trays and now this. It's an outrage. I should have been consulted about this, you know.'

'We only have five or six servants left, Constance, doing the work of forty,' Fergus replied wearily. 'It's too much, and some things will have to change.'

'I can't understand why there are so few servants.'

Fergus sighed. 'They are devastatingly ill, Constance, and from what Mrs. MacBain has told me, we are lucky no one has died.' The room bristled uncomfortably. 'It's a long and difficult recovery as well, so those that can are being sent home to recuperate. They'll come back when they have fully recovered.'

Constance took an enraged sip of tea. 'Well . . . then we should be hiring new servants to replace them. This is getting ridiculous.' She set her teacup down roughly on the tray. 'Just look at the state of these cakes. I don't know how much more of this I can take.'

'We don't have the money to hire more servants.' Fergus was close to losing his temper. 'So we must do what we can to help out until they return.'

'But making up our own beds?' Bella was, as expected, hugely insulted at the very idea. 'I wouldn't even know how.'

'Mrs MacBain will teach us,' said Fergus. 'Ollie, the footman will teach us how to light the fires—'

'You expect me to take instruction from a footman?' Angus spat. 'I am an Earl, for God's sake. I hardly need to look to the servants for instructions.'

'And why can't we use the other rooms of the house? That seems ridiculous. It's like living in a prison.' Even Cecil was affronted by the change; the Cards Room was on the no-fire list.

'You're perfectly welcome to use the other rooms, Uncle Cecil, there just won't be a fire, unless you build it yourself.'

It went on like this for what felt like hours to Fergus. Constance wanted to trade the beds for breakfast trays. Angus refused to wake up in a cold room. Bella simply sulked. It was exhausting.

Fergus eventually stood and held up his hands. 'Right, your fires will be lit tonight and in the morning. After that, you're on your own. If you would like instructions, Ollie will be giving a demonstration in the Blue Drawing Room tomorrow after breakfast. Which will be served in the Dining Room only.'

He looked pointedly at Constance. For one second, he thought she might throw her teacup at him.

For one long second, she considered it.

Ross appeared at the back door, which he rarely did, but he had the children in tow. Mrs MacBain stared at him, amazed and relieved. No one had yet told the family they were missing.

'Where were they? We've been searching since morning.'

'I found them in the Bird Loft, trying to set the racing pigeons free.' He glared at them. No one looked remorseful.

Mrs MacBain was aghast. The Loft stood in front of the barns. It was impossible to get in without being seen. If they'd have been at full staff, that is. 'How on earth did they get there?'

He shook his head. 'No idea, and they won't tell me. That lot,' he pointed to Elspeth's children, 'are pretending they don't understand English. Which is bollocks.'

'Ross! Language!'

'If they don't speak English, why'd they giggle?' He had a point.

'Thank you, Ross. This day . . .' She shook her head and herded the children into the hallway. 'Right, you lot, Iris is in a peck of trouble because of you. Up to the Nursery at once!'

Ross smiled and placed his hand on his cousin's shoulder. 'It'll be over soon enough.'

She nodded, smiling back at him weakly. 'Yes. I've forgotten what I was doing. We need venison from the game larder.'

'Do you want me to fetch it?' He started to walk off, but she caught his arm.

'No. Thank you. I'll do it. Gives me a quiet moment in the day.' He smiled and headed off. As she walked the few hundred yards to the larder, she mused about how the children managed to move around without being seen. It was maddening.

She was just leaving the game larder when the heavens opened up. She stood in the doorway for some minutes, hoping it would pass, or at least lighten. But when neither happened, she decided to run for it, hoping to miss the puddles. They got her in the end, though, and by the time she got to the back door, she was up to her ankles in icy water and mud. Pulling her foot out, she saw the shoe was wet but not too muddy. Why hadn't she put on her gumboots? She'd have to wear her other pair of house shoes, the ones that pinched. And then an idea came to her. No one wears house shoes outside.

Mrs MacBain walked swiftly through the house to the kitchen, leaving one wet footprint behind as she went. She just managed to grab Ollie before he went up to serve dinner.

'Ollie, when did you stop cleaning the shoes? Can you remember?'

Ollie stared at her. She was soaked. 'Oh, I'm not sure Mrs MacBain.' He turned to rush off with a tray of silver. She put her hand on his forearm.

'Think for a moment.'

He set the tray down and looked at her. 'Well, once Lady Georgina moved in, I couldn't get to them all, so I started doing half one day, half the next. But I stopped doing them completely about the time Mister Fergus and Mister Cecil had their row in the Armoury.' He thought for a moment and then nodded. 'Yeah, just about then.'

She did some mental mathematics. Constance's maid had

fallen ill just about then. 'And do you clean the ones in the Boot Room as well?'

'No. Not unless someone asks me to, that is.'

'Has anyone asked you to clean their outdoor shoes since His Lordship died?' she said, holding her breath, her heart pounding.

He shook his head, looking anxious. 'Do you need me to? I can do them tomorrow if you like.'

'That won't be necessary, Ollie. Thank you. Best get on now.'

She turned on her heel and headed straight to the Boot Room. As she went, she noticed the mud and rain she'd dragged in. The way things were going, someone would slip and hurt themselves. Cursing, she went to fetch a mop.

When she had finished cleaning, she returned to her hunch. Checking her watch, she saw that tea had just been served. That gave her half to three-quarters of an hour at most before the family were on the move again. Best begin with the wardrobes. She let herself into Constance's rooms first.

Constance loved shoes and spent a great deal of time collecting them. The more unsuitable for the countryside, the better. Mrs MacBain didn't understand the appeal. They were just shoes. They kept your feet from being cold, wet and dirty. Why each frock needed its own pair, she would never know.

Shaking her head, she opened the wardrobes and peered at the bottom shelves. Each pair had been neatly put away by the maid, heels facing out, lined up like keys on a piano. From what she could tell, none were missing. Mrs MacBain sighed. There had to be fifty pairs, she thought; several leather, yes, but most were silk, in pale colours, and heavily beaded. Lord, she thought, even her boots have heels. Not a single pair could have survived a trip to the weir and back.

She checked the wardrobes of the other ladies and reached

the same conclusion for each. Far fewer in number, but all put away neatly and all in perfect condition. The only wardrobe she didn't check was Her Ladyship's. But how to do that without disturbing her? That was something she'd have to think on. But for now, she headed down to the Boot Room.

Each family member had their own assigned area, to keep their things tidy. She rummaged through the ladies' footwear. Lady Inverkillen's and Elspeth's were well used, but only Elspeth's had fresh mud. Bella's were roughly cleaned but showed no sign of having been farther than freshly mown lawns. Constance's pile, however, was spotless. She wasn't much for the great outdoors, and only had a pair of water-proofs and some plimsolls for tennis. Mrs MacBain turned both over. Clean as the day they were made.

She hadn't really believed that Constance had suddenly become frustrated enough to kill her father-in-law, but this definitely put her in the clear. Lady Inverkillen, then, was the last man standing.

Mrs MacBain knew when, and how, and why, but she couldn't really prove any of it. *Now what?* she wondered, as she walked slowly back to her office. Short of asking Lady Inverkillen in person, there was no way to prove she'd been there and had been responsible for Hamish's death.

I'm a housekeeper, not a detective, she thought. *What am I meant to do now?*

Constance's face was flushed. 'And you expect me to do this every day?' She and Mrs MacBain were reviewing how to make up a bed the following morning, and she was finding it difficult to deal with the size of the covers. Her arms ached from the effort.

'It gets easier, milady. I promise.'

Constance sat down in a chair, frowning. 'I just don't know that I'll ever be able to do this. Lifting the mattress, tucking the sheets. And the pillowcases are absolutely impossible.'

'Luckily, we only do the pillowcases once per week, milady.' Mrs MacBain found it difficult not to roll her eyes. At least she could smile behind the mask.

'Well, I still think it's a ridiculous thing to have to do . . .' Constance descended into indistinct muttering, which Mrs MacBain suspected was on the wrong side of polite.

'I must get on, milady,' she said firmly. 'Lady Elspeth is waiting for me.' She wasn't, but Mrs MacBain couldn't afford to waste any more time with Lady Constance. If she'd made up the bed herself, it would have been quicker. If she'd cleaned the entire room, it would have been quicker. As it was, she'd spent thirty minutes instructing Constance and she strongly suspected the woman was faking incompetence.

She'd gathered the entire family two days previously to demonstrate how beds were made. The men found it physically easier but more of an affront to their masculinity. It had been three hours of demonstrations, corrections, tantrums and snide remarks. Mrs MacBain had known it wouldn't be a natural thing for them to do, but honestly, it wasn't that difficult. What would they do if she gave them a floor sweeper? It didn't bear thinking about.

Bella, too, was attempting to make her bed. 'How do they get it so damn tight?' she shouted at her empty room. She was finding it impossible. Every time Bella tucked the sheet under the mattress, another corner came loose. Or it would go slack and baggy in the middle. She'd been struggling with the damn thing for twenty minutes and was no closer to finishing. Mrs MacBain said it could be done in five minutes, but Bella couldn't see how.

Oh, sod it, she thought, I'm putting the damn blanket on.

She grabbed the tartan blanket and tried to throw it on the bed, not realising she was standing on it, and nearly swept herself off her own feet in the process. After some swearing, she managed to get it on the bed and was straightening it when she remembered that the second sheet was supposed to go on first.

Sodding second sheet . . . She really needed a cup of tea. No chance of that, she thought bitterly. Fine, leave the sheet for now and do the pillows. How hard can that be? Fifteen minutes later, a pillow went sailing across the room, knocking over a small side table.

Bella swore loudly. 'Why is this so damn hard?' she whimpered, close to tears. 'Bella, get a grip,' she scolded herself. 'You will not be defeated by a bed. If the servants can do it, you can do it.'

She shuffled to the end of the bed to grab the sheet, but her feet were immediately tangled up by the blanket on the floor.

More swearing, so much swearing. She yanked her foot free and immediately pitched forward, just managing to avoid hitting her head on the dressing stool. Her arm wasn't so lucky, and she howled in pain. Landing in a heap on the floor, she burst into tears.

What had she done wrong in her life to deserve this? She was the daughter of an Earl for God's sake. Did that mean nothing anymore?

It was then that she smelled smoke. She turned to see the corner of the pillow in flames. She had accidentally thrown it on the remains of this morning's pathetic excuse for a fire.

Bella jumped to her feet, shouting fire, but fell over again, tangled in the bed linens. She managed to extract herself and ran to pull the servants bell cord hard, several times. She

looked around the room. What did one do in a fire? She ran
to the hall just as the rug was catching alight and shouted
'Fire!' into the empty space. Where was everyone? This is
exactly why they needed servants, she thought furiously.

'Fire! F—Oh, yes, in there!' Ollie was sprinting towards
Bella with two red buckets in hand. He tossed the first one
on the rug and the second on the pillow. Sand. Is that what
those were for? How clever. Bella had never really thought
about the red buckets dotted around the Abbey. Well, beyond
watching Angus put his cigarette butts in them.

'Are you all right, milady?' Ollie panted, looking her up
and down as he stamped on the rug to make sure the fire
was truly out.

'Yes, yes I'm all right. How bad is it?'

They peered around the room. It wasn't pretty.

'It could have been worse, milady,' he said comfortingly.
'But you'll need a new room until this one is properly aired
out. I'll go and fetch Mrs MacBain.'

Bella sat on the sofa in the bay window, lower lip trembling,
tears threatening to spill again.

'Oh my word. Are you all right, milady?'

Bella looked up to see a panicked Mrs MacBain staring at
the fireplace, Constance smirking behind her. She straightened
up. 'It appears I've failed to make the bed.'

'So it would seem,' said Mrs MacBain, looking around the
room in amazement.

'Chin up,' said Constance. 'You're really getting the hang
of starting your own fire.'

Bella wished she had the flaming pillow to throw at her.

They were at tea that afternoon, discussing what would
happen with the county show that year, since they had so

few servants. It was always held on the Inverkillen Estate. There were stands to build and marquees to erect, not to mention the tea and cakes. Bella was on the brink of suggesting they simply cancel that year when Constance finally swept into the room, late and quite out of breath. The hem of her dress was muddy.

'You look a shambles! What's happened to you? No don't sit there!' Lady Georgina tried unsuccessfully to seat Constance farther away from her usual place. She didn't like to be so near to mud.

'I've been to the village,' she said, taking a gulp of the tea Hudson handed her. 'For my dress fitting. It was arranged ages ago and I couldn't reach Madame Elodie on the telephone to cancel so I had to go in. You know how she gets if you miss an appointment.' All the women nodded gloomily. She took another gulp of tea.

'But she wasn't there when I arrived. So, I went to Françoise's, hoping to have my hair done.' Another gulp of tea. Iris wondered how she wasn't burning her mouth. Bella wondered what had happened to her hair.

'But they're closed as well! I went round to Hambeldon's and then the post office, but no one was open. I saw a sign at the pub reading "Closed until further notice". It seems the entire village has shut down because of this illness.'

Lady Georgina rolled her eyes and tutted. Constance took the moment to help herself to a bit of cake.

'This has really gone too far,' muttered Lady Georgina. Then, motioning to Constance's hem, she said, 'And your dress?'

'Well, it started to rain on the way home, didn't it, so there wasn't much I could do. I'd have changed when I arrived, but I was so late, I thought it best to come straight in. I daresay my shoes are ruined.'

'Do you mean to say, you walked to the village?'

Constance nodded, munching on her cake. 'Well, I'd have taken the car, but I couldn't find Lockridge anywhere. I think we need to sack him.' She waved her free hand to signal the end of the conversation.

'That's a bit harsh, don't you think?' said Fergus.

'What is the point of having a chauffeur if one cannot take the car at a moment's notice? He should be sacked. It's as simple as that.' Constance waved her hand again. 'A countess should not be seen walking into the village. I should be driven in a car, as befits my status.'

'Oh, please,' he groaned.

'No, no. She's quite right there, Fergus,' said Lady Georgina.

Emboldened, Constance went on. 'And, as Countess, I should have the Stuart Suite. Victoria has had nearly three months to mourn her husband. Three months to sit in those rooms without coming out once. It's high time she rejoined the family and just got on with it. Angus and I are now the head of this family. And we deserve those rooms.'

Mr Kettering wondered if there was a way to slip out of the room unnoticed. Surely this was not a matter for his ears. He surveyed the room as more and more of the family started bickering – they had such short fuses – but he was dismayed to see that his only escape route would take him right through the middle of it all. If only they had been standing. Had they had been standing, he might have stood a chance.

Elspeth tried to broker a peace but was cut off by Bella, who insisted Constance was being beastly. There might have been a barb about her being childless, and then Constance crossed the room to slap Bella, bringing the entire family to their feet.

Mr Kettering saw his chance and slipped quietly behind the fray of warring family. His hand was on the door handle, so near victory, when he heard Constance announce that she was going to confront Lady Inverkillen about it once and for all. She shoved him out of the way and wrenched the door open, flying up the stairs.

As he bounced off the wall – my word she was strong for a small woman! – someone grabbed his arm and yanked him out of the room and into the Armoury. He couldn't have said who, but before he could think straight, he was rushing up the stairs to the first floor with the rest of the family. Hudson, still in the Library, sighed. Couldn't they have just one peaceful meal?

Constance arrived first, but only just. Fergus and Elspeth, hot on her heels, arrived just in time; Elspeth blocked the door while Fergus tried to restrain his sister-in-law. She was putting up quite a fight for someone so petite. Wresting herself free with a swift kick to Fergus's shin, she fell onto Elspeth, knocking her over. Cecil arrived just as Constance took hold of the doorknob. He managed to grab her arm, saying rather breathlessly, 'My dear, think this through.' Elspeth struggled to her feet and Cecil staggered aside, looking for a chair. It was quite some distance from the Library to the family rooms, he thought, still breathing heavily.

They stood for some moments, Constance, Elspeth and Fergus, squabbling in the corridor as the rest of the family arrived, all short of breath. It isn't every day an angry mob arrives at your door, demanding you relinquish your home, and Iris wondered what Lady Inverkillen was thinking. It was impossible for her not to have heard them but, just as it seemed Constance would listen to reason, she jerked back, catching Fergus off guard, who then fell backwards into the enormous flower vase. It tipped over, causing a tremendous crash. The clan fell silent, staring at the flowers, the dripping water, and shards of pottery strewn on the floor.

She knows we're here now if she didn't before, thought Iris.

Constance seized the moment and opened the door, shouting for her mother-in-law as she did. The family flooded through the door and stood, dumbfounded, looking around the empty sitting room.

'She's not here!' cried Constance, rejoining the family from the bedchamber. 'Why isn't she here?'

Angus and Elspeth pushed past Constance to see the bedchamber for themselves. Coming back into the room, Elspeth spotted an envelope over the fire. She picked it up. It said 'Read Me' in her sister-in-law's handwriting.

Lady Georgina arrived in the room and sat down, quite out of breath, and held out her hand for the envelope. Angus reached for it too, keen to assert his right as head of the family, but Elspeth grimaced at him and handed it to her mother.

'I've never even been in here,' said Bella, awed as she looked around the room. The walls were covered in silk with embroidered thistles rising from the floor. A rather ornate crystal chandelier hung from the frescoed ceiling. It was beautiful but utterly unexpected.

'Neither have I,' said Fergus, staring at the chandelier. 'Is that still lit by candles?'

'Well, these rooms were always off limits, weren't they?' said Angus. He was fingering a silver cigarette case on the writing desk.

'Why, though? What was so secret?' asked Bella, looking around. Elspeth asked Lady Georgina about the letter, which she handed back to her daughter, still breathing heavily from the run upstairs.

Elspeth read it quickly. 'She's gone away.'

'What?' Bella grabbed the letter and read aloud:

'It has become clear that my position in this family has been one of convenience and posturing, rather than affection and loyalty. It is a position I can no longer accept, and I refuse to have any further part in the deception. I have lived many years for the benefit of a family name that had little regard for anyone other than itself. I was asked to play a part, which I did, but without the benefit of knowing what was happening behind the curtain. To those that did know, I can only say this: I deserved better, and you know it. I am leaving Loch Down, to salvage what happiness I can. May God forgive you all for the hypocrisy so easily practised in this household.

'Victoria.'

'She wrote it the day after Father's will was read.' Bella sat down heavily on a sofa, stunned. Constance took the letter from her.

There was a long pause.

'So . . . she's been gone for three months, and none of you noticed?' asked Mr Kettering, more than a little bewildered and unable to resist asking.

Guilty looks flew around the room. There was a lot of uncomfortable shifting and a bit of indistinct murmuring about busy lives, not my job, leaving the grieving alone . . .

'I knew.' The room turned at the sound of an undeniably French voice. Auguste, who no one had ever heard speak English before, looked bored by it all.

Elspeth stepped towards her son. 'Darling, what do you mean, "I knew"?'

'What? Why didn't you say something?' sputtered Bella.

The teenager shrugged nonchalantly and then sat down in a chair. 'I 'eard the children one morning, out of the Nursery again – ' his eyes flicked to Iris apologetically – 'so I got up to catch them. On the way back to the Nursery, we saw Grandmère on the main stairs in her travelling cloak. She waved at us and then left.'

'But why did you not tell anyone, darling?' Elspeth was shaking her head.

He shrugged again and opened the book on the small table next to him.

'I can't believe she just left,' Bella was muttering to herself, slumped over the arm of the sofa. Iris felt she should comfort her but wasn't quite brave enough to try.

'What did she mean by "the hypocrisy so easily practised in this household"? What deception? I don't understand what she's talking about,' Constance asked the room, giving rise to more uncomfortable shifting and murmuring.

'She was clearly distraught. Grief does funny things to a person,' said Lady Georgina, not meeting anyone's eye.

'Indeed,' said Cecil, who was leaning against the door to Hamish's dressing room. He'd nearly recovered from the run. 'But perhaps a better explanation can be found in here.' He looked gleeful.

Fergus turned and gasped. 'That's father's private study! You can't go in there.' But Cecil did and Fergus followed.

No one had ever seen Lady Georgina move so quickly. But she was up and across the room before anyone could register what had happened.

'What have you done? Get out of there at once, both of you!' she shouted, but even as she did, she knew it was futile. It was never going to happen any other way. Pandora's box had been opened.

The room was just as Eva and Cecil had left it. The Rubens, all six copies of it, the unfinished painting from the Billiards Room, hundreds of sketchbooks – and the innumerable canvases of Maxwell. Hamish's well-guarded secrets were now on show to the entire family.

They moved slowly about the room, in a stunned silence. Some flipping through the canvases on the floor, others staring at the canvases on the easels. None quite understanding yet what they were seeing.

'I always wondered where those windows were. You can see them from the rose garden,' said Iris quietly to Mr Kettering, nodding to the north wall.

'Is that a skylight?' asked Angus staring up at the ceiling.

'It was built by the Fifteenth Earl when he added the portrait gallery.' Lady Georgina was looking at the ornate glass ceiling. 'It was designed by Robert Adam. He a was a distant cousin of the Countess's, apparently.' She had always liked this room, when it had belonged to her husband, that was. All these paintings. And what had he done to the walls? They didn't used to be white.

'All these paintings . . . I don't understand. Are these meant to be Father's?' asked Bella.

Lady Georgina looked at Fergus, sighed heavily, and sat down on a sofa. She waved her hand, and Fergus began to explain. They listened in silence for the most part, riveted by the story of the forgeries and selling the pieces on the sly.

When Fergus was finished, he sat down by his grandmother and waited. It was Angus, of course, that led the charge.

'How does he know all of this, but I don't? I'm the Earl after all!' He was angry and shouting.

'That's your concern in all of this?' Bella shouted back. 'Our mother has disappeared. Our father is an art forger. But heaven forbid Angus didn't know about it!'

'You didn't know about it either,' he said sulkily.

'Of course not, but I'm more concerned about why there are hundreds of nude portraits of our mother's lady's maid in our father's private study!' Her voice was almost a screech.

'I might be able to help you there, milady.' The room turned to see Mrs MacBain standing in the doorway. 'I don't mean to intrude. I heard the vase overturn and thought it was the children.'

She stepped into the room and glanced at Lady Georgina hesitantly, who nodded her head wearily. Mrs MacBain exhaled slowly.

'It's a bit difficult to explain delicately; I'm not quite sure how to begin.' She looked around the room and could see that tempers had already flared. 'Lord Inverkillen and Miss Maxwell were, um . . . in a relationship for many years. It started when they were at university together. After he married Lady Inverkillen, he brought Miss Maxwell here so they could continue to be together.'

The room was silent for some moments, Mrs MacBain watching their reactions carefully. Fergus and Angus were stunned. Cecil had a wry smile on his face, saying quietly to himself, 'Maxwell. Of course! Naughty boy.'

'That explains why he left her the annuity,' said Elspeth quietly. 'He loved her.'

Oblivious didn't begin to cover them, thought Mr Kettering. They saw nothing that happened in their own home. It was a level of self-absorption he had never encountered before, and it was astounding.

'All these years, and Mummy didn't know?' asked Bella, her voice hollow.

'She might have suspected something, I don't know, but once the will was read, the cat was out of the bag. She confronted Miss Maxwell the next morning, who confirmed it. I gather there was an argument.'

'I should hope so. Mummy should have sacked her on the spot!'

'She did, milady, but Miss Maxwell has nowhere to go, and with this sickness going around, we thought it best to have her stay here and continue to dress Lady Georgina.'

Lady Georgina tutted. 'This illness again. Honestly, you people are blowing it all out of proportion. Life didn't stop during the Spanish Flu, you'll recall.'

'Where is Her Ladyship?' asked Mrs MacBain, looking around the room. Constance handed her the letter, and she quickly read it.

'Oh my . . .' Mrs MacBain gasped, panic setting in. She had fled. Lady Inverkillen had fled. Surely, if she were innocent, she would still be here. Wouldn't she? What now? Oh, damnit! She'd have to involve Jarvis now. There was no way she could chase after Lady Inverkillen. Did they even know where she'd gone? How on earth was she supposed to get Roddy Jarvis to understand it all?

Lady Georgina watched her intently. She'd never seen Mrs MacBain with such a wild – and clearly irritated – expression. The woman was near to panic. It was an uncomfortable thought. 'You didn't know?' she asked cautiously, scanning the housekeepers face for a clue to what was happening inside her head.

'No,' stammered Mrs MacBain. 'No, I had no idea. The day after the will was read, she asked me to deliver all her meals on trays, here in the sitting room. I gave the order to Miss Maxwell.' The trays had been a ruse, clearly, to give herself time to disappear.

'Surely you noticed that the trays hadn't been touched?'

'What? Oh, but they had been.' Confusion swept over her face. She glanced at Iris, who looked terror stricken.

'It must have been the children,' said Elspeth, wearily. 'They knew Mama was gone, didn't they? And they must have seized on the trays, knowing they would go uneaten.'

Comprehension dawned on Mrs MacBain's face. 'Of

course. We thought it odd that her puddings were always finished. In twenty years, she'd not touched a single pudding.'

'And that didn't concern you? Or did you simply not care enough to check in on your mistress?' Angus stood and started to advance upon Mrs MacBain. 'You call that loyalty?' he thundered.

Mrs MacBain gaped speechlessly up into Angus's red face as he towered over her.

'Now, Angus.' Elspeth stepped between them and gently steered her nephew to a chair. 'None of us noticed either.' He started to object, and she held up her hand. 'You know as well as I do, we can go months without seeing the servants if we want. I remember one year when I didn't see Maxwell for our entire trip. And then just before we left for home . . . Oh! Yes, of course.' Her eyes slid to Iris.

Cecil looked confused for a moment and then slowly it dawned on him. 'Yes, that does rather make sense, doesn't it?' He turned and stared at the girl.

'What does?' said Iris. Her face was going flush and she felt slightly dizzy. Why were her feet numb, suddenly? And why was everyone staring at her?

Fergus grabbed one the faux Rubens and stared at it, stunned. 'Oh heavens! Miss MacLeod was right: she is pregnant. But if she's pregnant, that means . . .' He stopped mid-sentence and stared at Iris.

'She's their daughter,' said Elspeth.

'No! I didn't want it to happen that way! Oh my god, they're going to send me packing, aren't they?' Miss Maxwell was pacing agitatedly around her small room. The dressing screen threatened to topple each time she passed.

I must remember to lock that door, thought Mrs MacBain.

'No one wanted it to happen that way, but it has, Flora, and we must deal with what we have. Sit down, please. No one has been sacked.'

Mrs MacBain had settled Iris in her room with a strong shot of brandy in her tea and a hot water bottle. Then she had gone to find Miss Maxwell as quickly as she could.

'For better or worse, the family knows, so I suggest you stay below stairs for the time being. We all know they don't like surprises, and this was a doozy. I'll dress Lady Georgina, until we get a better idea of how she wishes to proceed. In the meantime, you need to speak with Iris.'

Maxell flopped onto the bed, hands covering her face. She stared at Mrs MacBain through her fingers. 'Oh no. I'm not doing that. She hates me. Surely, she does. I've lied to her for years. I left her at an orphanage, for heaven's sake. I'm sure she hates me. Why wouldn't she? No, no . . . No, I can't bear to speak to her about it.'

Mrs MacBain sighed. 'Of all the people in this house, she is the one least capable of hate. She's confused, rightly so, but hate has not entered her mind. But if you refuse to speak to her, she'll feel rejected, and you'll lose your only chance to be her mother. Go and speak to her. Heaven forbid Angus and Bella get to her first. She needs all the friends she can get just now. Be one of them.'

Mrs MacBain crossed the room and opened the door, waiting for Maxwell to join her.

At length, Maxwell stood and walked slowly to the open door. This must be what condemned prisoners feel like, she thought.

Iris heard a soft knock at her bedroom door. It was partly opened, and she could see that it was Miss Maxwell. Her mother. Golly, that was a strange thought. Not knowing what she wanted to do, Iris hesitated, and she could see that Maxwell had noticed, and was devastated.

'Please, Iris! Please let me in to speak with you. I know you must have questions and I'd like to get this all out in the open. Finally.' Still she held the door between them. 'If after we've spoken you want no more to do with me, that's fine. I'll not bother you again. But let's get it all out in the open so you can choose what to do. No more secrets.'

Iris took a stuttering breath and opened the door fully. She did not move to let the older woman into her room, however. She looked at Maxwell, as if seeing a stranger at her door. It was a curious look, not an angry one. Maxwell let it wash over her.

'I'm not angry,' Iris said finally, 'so you can stop looking at me like that. But I'm not ready to speak to you yet. There's just been too much happening to process this. You, my mother; him, my father. I need time to think before we can speak.'

'But we will speak?' asked Maxwell, hopefully.

Iris hesitated and then nodded very slightly. She closed the door softly.

They weren't out of the woods yet, but there was definitely a promise, and that was enough for Maxwell for now. She shuffled back to her room, feeling like she'd aged fifty years within the last hour.

Fergus was standing in front of the fire in his former bedroom, discussing the revelation with Lady Georgina.

'Did you know?' he asked. 'About Iris, I mean?'

His grandmother regarded him with an air of maddening superiority. 'Of course I knew. You think I chose her at random? Like some puppy from a village fair? No, Sister Margaret sent me a letter, asking me to come for tea. I presumed she wanted a donation but as soon as I walked in, I spotted Iris across the room and knew why I was there.'

'There are no secrets in a Scottish village.'

'No. Especially when the secret is a walking copy of Hamish. Thankfully, Sister Margaret is a generous soul. She thought it would be better to have Iris here at the Abbey than walking around the village, advertising Hamish's indiscretion.' She sounded weary. 'Small mercies are not to be underestimated.'

'Did you know Father and Maxwell were . . .'

'I turned a blind eye to the dalliance. All men carry on with the maids, that much I know. But I presumed it would exhaust itself, like all his other passions did. Clearly, I should have kept a better eye on the situation. Poor Victoria. But the secret stair was as much a surprise to me as to you.'

Fergus poked at the fire in silence.

'So, what do we do now? Do we legitimise her, make her part of the family? Do we send her away?' Fergus wasn't sure how he felt, but he did know that direction needed to be given to the family straight away. Otherwise . . . well, he didn't want to think about how his siblings would treat her now. 'We cannot continue as we have.'

'No, we can't. Well, she's not the first illegitimate child in the family but traditionally, it has only been the boys who have been recognised.'

Fergus was shocked by the blithe statement, and instantly wondered to whom she was referring.

'Hamish obviously wanted her taken care of and, distasteful as it is, I think we must honour that wish.' They both stared into the fire for some moments. 'If, that is, she wants to be part of this family. She may well want to run for the hills. We haven't exactly been warm to her over the years.'

There was an understatement. Fergus poked at the fire again for a moment.

At length, he turned to his grandmother and said, 'They'll take their direction from you, but it must be done tomorrow, first thing. Otherwise . . .' He leaned over and kissed her on the forehead. 'Good night, Grandmama.'

After he left, she sat staring at the fire until it nearly went out. Then she rang for Mrs MacBain.

Iris wisely stayed out of sight. She hid in the Nursery, knowing she'd be safe there. As she watched the children play, her mind drifted to all the conversations she and Maxwell had had over the years. She had always known she was a favourite of Maxwell's, and now Iris understood why. But try as she might, she could only think of once when Maxwell had given any real indication of maternal affection. Maxwell had gone teary eyed when Iris had donned her first ballgown. It was another of Bella's cast-offs, but Maxwell had tailored it to fit perfectly. It fitted so well that Bella had demanded it back. Bella. Who was now her sister? How strange life could be.

Bella, for her part, still felt stunned hours after the revelation. And also insulted on her mother's behalf. How could her father have done this to them? And then flouted it so openly. Well, not openly, exactly. It had taken a good deal of effort, all that deception and sneaking around. And Maxwell, hiding in plain sight, a trusted part of their household. So deceitful. She thought of her father, closeted in his bedroom, concealing the truth from the world. Worse still, from his wife. She crossed to the window and looked out at the rain. Angus and Hugh were running across the lawn. *Where on earth are they going in this downpour*, she thought irritably. They disappeared into the Tennis Pavilion. Bella felt her chest tighten.

Ollie nearly dropped the dish of scrambled eggs. It clanged loudly and Hudson glared at him, and Ollie nodded to the back of the room in explanation. Lady Georgina had come to breakfast.

'Do be careful, that's quite valuable, you know. Georgian silver. The first George, not the one who lost the American Colonies.'

The room was startled. No one could remember Lady Georgina ever having been at breakfast. Fergus leapt to his feet and ushered his grandmother to a seat.

'I see Iris isn't down yet. Good. That gives us a chance to speak first. Mr Kettering, if you don't mind finishing your breakfast in the Morning Room? I'd like to speak with my family.' He immediately stood to leave, and Ollie rushed to load his dishes on to a tray.

That's one distraction out of the way, she thought. 'Fergus, please see to the door. It won't do to have Iris wandering in unexpectedly. Sit, all of you.' They did as they were asked, most of them with gaping mouths and wide eyes. She asked Hudson for a cup of tea. As she readied it, they sat in silence, watching her, equally fascinated and terrified. At length, she took a long sip and set it down carefully.

'You are to treat Iris as a member of this family,' she started, calmly and firmly. 'It is clearly what Hamish wanted, and you will do as you've been asked.' She held her hand up for silence. Not that anyone had spoken. They were too stunned by her appearance to object to what she was saying. 'She will not be called Lady Iris, that's a step too far. But she will be treated with dignity, as befits her status as the youngest daughter of an Earl. What's done is done and she is a now member of this family.' She took another long sip and looked over the rim of her teacup. Anger and distain stared back, but no one argued. 'And do try to be kinder to her than you are to one another. Hudson, I'll have bacon and toast please. Is this Darjeeling? It's a nice change from English Breakfast.'

Lady Georgina carried on as if nothing unusual had happened yesterday. Fergus's eyes swept the room. He was hugely relieved she'd listened to his advice – and from what he was seeing now, not a moment too soon. Dangerous clouds were sweeping over Constance's face. Angus was muttering to himself as he buttered toast into oblivion. Bella was strangely calm, concentrating on stirring her tea. The French corner went back to their papers. It didn't really affect them, he supposed. Fergus opened the door and went to help himself to scrambled eggs. Can it really be this easy? he wondered.

Mrs MacBain had found a spare twenty minutes that afternoon. How, she didn't know, but she was thankful for them. She was on the family floor, sweeping through the bedrooms to check how everyone was faring. The men had adjusted well to making their own beds and fires. Of course, they'd all been in the army, so knew what to do. The ladies, however, had produced mixed results.

Lady Elspeth was managing but Bella had given up entirely. The first week, she simply left the bed linens in a heap in the middle of the bed. By her second week, she'd managed to straighten them a bit, but it was never a tidy job. She was clearly still incensed at being asked to do the work.

Constance, for her part, fared better, but her hair was an absolute disaster. She'd managed to get Françoise to come to the house and cut her long hair into a wave some weeks ago.

It had looked charming on her until her maid fell sick. Now she had to do it herself and clearly wasn't up to the task. The back stood up in odd sections and the front hung limply about her chin. She'd taken to tucking it behind her ears, which then flipped out at uncomfortable angles. This week she was experimenting with scarves.

Mrs MacBain was coming out of Angus's dressing room when she heard the sound the first time. Muffled shouting. It must be the children, she thought absently, and continued down the corridor. When she exited Lady Bella's dressing room, she heard it again, louder this time.

Glancing around, it was some moments before she realised that the sound was coming from behind the locked water-closet door. It was Eva. She'd been caught without any bathroom tissue.

'How can that be?' said Mrs MacBain with mounting frustration. 'I set a new roll out this morning.'

'Well, there isn't a square to spare in here now, Mrs MacBain! Do something!'

Mrs MacBain ran swiftly to the men's at the far end of the corridor. It too was empty. Wondering what on earth to do and cursing the lack of hall boys, inspiration struck; she dashed into Constance's bedroom, hoping to grab a box of tissues from the dressing table. Just as her hand touched the box, her eyes were drawn to the rest of the table. It was covered in jewellery: diamonds, pearls, sapphires; all neatly laid out on the top of the dressing table. Stunned, she stopped to look around the room. Constance had clearly raided Lady Inverkillen's dressing room and helped herself to the family jewels. Brooches lined the windowsill neatly. Necklaces shared hangers with her dresses. And no less than three tiaras were tucked in with the hats. *The cheek!* But then Mrs MacBain remembered why she was there. Dashing back to the hall, tissues in hand, she knocked softly at the water-closet door.

'It's me, milady. I have some facial tissues for you, which should do nicely. Can you open the door? We're quite alone.' Mrs MacBain heard some muffled swearing and then the door opened slightly. She passed the box to Eva, who snatched it out of her hand, and stood back. As she waited, she reviewed her morning's work. She had absolutely, definitely stocked each room as soon as the grocery delivery arrived. Where could they all have gone?

When Eva came out, Mrs MacBain set about apologising, but Eva wouldn't hear a word about it. She simply sniffed at Mrs MacBain. 'See that it doesn't happen again,' she said, with as much dignity as she could muster. She then turned on her heel and walked towards the staircase to the guest floor.

Mrs MacBain sprinted down to the kitchen to find more rolls, praying they had some partials left. Someone had clearly gone around all the bathrooms and taken all the lavatory paper, but who and why? Several faces fought for first place on that list. She shook her head and started back up the servants' stairs. More to the point, who, knowing there was a shortage, wouldn't check before sitting down?

It was nearly eight o'clock the next evening and the children were missing. Again. Iris had searched all day without finding them. Hudson would be leading the family into dinner soon and she needed their help, whether or not they were ready to face one another. Taking a deep breath, she walked into the Library to face her family.

'Excuse me.' It was barely above a whisper, and no one heard her. Screwing up her courage in both hands, Iris stepped fully into the room. Elspeth was the first to notice her.

'Iris, how lovely to see you.' Elspeth looked at Iris's day dress with mild surprise. 'Are you not joining us for dinner?'

'Um, no.' Iris could hear some snide remarks being made, and her courage began to shrivel. She closed her eyes and blurted it out, 'I've lost the children.'

'Oh, you useless girl!'

'Bella!' Both Fergus and Elspeth admonished her.

'What? How hard can it be to manage three children?'

'Six,' corrected Elspeth. Bella glared at her aunt.

Lady Georgina took charge. 'What do you mean by lost, Iris?'

'They disappeared when I went to get their lunches. I've searched everywhere and can't find a trace of them.'

'That was hours ago!' Fergus cried, jumping to his feet. 'Do we need to search the grounds? Where have you looked?'

'That's just the thing; they're in the house. I can hear them. I just can't find them.'

Fergus stopped pulling the bell cord and turned to Iris. Her statement puzzled everyone.

'That makes absolutely no sense at all,' Constance snapped. She wondered if the girl was going mad, after all the revelations. Who knew what ran in the maid's family?

They fell silent, listening intently, but heard nothing.

Elspeth jumped up. 'Of course. The Stuart passages.'

'The what?' The room turned to her, confused.

'It's how I used to escape Nanny. The current rooms were built inside the old sixteenth-century walls, and in several places, the newer, smaller rooms created passages and back corridors. There are hidden doors all over the house.' Surprise and confusion swept the room. She stepped to the side of the bookcase and opened a hidden door. 'How do you think the servants move around the house unseen?'

Angus shrugged and lit a cigarette. Of course, they'd seen

the footmen disappear countless times, but one never thought about where they went. Why should one? They were servants; it's what they did. A defeated look set into Lady Georgina's eyes and she rang for Hudson.

'We'll need to search these passages, then. Ah, Hudson, can you arrange for some torches? The children are missing again.'

Hudson sighed quietly. At least the staff had already eaten dinner. Clearly it was going to be a long night.

'Elspeth has been telling us about the back passages throughout the house. I think it safe to assume the children have found them.'

Hudson paused, and then nodded softly. 'Yes. That would explain a lot, milady.'

'So, you've never seen the children in them?' Lady Georgina asked.

'No, milady.'

Lady Georgina sighed and looked to her daughter. 'I suppose it's too much to hope that there is only one set of passages?'

Elspeth looked remorseful and shook her head. 'The house is riddled with them, Mama. Hamish and I spent years exploring them all. And we never once ran into a servant.'

Yet another thing I was excluded from, thought Cecil. They had only ever included him to get him into trouble, it seemed. The revelation made him feel unexpectedly sad.

'Right, let's split up.' Fergus took charge. He divided everyone into pairs and assigned them part of the house, careful to give the family floors to Hudson and Mrs MacBain as he strongly suspected both Constance and Bella would use the opportunity to snoop instead of search. Angus and Constance would search the staff quarters and attics of the east wing, Hugh and Bella the same in the west wing.

Constance immediately objected to having the attics.

Shouldn't she have a more distinguished floor? She was the senior member of the family; she should be searching the main floors, clearly. Eva could search the attics. Bella, for once, agreed. She wanted to search the family floors, too. Predictably, they all started to squabble. Lady Georgina stood and banged on the fireplace with a brass candlestick she'd always hated. It was immensely satisfying, and she couldn't help but smile as she returned the dented piece to the mantle.

'You will do as Fergus said,' she ordered. 'Start in areas we know the children have caused mischief, like the Fencing Studio and the Minstrels' Gallery. Hudson, can you bring me a chair so that I can monitor from here? When they are found, I shall ring the dressing gong.'

A loud gasp went up. No one struck the gong but him. No one. The room went quiet and all eyes went to the horrified butler.

'Hudson, the mallet please.' Lady Georgina said it in a slow and deliberate voice, stretching out her hand as she did so. Iris realised she was holding her breath. After an eternity, he slowly, reluctantly, handed it to the Dowager and shuffled off in shock, leaving Fergus to fetch her a chair.

They each went off in their pairs. Lady Georgina could hear some grumbling floating down from the upper floors, but she was pleased that it was fading away. There had been far too much grumbling these past few weeks. She settled into her chair and immediately wished she'd asked for tea before Hudson had left.

After several minutes' walk, Angus and Constance were finally in the attics. Neither could say they'd ever been there before.

'Ugh! It's positively filthy up here. What exactly are we looking for?' asked Constance, trying her hardest not to touch anything. When they were back to normal life and she was firmly in charge, the attics must be cleaned regularly. This would never do.

'How should I know?' her husband snapped. 'Today is the first I've heard of secret passages.'

He shined the torch around the attic. There were a few storage rooms, but mostly the rafters were exposed, and furniture was stacked in the open, covered with dust sheets. There had to be a light somewhere, he just couldn't find it.

'There,' said Constance suddenly, pointing to the floor in front of him where unmistakeable footprints had disturbed the dust.

'Well done!' he said. 'Let's follow the trail.'

But their jubilation faded quickly when the footsteps led to a brick wall.

'We've literally hit a brick wall,' said Angus, scanning the areas around them.

'Well, this can't be it.' Constance was tapping on the wall. 'I'd say this is exactly what a secret passage looks like.' Angus suspended the torch in a rafter so that they could both see. After some minutes, Constance pushed on a single brick and the door slowly swung open to reveal a set of stairs. She cried out in triumph. 'How clever!' said Angus, grabbing the torch and peering into the passageway. He looked at Constance and grimaced. 'Let's go.'

'Can we leave it open though? Just be sure we can get back out.' Constance had just finished reading *The Cask of Amontillado* and the entire idea made her nervous. But Angus was far off in the darkness and didn't hear her. Constance stepped in, hoping it was cleaner than where they'd just been.

The passage curved at one point, she thought, but it was dark and difficult to be sure. There were some more stairs, rather steep, and then it went flat for quite some time. Constance swore. she could smell earth. Ten minutes later, they finally stopped in front of a rather short door. Angus stooped to listen.

'No voices,' he whispered, 'but there is a sound. Not sure what it is.'

The door slid to the side and they stepped through, Angus banging his head on a ceiling of sorts. He carefully helped Constance out and they stood together, looking at an ancient inglenook fireplace that Angus had never seen before.

'Where are we?' Constance asked in a hushed voice, stepping into the room. It seemed to be a very old kitchen. Stone walls, stone floor, and an ancient bed in the corner. There was a puzzle on the table, half finished.

'No idea. I think we're in someone's quarters,' said Angus slowly. He walked to the only door and peeked out of the small side window. He groaned. Constance stepped quickly to his side and glanced out. Where she had expected to see children, she had a clear view of the waterwheel. They were in the Distillery.

She looked to Angus stonily. 'What exactly do you do all day?'

Mrs MacBain and Hudson were searching the family floors, each convinced they would find nothing. Surely if a door existed, they'd have found it by now. These rooms were cleaned daily, with great attention and care. Mrs MacBain tried to view the rooms with fresh eyes, but it was difficult.

They were in Angus and Constance's rooms. Hudson searched the sitting room, Mrs MacBain the bedchamber. She'd found nothing. Not at the back of the fireplace, or the bookshelves. She carefully checked behind the curtains, in case she had missed a button or a lever of some sort. Nothing. She moved on to Constance's dressing room.

Hudson stepped into the bedchamber, saying, 'I'm all finished. If there is a passage, I cannot find it.' The room was empty. 'Mrs MacBain?'

'In here,' called Mrs MacBain.

Hudson crossed the room, scanning the walls for any hint of a door, just in case. Satisfied there was nothing, he proceeded to Lady Constance's dressing area. He hesitated; it was an improper place for him to be, a lady's wardrobe, but desperate times called for desperate measures. He had just turned the corner into the dressing room when Mrs MacBain opened a wardrobe door and was knocked over by an avalanche of lavatory paper. Hudson burst out laughing.

'Right, let's start in the Nursery and see where it leads,' said Fergus. 'Elspeth said there was a secret door behind the blackboard.'

Eva was riveted by the entire idea of secret passages. They went to the blackboard and tapped it for a few moments, until Eva spotted a worn spot on the bottom. She pushed it and it swung open silently. They were staring at a stone passageway with ancient iron braziers. The floor was quite worn, and they saw sweet wrappers dotted along the way. They looked at each other grimly. At least they were clearly on the right track.

They followed it for a few moments before they came upon a door. Pushing it open, they found themselves in the main corridor.

'So, you escape Nanny to here. Then what? How do you get out of the house from the second floor?'

'There must be a second passage here.' They tugged the portraits and pulled back the rugs but found nothing. It was only as Eva was replacing the rug that she spotted it; under the console table, with a rather ugly urn sitting on top. The leg of the console table hid a lever, which Eva pulled. The panel slid up to reveal a metal chute. They stared at it, and then each other.

'You don't suppose . . .' she began.

'Only one way to find out.'

Eva snorted. 'I'm not climbing in there without knowing where it ends up.'

Fergus poked his head in and laughed. The sound echoed back to him.

'There's a sticky handprint on the wall. I think we'd better see where it leads.' And he climbed in, feet first. 'Wish me luck!' he called as he slid out of view. Eva could hear a bit of thudding and swearing as he descended. Eva wasn't sure if she wanted to follow.

It felt like a long slide to him, with a few curves. Fergus banged his head more than once, before he shot out into the laundry room. Picking himself up from the floor, he shouted up to Eva to let her know he was fine, then went to a door on the other side of the room. It opened up into the service yard. No wonder they never saw them escape, he thought. How seriously intrepid of the little brats. Part of him admired them for it. Well, there was no sign of the children in the laundry room, and it didn't seem like Eva was going to follow him. He locked the door and made his way towards the hallway. As he was passing the jam larder, he swore he could hear giggling, but he couldn't tell where it was coming from. It was maddening! Poor Iris, having to chase them all day. He stopped and listened. Ollie the footman rounded the corner and Fergus shushed him, pointing to the walls.

Giggling. They both heard it. The children were having a grand time together, completely unaware of Fergus and Ollie. Both men looked around carefully but found nothing. There must be another passageway somewhere. They started to feel the walls, pressing gently, when Ollie suddenly stopped. He was listening to the dumb waiter. Fergus walked over and listened. Definite giggles.

'They're in the dumb waiter?' Fergus whispered.

Ollie shook his head, saying that he was sure it wouldn't hold six children. He very slowly opened it and stared in amazement. There was a door at the back of the shaft. As many times as he'd used the thing, he'd never noticed it. 'How do they even get in?' he whispered back. They stood there for a few moments, flummoxed.

'If we can figure out where it leads to, perhaps we can get in that way.' Fergus had never been in the basements. 'What's on the other side of this wall?'

Fergus stood guard at the dumb waiter while Ollie went off to investigate. Cecil and Auguste appeared, and Fergus shushed them and stepped some feet away from the dumb waiter to ask them how they'd got there. They told him how they'd found a tunnel behind the suit of armour belonging to the 4th Earl. It had been a tight squeeze, but they'd managed, and it had led them to the cold store next to the garage.

Ollie returned and said he felt sure it was a room, not a passage. Mrs MacBain's bedroom was on the other side of the wall, and Ollie was pretty certain she'd have known if the children had been there.

'Oh, yes,' said Cecil. 'I seem to remember there are several priest holes in the house. But behind a dumb waiter, that's devilish. Pardon the pun.'

They debated for some moments what to do. If it was a passage, the children might scamper. But if it was a room – well, they had them cornered. It was a coin toss, really. And they were just about to literally toss a coin when Bella and

Hugh appeared, rather scuffed up and looking quite cross. No one wanted to ask.

'My lord that was disgusting! I'll need a bath before dinner,' exclaimed Bella loudly before anyone could shush her. Fergus and Ollie winced. They heard a small voice gasp, 'It's Mummy!' followed by the other children shushing.

Fergus leaned across the dumb waiter and knocked on the door.

'What's the magic word?' a small voice asked after a short pause.

Fergus grinned. 'Please.' Truly, children were such wonderful creatures.

'That was yesterday's word!'

So near yet so far. How did the door work? Fergus felt more and more chagrined that children could work it out, but six adults could not.

They spent several minutes cajoling, begging and bribing the children, but to no avail.

'Leave it to me,' a voice said, startling the assembled group. They turned to see Mrs Burnside leaving, only to reappear a moment later. She waved a tray of freshly baked sausage rolls in front of the door and said loudly, 'Oh dear. I have all these sausages rolls for the children, but I can't find them anywhere. What should I do with them?' She winked at the family and waited a moment. Furious whispers came from the children. 'Yummm . . . Maybe we should eat them ourselves since the children aren't here.'

After a few moments of tense silence, the door slowly lowered. Of course, it was a drawbridge. Small faces grinned out at Fergus. He shook his head and tried not to smile.

'Here we are! We want sausage rolls!' They scampered to the kitchen in a loud swarm behind Mrs Burnside. Fergus looked in to where they'd been squirreled away. It was a hidden room, quite sizable, furnished with two camp beds, a bookcase, two ladderback chairs and writing table. It even had a small ceiling light. Fergus burst out laughing as he looked at the table. It was groaning under the weight of stolen puddings, jars of jam, scones, and an entire wheel of cheddar.

Goodness, he thought, they really are a handful.

Fergus went to tell Lady Georgina that the children had been found, and she immediately sounded the gong and asked Hudson and Ollie to serve brandies in the Library. Everyone was animatedly discussing the various secret passages they'd found. Angus and Constance were the last to arrive.

'There you are! We found them in the basement.' Fergus handed his brother a snifter of brandy.

'Didn't you hear the gong? We've been waiting for you for ages.' Lady Georgina sounded annoyed. Mostly, she was hungry.

'No, we didn't hear it, because we weren't in the house,' said Angus. He took a sip of his brandy. 'We ended up in the Distillery.'

'The Distillery?' nearly everyone gasped in unison.

'Yes. There's a passage from the attic, down a lot of stairs, through a tunnel and into the back of MacTavish's Inglenook.' Angus set down the snifter and took out his cigarette case. 'Couldn't figure out how to get the wretched thing open again, so we had to come back through the woods. Damned slow with those shoes of hers.'

'They are ruined, by the way.' Constance grabbed a snifter and collapsed on the sofa.

Mrs MacBain felt the hairs on the back of her neck stand up. 'Which attic, My Lord?' she asked, turning around to face Angus.

'Hm?' Angus finished lighting his cigarette and looked at Mrs MacBain. 'Oh. The east wing, lots of storage rooms, but at the very end a brick wall that opens up if you push on the right brick. Oh, I found our rocking horse up there, Bella. We should move it back to the Nursery for the children.'

Mrs MacBain set the silver tray down and said to Lady Georgina, 'I'll just go see if dinner is ready.'

But Mrs MacBain didn't go to the kitchens. As quickly as her skirts would allow her, she was in the attic of the east wing. The lights flickered on and she walked to the far end. There was the rocking horse, and there was the brick wall, just as Angus had described. It was still open to the passageway. And it stood next to Maxwell's room.

Mrs MacBain took a deep breath and stood very still. After a moment, she closed the door to the passageway and started to make her way down the stairs. She just needed one last piece of the puzzle. She looked at her watch. There should be just enough time to find it.

Ten minutes later, she entered the kitchens and watched Miss Maxwell and Mrs Burnside revive dinner. 'Are we all ready, Mrs Burnside? The family is in the Library and Lady Georgina is quite sharp. You know how she gets when she's hungry.'

'We're nearly ready.' Mrs Burnside turned back to her preparations. She didn't like chatter when she cooked and finding the children had put her off her usual rhythm.

Mrs MacBain stood watching for a few moments. 'Fine. I'll let Hudson know to seat them now. Oh, Miss Maxwell, I wonder if we could have a private word when you're finished?'

Maxwell stopped pouring sauce on the pheasant and

looked at Mrs MacBain, surprised. 'Of course, Mrs MacBain. We shouldn't be more than, what, fifteen minutes?'

Mrs Burnside nodded, not taking her eyes off the garnishing she was doing.

Mrs MacBain walked slowly to her office, settled into her armchair and stared into the fire. She was deeply lost in her thoughts when Maxwell knocked at the open door. 'You wanted to see me, Mrs MacBain?'

'Yes. Please come in, Miss Maxwell. Why don't you shut the door?' She gestured to the chair opposite her. They were silent for some moments. Mrs MacBain didn't know how to begin.

'Something's been bothering me since we spoke in His Lordship's studio, and I hoped you could help me with it.'

'If I can.'

'There were a lot of canvases in the room, and while I didn't get a chance to look at very many of them, one particularly stuck in my mind.' She uncovered the unfinished painting of a woman standing at the weir. 'I presume that's you?'

Maxwell was startled to see the painting, and her eyes darted back and forth between it and Mrs MacBain. She was clearly trying to work out what Mrs MacBain knew but the housekeeper gave nothing away. Servants know how to control their reactions. After some moments, Maxwell nodded mutely.

'I realise it's unfinished, but that appears to me to be a present-day portrait, not one of you when you were younger.' Maxwell shifted in her chair but said nothing. Mrs MacBain said a silent prayer. 'You were with him at the weir, weren't you, on the day he died?' She held her breath, unsure what she wanted to hear.

There was a long silence, then Miss Maxwell simply said, 'Yes.'

'Flora! Why did you never say anything?' Mrs MacBain was

shocked. She had several things she wanted to say, none of them quiet, but she held her calm, knowing that shouting would get her nowhere. She wanted to throttle the woman but forced herself to keep her voice gentle. 'What happened that day?'

Maxwell considered Mrs MacBain for a long moment, clearly weighing up something in her mind. When she finally spoke, she was calm but mouse-quiet. Mrs MacBain set the painting down, trying her best to look supportive.

'He needed to talk to me about Iris, so we went down to the weir. I should have known it wasn't going to be a good conversation. He always took me to the weir when he thought I'd shout.' She paused and shifted in her seat. Mrs MacBain waited silently. 'Hamish had arranged a governess position for Iris while they were at the ball, and she was due to start in a few weeks, with the McDonald family.

'McDonald?' Mrs MacBain racked her brains. 'I don't know that name.'

'No, you wouldn't, because they're from Ireland.'

'Oh.' Mrs MacBain nodded silently, understanding dawning on her.

'I knew he was looking for a position for her, but I thought it would be in Edinburgh or Yorkshire. It never occurred to me he would send her abroad. If she goes to Ireland, I'll never see her again. She doesn't know I'm her mother – or didn't then, at least. Why would she have kept in touch? And when would she come back to visit? It caught me by surprise when he told me. I was angry and we were shouting.'

Mrs MacBain struggled to remain silent. Her head was whirring with questions, most of which would require shouting of her own, accompanied by a sharp slap to the back of the head. *Deep breaths, Alice.*

'So, you went to the river, he told you Iris was going away, and then what?'

'I was angry he hadn't consulted me first; but mostly, I couldn't bear the thought of never seeing her again. Ireland is so far away! He told me I was being ridiculous. Servants, he said, can't afford to be sentimental. Oh . . . I just snapped. In all the time we've been together, he's never called me or treated me as a servant. I lost it. Nearly punched him, so I waded out to the weir, just to put some distance between us.'

'How did he end up in the river, Flora?' *Gently, gently, Alice.*

'It was my fault. I nearly got taken out by a salmon and fell into the pool. And these skirts, they're so heavy; I was being dragged down, so I tried to take them off. Hamish must have thought I was drowning and jumped in after me, idiot man.'

'He couldn't swim, could he?'

'No. I begged him to learn for years, but he always refused. So how he thought he could save me . . .' She paused, tears starting to spill out of her eyes. 'He sank like a rock. I managed to get him to the surface but then the current swept us down the river. It took every ounce of strength and energy I had to swim to the bank. I must have fainted. When I came to, I was in the Distillery.'

'How on earth did you get there?'

'Ross found me on the bank. He took me up to MacTavish and then went to find Hamish. He came back about four in the morning and told me he couldn't find him.'

'And no one saw you come back into the house because MacTavish sent you through the tunnel that connects to the attic by your room.'

She nodded, tears falling thick and heavy now.

MacTavish's words flooded back to Mrs MacBain. *The poor creature's been through enough. Let her grieve in peace.* It was a horrific thing to have gone through. Mrs MacBain let her cry.

'I'm sorry, Alice.' Maxwell sniffed and took some deep breaths. 'I know I should have said something, it's just, how could I explain why I'd been there? We'd been so careful not to be found out. And it was all for nothing.' And she finally broke down into wracking sobs.

Mrs MacBain put her arm around her and rocked her soothingly. In spite of overwhelming evidence to the contrary, it had been an accident after all.

Mrs MacBain was in her dressing gown, sitting in front of the fire in her room. It had been a long day and while she was exhausted by it all, her mind was whirring. Roddy Jarvis had been right: it had been an accident, except he had no idea what had really happened. But she did.

She slowly braided her long hair as she thought back to everything she'd learned. The forgeries, done by His Lordship for decades. That alone was enough of a bombshell to keep Scotland talking for decades. But then there was Lady Inverkillen and Garvey, Maxwell and Lord Inverkillen. Iris. Anyone who said there were no secrets in a small village had clearly never been to Loch Down. She shook her head and let out a long sigh.

Her mind went back to Maxwell's story. It had been an accident; she didn't doubt that. But did she owe Jarvis the truth? That she couldn't say. It wouldn't change the official ruling. And there was every chance he'd get the wrong end of the stick and arrest Miss Maxwell for murder. What proof could she offer him to prove Maxwell's innocence? It was all hearsay and circumstance.

Plus, she thought reluctantly, she didn't want to involve the family any further. They didn't know Maxwell had been at the river, and it was only Elspeth that heard the shouting.

And, well, much as she hated the idea, a little white lie would put that demon to rest. However it had happened, it had been an accident and Hamish was gone. Telling them would only stir up trouble, and Maxwell still needed a letter of recommendation for her next position. If she wanted another one. Mrs MacBain wasn't sure she would.

The fire burned low and Mrs MacBain shivered. It was late and the house was quiet. Tomorrow would be another busy day. Did she really have the strength to have this conversation with Jarvis?

Crawling into bed beneath her mother's quilt, she put out the lamp. *It's not my story to tell* – isn't that what MacTavish had said that night? Maybe it wasn't hers to tell either.

It was a fitful night's sleep, but when she woke at dawn, her mind was clear. There was absolutely no reason for full story to come out. The truth would stay with her.

The next day was Tuesday, which meant a meeting with Lady Georgina. The Dowager had finished her meeting agenda and was tidying papers and reaching for her writing pen when Mrs MacBain cleared her throat softly.

'Was there something else, Mrs MacBain?'

She tried to keep her nerve. 'Given the troubles of yesterday, milady, I wondered if it might be best to close the Nursery and move the children into one of the main rooms of the house.'

'Close the Nursery?' What started as surprise quickly turned to shrewd suspicion. 'And what do you mean by "main rooms", exactly?'

'I was thinking the Library.'

'The Library! For the entire day?'

'Well, yes. It would make it easier for the family to help

Iris watch them. People can read, or . . . whatever.' After fifteen years of service, she still didn't understand what it was the family did all day. But this wasn't the time to ask. 'A second or third set of eyes wouldn't go amiss. Iris is lovely but she's no match for those children.'

'No, that much is true. We shouldn't have asked her.' She thought for a moment. 'But the Library?' she said plaintively. 'Couldn't it be another room?'

'The only rooms large enough are the Library and the Map Room, and I think the Map Room is far too tempting. All those drawers and globes; the sextant collection alone would be impossible for them to resist.'

'Agreed. But I can't be expected to sit there all day. I'm already running two households.'

'With respect, milady, you've raised your children. It's time for the actual parents to do their duty now.' The women exchanged a sardonic look.

'Fine. They're in the Library during the day.' Lady Georgina sighed. 'But presumably, they'll still be taking their meals in the Nursery?'

Mrs MacBain hesitated. 'Given that there is an entrance to the tunnels in the Nursery, I think it would be best to have the children eating with the family as well.' She held her breath. It was a big ask. She knew it. Lady Georgina knew it. It was a practical idea for one and an audacious idea for the other.

'But children, in the Dining Room.' Lady Georgina was aghast. 'It's wildly inappropriate. What if word got out?'

This, coming from a woman who had famously seated her beloved Scottish Deerhound at table with the Duke and Duchess of Ardenloch. White tie and diamond tiaras for thirty. The dog had worn a lovely pearl choker.

'Until we know where all the entrances are, they'll keep disappearing on us.'

'Yes, I suppose they will,' Lady Georgina agreed reluctantly. 'But nineteen people in six rooms . . . It'll be like a Victorian tenement.' Walking to the French doors, she stood looking out, tutting and shaking her head. 'And all of this because Nanny died. Extraordinary.'

Mrs MacBain took that as a yes and left as quietly as she could.

Places were set for the children at one end of the luncheon table. The seating had been battled over all morning. Hugh and Fergus wanted half at each end of the table and Bella and Constance had argued for all of them at a single end of the table, whereas Lady Georgina felt this was entirely the wrong thing to do.

No small amount of time had been dedicated to the menu that morning because Lady Georgina felt it should not change. 'It's such short notice. Cook won't have had time to prepare anything for them.'

'If the children are going to be at table, they should eat as the adults do,' seconded Bella. Even though Angus agreed with her, Bella scowled at her brother. 'I hardly think you should have a say in this matter, given you have no children of your own.' Constance glared at her sister-in-law and Elspeth jumped in to keep the peace.

'Let's just get though luncheon and see how the children do, shall we?'

Luncheon finished in tears, but at least the family finally understood the issues.

Elspeth's children, being older, were merely unhappy to have poached salmon on spinach, but they ate it. Well, they picked at it, and pushed it around their plates. Bella's children, however, staged a mutiny. They wanted chip sandwiches. It was Tuesday and Tuesday was always chip sandwiches and peaches. Someone slid under the table and wailed in a tiny but piercing voice. 'I love peach day! Why did peach day go away?' Two others crawled under the table, trying to comfort the poor thing. A new potato went sailing past Lady Georgina's face. The boys were using their parfait spoons to catapult food across the table, each hiding behind salmon fortifications. It had horrified Hudson, who slipped on some spinach and nearly dropped a decanter of wine on Mr Kettering. Thank goodness they hadn't used the good linen tablecloths.

After luncheon, Iris took the children for a long, exhausting walk while the family gathered in the Library with Mrs MacBain to discuss how best to proceed.

'Well, one thing is clear,' began Elspeth, 'none of us would like to suffer through that again.' The room nodded, slightly shell-shocked.

'I told you that seating them together was a mistake. They draw strength from their numbers,' Lady Georgina said grimly. 'Better to vanquish them by breaking them up.' For dinner, they would be seated between the adults.

Mrs MacBain nodded. 'If I may say something? I don't see the children sitting quietly through a two-hour, five-course meal each evening. I'm sure they will be on their best behaviour tonight, but I have a feeling that tomorrow evening will be difficult and the following night impossible.'

'Just what are you suggesting, Mrs MacBain?' demanded Constance. She was near the end of her patience with the matter. As mistress of the house, she should have been the one setting the menus, but Lady Georgina refused to give up control. The whole thing was very unsatisfying. This was not how she had envisioned being Countess of Inverkillen.

'Well, milady, if we could limit the meal to three courses—' The room erupted, and it took some time for Mrs MacBain

to regain the floor. 'Three courses and serve nursery food—'
Outrage again.

'I'm not eating nursery food in white tie!' shouted Angus.

'I'm not eating nursery food in any tie,' thundered Cecil.

Mrs MacBain sighed audibly and began again. 'If we can
serve the children nursery food, you can be served your usual
foods, but in three courses, then dinner will be slightly shorter,
and I think that would pacify the children.'

'First we had to change our lives to suit the servants and
now we have to accommodate the children? What is
happening?' Bella threw her handkerchief onto the sofa and
stood to pour herself an angry cup of tea. She was stirring
so violently that Hudson worried the teacup might shatter.

Mrs MacBain wanted a lie down. She had the beginnings
of a headache.

Fergus stood to help her. 'Mrs MacBain is right. We might
get the consommé past them but slivered brown trout with
roe and watercress is going to be trouble. If we serve them
the foods that they are accustomed to, we might just have a
pleasant evening.'

'I still don't think children should be catered to in this way.
If they want to be adults, let them eat as adults,' argued
Constance.

'They don't want to be adults, Constance. They want to
be pirates tearing through the hidden passages, stealing
sweets,' Fergus said with exasperation, setting his teacup
on the silver tray and rolling his eyes at Hudson. 'We want
them to be adults. We are asking a child of six to wear
Sunday best and eat with a fish fork. It's a ridiculous thing
to ask.'

'If we hired a new Nanny, we wouldn't have this problem!'

'Bella, we've been through this . . .'

It went on like this for forty-five minutes. In the end Mrs

MacBain was no closer to a decision on the menu. She caught Fergus's eye, pointed to her watch and left the room. It was for them to decide.

That evening at eight o'clock sharp, Iris brought the children into the dining room in their finest clothing and seated them at the table, interspersed between the adults. They were very excited to be there. The adults were decidedly nervous. Lady Georgina, seated at the centre of the table in Lady Inverkillen's usual place, appraised each child sternly, and nodded at Hudson, who began service.

The adults skipped the consommé and began with fish. Then on to game, and finally a compressed final course of everything-else-all-at-once. The children began with what looked like star- and heart-shaped canapés.

'What are they eating, Hudson?' asked Constance, mystified, staring at the child next to her as if she were cheating at cards.

'I believe those are cheese toasties, milady.'

'Cheese toasties?'

'White bread with melted cheese.' When she looked puzzled, he continued, 'A bit like the crouton on a bowl of French onion soup, milady.'

'Oh yes, I see. I rather love that part of onion soup. Perhaps we should ask Cook to prepare that for all of us tomorrow?' She glanced around the table for support but found only disbelieving looks.

The next course was delivered to the children and Elspeth was riveted by her daughter's plate. 'What are they eating now?' she asked Hudson.

'Fish pie, milady.'

'*Maman, c'est vraiment bien. Manger un peu.*' A fork was hoisted to Elspeth, expecting her to try a bite of their food, which was currently dripping on the linen tablecloth.

She took a nervous bite. 'Oh! *Oui, chérie. Merci.*' She took another. 'Oh, I say, that is rather good.'

The children happily tucked into their plates, chirping away as happy children do. The adults helped themselves from the serving dishes proffered on the arms of the servants. But as the children were nearly finished before any of the adults had even started, Fergus wondered how long before they, too, had prepared plates set in front of them.

Noticing this, Iris gathered the children in a corner of the room and gave them colouring to do 'while the mummies and daddies eat their dinners'. She promised pudding if they were well behaved.

'How did you know they would finish before us?' Mr Kettering asked her, impressed, and not for the first time.

Iris blushed. 'I didn't. I just grabbed the paper and pencils on our way here, for backup. Always be prepared. I hadn't thought much beyond that, really.'

The rest of dinner went well. The children were delighted with the puddings and cheese and munched in happy silence. It had been the only silence of the meal. When they were finished, Iris took the children up to bed and the adults went through to the Drawing Room, each agreeing it hadn't been as bad as they'd anticipated.

Downstairs, Mrs MacBain and Mrs Burnside toasted each other with a well-earned cup of tea.

Fergus came down to breakfast slightly later than usual the following morning. He could see the children had been and gone already; there were no sausages left. As he was buttering his toast, Angus let out a loud and vicious laugh.

'Ha! I see Lord Eltenbrae's finally kicked the bucket! Grandmama will be delighted. Does he even have an heir? A legitimate one, that is? I can't remember.' He threw the paper on the table. 'Tennis, Hugh?'

Fergus scrambled for the paper. There it was, on the front page of the *Scotsman*: LORD ELTENBRAE DIES. Fergus sat down heavily. The offer to buy Loch Down was still active, as far as he knew, but no one had been able to shift Lady Georgina's mind on the matter. What had happened to the man? He read for some minutes before he found it: Lord Eltenbrae, his son and two housemaids had been feverish for several days, and only the housemaids had survived. Virulent Pernicious Mauvaise was cited as the cause.

He groaned audibly. *Our last hope*, he thought, *snatched from us again by this damned illness*. He was starting to think they were cursed.

It didn't take Lawlis and Imogen long to get to the Abbey that morning. Hudson escorted them into the Map Room. Lady Georgina was waiting for them with Fergus. He looked defeated; she looked elated.

'What on earth do we do now?' asked Fergus as soon as the door had closed behind them.

'Couldn't believe it when I read it,' said Lawlis, shaking his head. 'But in all honesty, even had we accepted the Eltenbrae offer, it wouldn't have completed before this. So let's not beat ourselves up.'

'What do we do now, Andrew?' asked Lady Georgina. She glanced down at Imogen's shoes as she spoke. They clearly weren't up to her standard. Imogen tucked them under her chair.

'We proceed with the auction. It's all we have left. I've been speaking to Mr Kettering about the value for the art and objects, and I think we're nearly at a final figure for the reserve on the Estate.'

'And what if we don't make that reserve?' Fergus looked pained as he said it.

'It doesn't bear discussing just now,' Lawlis replied, equally pained. 'I don't know if the family is prepared for this next step. If not, you'd better start getting them used to it. Cleaverings are arriving next week to start tagging items and staging sales areas.'

Imogen looked to Lady Georgina and explained, 'They'll be moving things around, gathering like objects together. It's quite disruptive to everyday life, and people often find it upsetting. If the family could move to Drummond House, it would better.'

Fergus shook his head. 'That's a non-starter, I'm afraid. We still have servants convalescing over there.'

'Then you'd best prepare the family for what's about to happen.' Lawlis stood. 'I'll ask Cleaverings to work with Mrs MacBain, keep the disruptions to a minimum. But this won't be pretty.'

Fergus turned to his grandmother after Lawlis and Imogen had departed.

'Through the looking glass we go, Alice.'

She raised a sardonic eyebrow. 'Really? It feels more like *The Fall of the House of Usher* to me.'

The following week, Cleaverings arrived at eight o'clock and thoroughly disrupted breakfast. Constance was irritated that she had neither been consulted nor informed. Angus was upset until he was assured they wouldn't be going anywhere near the Tennis Pavilion. Lady Georgina came down at her usual time and chased several porters out of the Music Room. They were off to a rocky start.

Iris and Mr Kettering were drafted to help the effort. Iris ushered people to and from various rooms of the house, almost like a mountain guide. Mr Kettering, for his part, was in charge of the paintings, artwork, and helping sort the authentic from the reproductions. As discreet as he tried to be about the issue, it didn't escape the notice of the Cleaverings' experts, all of whom had been well trained to control their reactions in front of the families. 'It won't do to upset them further, just carefully separate fact from fiction.'

Below stairs, Mrs MacBain had the remaining staff hard at work. Hudson alone was left to deal with the family. Ollie, Mackay and Maxwell helped sort linens, silver, crystal; anything that could be valuable was set aside for Cleaverings to decide upon. While it was sad to be doing it, Mrs MacBain was immensely satisfied by the clear-out. She could never have got the house this clean and tidy under normal circumstances. And the chance to empty the overstuffed cupboards and cabinets gave her an almost indecent thrill. Why did people need so much? she wondered, tossing a heavily repaired table felt onto the rubbish pile. The house could easily function on half of what the family had amassed over the centuries.

Upstairs, it didn't take long for Cecil to annoy everyone on the staff of Cleaverings. He followed them around the house, insisting on explaining the detailed history of each object they viewed. *Poor sods*, thought Eva. She felt sorry for them, having been on the receiving end of that very tour herself.

'That is not just any silver bowl you are holding, young man. It is the silver bowl the Eighth Countess used to repel the English forces as they attempted to requisition the Abbey before the battle of Flodden. It was dented on the forehead of the Commander himself. She was a formidable woman, you know.'

'Those books were given to the Eleventh Earl by Charles the First himself, after an afternoon's stalking. There is an inscription and royal seal in the first book. They shared a love of ornithology.'

'Of course, that was given to the family by . . .'

On and on it went until the head of Cleaverings was forced to step in. 'Sir, while I appreciate you are trying to help, firstly, it is not, in fact, helping; and secondly, while these artefacts may be exceptionally valuable to the family, unless that bowl also includes a letter from the Commander apologising for the incident, it is merely a dented bowl.' Cecil drew an outraged breath but was deftly distracted. 'But I do admire the foresight of the Eighth Countess to purchase Sheffield silver several hundred years before it was invented. Now, if you'll excuse us . . .'

Cecil was expertly escorted from the room with his mouth slightly agape.

That evening, Constance was late in coming down for dinner. As she entered the Library, Bella gasped. 'What on earth are you wearing? You look like a chandelier.'

The room turned at Bella's horrified statement, following her gaze to Constance, who was positively coated in jewellery. The entire family stared. She had managed to don three broaches, a pearl choker with a sapphire pendant the size of a walnut, and she was wearing earrings so large they rested on her shoulders. The tiara she'd chosen had been heavier than expected and had required her to walk slowly and cautiously in order to keep it aloft. Not that Constance would admit it to the family, but if she were honest, she was regretting the choice; all the finery was already making her neck and shoulders ache.

'Jewels have always been worn at dinner,' she replied petulantly.

'Yes,' said Lady Georgina, dazed, 'but not all of them at once.'

Constance tentatively touched the back of a chair feeling her way to the front, rather than look down. She slowly and awkwardly tried to sit. The tiara slid dangerously backwards on her head and Constance reached quickly to steady it, rattling as she did so.

'Oh, do go and remove some of it,' snapped Lady Georgina. 'You look ridiculous. And if you damage that tiara, I shall never forgive you. It was given to us by the Russian Imperial family, for safekeeping.'

Constance abandoned her attempt to sit when Hudson entered to announce dinner. He stared at Constance, clearly disturbed by the display. With great effort, he dragged his attention to the rest of the family, finding Lady Georgina with a smirk of amusement on her face.

'Dinner is served, milady.' He bowed, although his eyes strayed back to Constance.

'Thank you, Hudson. Shall we?' The family filed out of the room, leaving Hudson to wait as Constance shuffled slowly to the door. It was interminable.

'Perhaps I can carry the tiara to the Dining Room for you, milady?'

Constance glared at the butler for some moments before finally issuing a very soft, 'Yes, please.'

This was not how she had envisioned being Countess of Inverkillen.

The day of the auction approached, and the family worked hard not to notice. But as the hour drew nearer, they gathered, one by one, in the Armoury. Chairs had been set up and Cleaverings were using the guest stair landing for a podium. People had been wandering around the house all morning with the sale booklets. Frank discussions were had by total strangers about the desirability of the family's possessions.

Lady Georgina settled into a seat near the Library doors, reading the booklet and remarking spitefully that Cleaverings had underestimated the value of every single item. Constance came into the room, muttering loudly, 'Vultures. All of them.' Cecil was unhappy with the details in the book. He had done his best, he said, but they simply wouldn't listen to him. The more they read, the less happy they were, but what bothered them most was the number of water closets Cleaverings had listed. They discussed it for some minutes, before Cecil announced he was going to speak to the Auctioneer about their mistake.

'I can assure you,' said Fergus, loudly and suddenly, 'we counted them carefully.' No one believed him, of course, and the litany continued.

Top of the green stair. At the end of the stone hallway. Under the stair at the entry. That one from the tennis courts. No not the terrace doors, the door next to the rose bush. The one near that stained-glass window on the second floor. Does that count since it's only a loo and a basin? Outside the Portrait Gallery. Off the Glasshouse. Don't forget the Boot Room. Ha! Two at the Ballroom. Is there one at the Banqueting Hall? I can't remember. How many is that? Doesn't the Fencing Studio have one?

It went on for some minutes, each insisting they alone were correct, completely oblivious that the auction was attempting to begin in front of them. An usher tried to shush them; Bella glared at him. Mr Kettering suggested they move to the Library, but Constance waved him away like a midge. Throats were cleared. Polite entreaties were made. All unnoticed or ignored by the family. On and on, each assured their total was correct, speaking louder and louder, in order to be heard over the rest of the family. The auctioneer finally had enough. He banged the hammer on the desk as loud as he could and, once he had their attention – it took a moment – he ordered them from the room.

Hudson stepped over to the family to guide them out. 'If you'll come with me, I've prepared tea in the Morning Room,' he said discreetly.

Mute with indignation, Lady Georgina rose and followed Ollie, the footman. The family went slowly, muttering and glaring at those gathered in the room. Iris was tempted to stay, having never been to an auction, but Hudson gently cleared his throat and pointedly tilted his head to the door.

She sighed and got up. 'Yes, all right,' she muttered. 'But please don't leave me alone with them.'

In the Morning Room, a housemaid was pouring tea. Philippe and Auguste were playing chess in the bay window. Angus and Hugh were at the fireplace, pulling cigarettes from a silver box on the mantle. The ladies were seated in front of the fire. Iris took a cup of tea and moved to her usual spot, as far out of the way as she could get.

They were discussing dinner that evening. Lady Georgina had decided that they would have one last dinner together. She asked Hudson if it could be arranged, given that she could see a man walking to his car with a vase that had once stood in the Library.

'Must they take everything right now? Can't it wait until tomorrow at least?' Bella sat down roughly in the chair by the fire and tried not to burst into tears.

Everyone was quiet and the auctioneer could just be heard from the Armoury.

Elspeth looked towards Fergus and broke the silence. 'What will you do about the wedding?'

So much had happened, the impending nuptials had been quite forgotten. Not least by Fergus. He was ashamed of himself at the thought. He looked at Eva, thinking what a poor specimen of a husband she had chosen. He would have to do better.

'I suppose we'll do it in London. On a much smaller scale, obviously,' he finally said. 'Don't you think so, darling?'

Eva turned from the window to look at him but said nothing. She looked apprehensive.

'How can they marry?' The room looked around, confused as to who was speaking. It was Auguste. 'Is not, how do you say in English . . . *bigamie*, is it not illegal 'ere?'

'Bigamy?' Elspeth turned to her son, wondering if he had the right word. 'What are you talking about, darling?'

'Lady Eva, she is already married.' He turned back to his chess match, completely unbothered by the entire room, including his father, staring at him, utterly confused.

'Eva, why does he think you are married?' asked Fergus, just barely quelling the panic he felt.

Eva looked absolutely terrified and wouldn't meet his eye. 'I've no idea. Children, you know, they make things up.' Her voice reached a rather high octave.

Auguste looked around at her, scowling. 'But I saw it. You and Oncle Cecil were married last week in the Chapel. I was in the choir loft sketching the . . . how you say . . . *gargouilles*. Ha! *L'echec et mat!*' He looked triumphantly at his father.

Fergus looked from Cecil to Eva, not understanding. The family looked from Eva to Fergus, not understanding. Eva looked from Fergus to Cecil, understanding perfectly.

'Is this true, Eva?' Fergus's voice was barely above a whisper. 'Uncle Cecil?'

Cecil looked slightly chagrined but said nothing.

'Let me get this straight,' began Lady Georgina, slowly and with slightly too much sing-song in her voice. 'Just to be perfectly clear: not only did you marry a woman barely half your age, but you did it secretly, in the midst of a family crisis that might see us penniless and homeless, and the cherry on the top is that you stole her from your nephew. Do I have that right, Cecil?'

'I . . . I . . .' Cecil began stuttering. Lady Georgina resembled a wounded tiger just about pounce. He stepped back slowly, staring at his mother.

Fergus's whole body was trembling. Iris could see him struggling to keep control of himself.

'Get out.' It was so quiet, she barely heard it. And then Fergus stood, clenching his fists at his side, doing all he could to keep calm.

'I said get out. Both of you. Leave this house immediately and never return. Oh wait, none of us will return because we no longer own this house! Somebody in there now owns it!' His face was purple, and he was shaking violently. No one had ever seen him this angry before. Angus discreetly moved the fire poker out of reach.

'Look, I knew you'd be angry but given the flirting you've been doing with that secretary, I had rather hoped we could let it go,' Cecil said, hoping a dose of charm would get him out of this. Charm usually diffused sticky situations, in his experience.

But Cecil had breached the seal, the last remaining grasp on any sense of decorum in the family. Fergus lunged at him, rugby tackling him to the ground and pounding his shoulders repeatedly against the floor. Angus and Hugh leapt in and tried to pull Fergus off, knocking over a table and vase full of flowers in the process. Philippe and Auguste grabbed Cecil, pulling him to the other side of the room, but he kicked out and managed to knock over a chair and a lamp table in the process.

The ladies, for their part, were no better behaved. Bella charged at Eva, hurling insults, and Constance was attempting to wrench the engagement ring from her finger, shouting about family jewels. Lady Georgina was beating Eva about the head with a cushion. Several pieces of furniture went flying, and a bronze casting of a dove landed on Constance's foot. She howled in pain.

It wasn't until Hudson thundered on the dressing gong that the action ceased. Iris felt like a bystander in a farce. And to cap it all, the entire auction had gathered and was peering through the open door, watching with their mouths slightly agape.

'What in the name of all that is holy is happening here?' Mrs MacBain shouted, aghast. No one had ever heard her shout before, and it was enough to shock them all into silence. 'Sit down. All of you. Now!' She swept into the room with Lawlis, Imogen and Mr Kettering behind her and proceeded to sort the various warring parties into separate corners of the room. She removed the cushion from Lady Georgina's hand and returned it to the sofa.

The family did as they were told, meek and chastened. Iris crawled carefully out of the window seat where she had been hiding and stood staring at the destruction. There were feathers and broken glass everywhere.

Imogen pushed the auctioneer and the gathered public out of the room and gently closed the door. She turned around and nodded at Mrs MacBain, who turned her stony gaze on each family member in turn.

'I don't even know where to begin.' She cast around the room, looking for one calm and sane face among them. 'Now . . . Iris, what is this all about?' A few plaintive voices started to speak, but Mrs MacBain held up her hand and they ceased instantly. 'I asked Iris.'

'Well, um, Cecil just told us that he and Eva, um, were married last week.'

She stared at Cecil, her mouth falling open. 'What?' she gasped. If she had expected anything, it certainly wasn't that.

'And the news wasn't well received, as you can see.' Iris sat down, unsure what else to say.

Mrs MacBain surveyed the room, looking from Cecil to Eva to Fergus and back again. 'No. I can't believe it,' she said shaking her head.

'Believe it.' Eva stood, trying to look dignified in the disarray of it all. She still had feathers from the cushion in her hair. 'The Vicar married us last week. I am now the Marchioness of Drysdale,' she announced in a ringing voice, looking positively triumphant.

There was a stunned silence, before Hugh started laughing.

'Ha!' Angus snorted. 'This will be good.'

'Oh, dear . . .' whispered Bella, shaking her head.

'That can't be right.' Mr Kettering looked confused. Or perhaps concerned. Iris couldn't tell which.

Eva's victorious smile wavered. What was she missing? 'Of course it is. Cecil is the Marquess of Drysdale and now that we're married—'

'Oh, my dear,' Elspeth said, shaking her head and looking pityingly at the girl. 'That is not how the title works.'

Eva stared at her, her mind whirring. 'What?' She turned to Cecil, who looked even more chagrined.

'My late wife was the Marchioness in her own right,' he said simply. She looked at him blankly. 'When the female holds the title, in her own right, the title is never extended to the husband. Surely you knew that?'

'You're not the Marquess?' she asked, the colour draining from her face.

'No. Sadly, some ratty little tradesman in London is.'

'Hey, now!' said Mr Kettering, looking quite offended.

'This can't be happening.' Eva's voice wavered, and she went awfully pale. Hugh moved near to her, just in case she fainted. 'Please say it's all a mistake.'

'I really thought you knew,' Cecil said, as kindly as he could.

'Oh, dear god, what have I done?' Eva sat down hard in the window seat. Iris just had time to move out of her way.

'You married him for a title?' It was a bitter cry from Fergus, who was staring at Eva as though he'd never met her before. 'Is that the only reason you married him? If you loved him, I could forgive you. But for a title? Oh my god. What a close shave I've had. I need some air.' Fergus walked quickly out of the room, leaving the door open behind him. The crowd parted to let him pass through the Armoury.

'I am not a ratty little tradesman.' Mr Kettering was staring at Cecil, clearly very offended.

'What? No, of course not. My apologies, Mr Kettering,' Cecil began to apologise but wasn't sure why he needed to. 'I didn't mean you, obviously . . .'

'You're in a profession, Mr Kettering, that's not the same thing . . .' Elspeth tried to smooth the situation.

'No, it's not that,' said Kettering. 'You see, I am the Marquess of Drysdale and I am not a ratty little tradesman!' Stunned silence filled the room. Iris felt dizzy. 'The title came to me some months ago, completely out of the blue. I'm still not quite used to it.' He glanced at Iris, looking almost apologetic.

'You!' Cecil turned an ugly shade of purple and took several steps towards Kettering, the glass from the broken lamp crunching beneath his shoes. 'You have my fortune. You have my houses. What else are you here to take from me?' Auguste and Henri moved to protect Kettering, who stood his ground, looking wary. Eva stared at him, confused, and her mouth fell open slightly. Angus and Hugh erupted in further laughter, with Bella not far behind them.

'My dear, the most important thing about the aristocracy is knowing which family owns the title.' Lady Georgina stood and regarded Cecil. 'You and your bride will stay in Drummond House this evening, but I expect you gone on the early morning train. And Cecil, the silver has been counted.' She swept from the room without a second glance.

Elspeth stood and followed her, causing the rest to file out of the room, issuing snide little comments as they went.

Schoolboy error my dear but spectacular style. Perhaps a copy of Burke's Peerage *for a wedding gift? I told you she was a gold digger. Yes, but she should have done her homework. I really should put this in my next novel – seriously good material here. Bad luck,* mon cherie.

Mrs MacBain shut the door behind her, leaving Eva and Cecil to have their first marital spat.

Lawlis and Imogen came back late the following morning to discuss the auction results with the family. Unsure who they were going to meet, they simply presented themselves at the front door and asked Hudson who was available. To their surprise, he announced that Fergus was in the Library with Lord Drysdale.

'Lord Drysdale? Oh, you mean Kettering.' Lawlis was thrown for a second, disturbed at how quickly Hudson had made the switch. But he supposed 'unflappable' was the most important thing a butler could be. Especially with this family.

Upon entering the room, Lawlis could see they were joined

by Iris and Lady Georgina. Still no Angus. What did that boy do all day?

'Good afternoon. I don't come bearing good news, I'm afraid,' he began.

'Why is it that whenever someone professional comes to the house, it is never good news for this family?' asked Lady Georgina.

Lawlis forged on, scowling at her. 'I don't think anyone will disagree when I say that yesterday was a complete disaster. Because of this illness, we didn't have a good turnout to begin with, and those that did come didn't bid for much. There were a fair number of villagers that came to snoop around the Abbey. And then, of course, we had the scuffle in the Morning Room.'

Fergus looked chastened. Lady Georgina picked at an invisible thread on her skirt.

'Needless to say, we never even got to the house. We only have three weeks left, and it's not looking good.'

'I don't understand why so few people attended.' Mr Kettering seemed to take it as a personal defeat. 'Your collection is quite astonishing, even without the authentic pieces. But there was not a single agent from the nearby estates. No one from Edinburgh, or from London. I was quite vocal about it with my colleagues.'

'Could word of the forgeries have leaked out, perhaps? Scared them off? Maybe we need to do some damage control,' Imogen suggested.

Lady Georgina's head snapped up. 'No one could have possibly known. This family didn't even know. And may I remind you that every single one of those estates has done the exact same thing.' She turned to Hudson. 'Has there been talk in the village, Hudson? I know the servants gossip about us and if they did it in the village, word would spread quickly.'

'It would be unlikely anyone said something indiscreet,

milady. Given we have so few healthy staff, no one has had time to leave and even if they had, the village is entirely shut up. There would be no one to tell.' Imogen thought he looked a bit hostile underneath the mask, but she couldn't be sure. She wouldn't blame him; it was an insulting accusation.

'Be that as it may, someone could very well have put it in a letter,' said Lady Georgina. 'This is exactly why my mother always read the servants' letters each week. I counselled Hamish to do the same when he inherited the Estate but he refused to listen.'

'Grandmama, you cannot read people's letters,' said Fergus, appalled. 'It's an invasion of privacy!'

She sighed heavily. This new generation was so touchy. 'Can't I? In my own home? I suppose I can't search their quarters either. Hm?'

Hudson and Ollie, the footman, stared at each other, terror in their eyes. The idea of Lady Georgina reading their letters was disturbing enough but rifling through staff belongings was beyond the pale.

'If we could get back to the matter at hand,' Lawlis interrupted, attempting to cut short what he feared could easily become another shouting match. 'It doesn't matter why; it only matters that we haven't raised enough in the auction and the house remains unsold.'

'We need another plan,' said Fergus, 'and we need one quickly. Three weeks is no time at all. We've already lost two offers to this illness and I doubt Cleaverings will agree to another auction. Lawlis, is there no one else you can speak to about a private sale?'

'Unless I can widen the net to include the Americans – ' He paused looking at the pursed lips of Lady Georgina. ' – I've exhausted my address book, I'm afraid. We just need one decent offer.'

'Can we go back to the people who bought the Distillery?' asked Fergus. 'Maybe they've changed their minds?'

'We can try, certainly. But approaching them puts us in a weak position for negotiation. Plus, I had the impression they bought it as a long-term, hands-off investment. But who knows? I'll telephone in the morning if you wish.'

Fergus and Lady Georgina nodded.

'Right then, we're finished for today. Mr Kettering – I mean, Lord Drysdale – have you wrapped everything up here?' Lawlis stood up, ready to leave.

'Yes. I have a train booked for this afternoon.' He looked quickly at Iris and then back again at Lawlis. 'I'll drop my report to you before I leave, if that suits?'

Lawlis nodded and left with Imogen. Iris looked at Fergus watching her leave and smiled.

'Well, Lord Drysdale,' said Fergus, shaking himself back to life, 'you've been here so long, you almost feel like family. Although, given this family, that might not be much of a compliment. Thank you, for all your help.'

'It was my pleasure.' Kettering was slightly flushed at the attention. 'I wish you all the best of luck.'

Lady Georgina slowly stood. 'Have a safe journey back, and thank you for your expertise.' She extended a hand timidly, as if she'd never shaken a man's hand before. Mr Kettering stood and bowed his head, relieving her greatly.

'You might make a suitable Marquess yet,' she said, in what was clearly supposed to be a compliment, and she swept from the room.

Mr Kettering asked Iris to join him for a quick walk before he left. There was something he wanted to speak to her about. Flustered, Iris agreed, and they started out into the grounds. The gravel drive crunched underneath their feet as they set out from the house. It was good to get out of the madness, thought Iris. Maybe that was why Elspeth went walking each evening. She decided to add it to her daily routine, too. Not that she would be here for long; she'd applied for several posts as governess. She no longer knew how to feel about that.

They walked some minutes in silence, neither in a hurry. It was turning into a beautiful day. Iris stopped to watch the mist over the loch and turned when Mr Kettering cleared his throat.

'So much has happened since I first arrived.'

'Yes, it's a whole different world now,' she replied, shaking her head.

'I've enjoyed our time together, Iris. Very much.' Mr Kettering was staring at the ground in front of Iris's feet, blushing slightly. 'You are a remarkable young woman and I . . . well . . . I'll miss you.'

Iris gasped softly. 'I'll miss you too! And, well, it will be a bit empty without you. I hadn't realized how lonely I was before you came.' Iris felt dizzy. She hadn't planned to say any of that, and she blushed furiously. What must he think of her?

'I'm so glad to hear that.' He stopped walking and grimaced. 'Not that you're lonely, not that part. No, erm . . .' He grimaced and shook his head. 'What I mean is . . .' He turned to her, looking uncomfortable but resolved. 'I wanted to chance to speak with you about the future. Your future.'

Iris looked around at him, surprised. 'My future?'

'Yes, well, a lot has happened recently, and I wondered if you'd had a chance to consider what you'll do when the house sells. It will sell, you know.' He looked at her with such sympathy. He really was so very kind. Iris set off again, heading into the woods, and he hastened to follow her.

Kettering continued. 'I have been so very impressed with you since arriving at Loch Down.' Iris flushed and looked down at the ground. 'Your knowledge of the works here, your observations, the detailed notes you kept; it's all very impressive, especially for your age.'

Iris could feel tears brimming in her eyes, and she turned away so that he wouldn't see. She really didn't want him thinking of her as a child – some little thing to placate, pat on the head and shoo away. And that was what this talk was sounding like. She wondered what to say to change his impression of her, but she drew a blank.

'But given you've had not training or education in art history, I'm simply amazed by you, Iris and I wondered, um, if there was any chance that I could get you to, erm, come and work with me.'

Iris stopped walking and looked at him, not knowing what to say. Her heart soared.

'You'd need a proper degree, of course,' he said hurriedly, 'but that can be sorted. Really, I just wanted to know if you would be interested at all.'

'Of course I'd be interested!' She nearly shouted it. 'I was so worried you'd leave, and I'd never see you again. Or speak to you about art and history and honestly, these have been the best weeks of my life, with you. I couldn't bear spending the rest of my life as a governess. Oh, do please let me come work with you!' She was nearly clapping her hands, she was so overjoyed.

Mr Kettering looked at Iris, whose enthusiasm was fast overcoming his very English nerves, and his face broke out in a beam. He fumbled for her hands and then slowly leaned forward to kiss her.

Iris had never been kissed before and had she any spare brainpower at that moment she would have thought it was a wonderful thing to be kissed, especially by Mr Kettering. When she opened her eyes, he was looking at her, entirely too seriously. Iris squirmed. Had she done it wrong?

Just when the silence was getting too much for her to bear, he broke into another dazzling smile and said, 'Also, I'd quite like to marry you.'

'Does this mean she'll be a Marchioness now?' asked Ollie.

'Goodness, I hadn't thought of that. I suppose so,' answered Mrs MacBain. She passed a tray of cakes around.

Mrs MacBain had gathered the staff – what was left of them – after Iris told her the good news. If they'd had any champagne, they'd have popped it open and toasted the happy couple. But as it was, Mr Kettering had a train to catch shortly and Mrs MacBain felt, quite rightly, that they should see Mr Lawlis together about Iris's wardship as soon as possible. This family could be unpredictable, and she wanted to be sure Iris was free to do as she wished. Now was not the time to be reckless, she said, so she put them in a car without a celebration and sent them off.

'She'll outrank them then, won't she? All of them, even the Dowager.' Ollie cracked a huge smile and stared happily into the distance.

'Ha! They won't like that,' said Mrs Burnside, laughing. 'I'd love to be there when the news breaks, though.'

'No, they won't like it at all. Especially Bella. And no one is to mention it at all until Iris tells them, understood? Not a word of it above stairs.' Everyone nodded and continued laughing and eating cake.

It was a good day.

August

Lawlis and Imogen were on their way back up to the Abbey, hoping to be delivering good news for once. They had ten days before the death duties were due, and Lawlis was as near to panic as Imogen had ever seen him.

Hudson let them in the door. As they donned their masks, Imogen looked around, wondering if this would be her last visit. Hudson led them to the Map Room, where Fergus was waiting. He could sense their excitement as they walked into the room and stood up from his chair expectantly.

'We have another offer!' Lawlis said triumphantly. 'And, by Jove, it's a good one!'

'Thank you, Hudson, that will be all.' Fergus dismissed the butler and shooed the dogs off the sofa. Thinking the better of it, he moved to the reading desk on the opposite side of the room. 'An offer? Really? Are they Americans?'

'Erm . . . I don't know. It's the same group that bought the Distillery.'

'Wait, we don't know who they are? How is it possible we've got this far, and no one's asked who bought the Distillery?'

Imogen had wondered that as well. But she was just a secretary; what would she know?

'I was approached by a solicitor, who handled everything for his client. We don't know who they are, but they are very happy to take the Abbey, contents and all.' Lawlis rocked back on his heels and savoured his moment of triumph. 'It's enough to take care of the death duties and keep Lady Georgina in relative comfort. They only have one condition.'

'Condition?' Fergus felt his stomach lurch. Not again, not so close to glory. 'What do they want?'

'They want to retain you as manager.'

Fergus was now thoroughly confused. After some time, he spoke. 'They want me to be the butler?'

Lawlis laughed. 'No. Whoever bought it – and I gather it's a consortium of investors – wants to turn the Abbey into a hotel. And they want you to stay on board to be the manager of the entire operation.'

Fergus doubled over as if he'd been punched. Wasn't this exactly what he'd proposed to his father and Angus, only to be told it was ridiculous? But here they were, and they wanted him to run it for them. Run it, not for his family, but for this group of investors, strangers, probably foreigners. Fergus felt dizzy – with anger, with bitterness, with indignation.

'This is what you wanted, isn't it?' asked Imogen, touching his knee lightly.

'No. No this is not what I wanted. What I wanted was to be doing this exact thing for my family. What I wanted was to avoid the last few months of humiliation, trauma and shouting. What I wanted was to raise my children in the same home I was raised in. Not to manage it as a hotel owned by someone else, because my father and the people surrounding him were all idiots!' He swept a pile of papers off the desk and walked to the window.

Lawlis and Imogen fell silent, staring at Fergus's back and then at each other, unsure what to do next. They had hoped for a happier reaction.

'I'm sorry. Please forgive me,' Fergus said quietly after a

minute or two. 'I genuinely thought I'd be happier when the offer finally came through. But this is a bitter pill to swallow. Not just to lose my family home, but to lose it in the exact way I proposed saving it. Bitter is the only word I have.'

He turned to look at them. 'Please forgive me, Andrew. It was rude and thoughtless of me. I know what you have done for this family, how you have fought to keep us afloat, and I appreciate your efforts enormously. I don't think you're an idiot. But this was never going to be an easy moment and I didn't behave well. Please forgive me.'

Lawlis shifted in his seat, wondering what to say next. They needed to go over the offer in detail so he could respond, but it didn't appear Fergus was in the mindset for that. He wondered how long the buyer would wait. And how long Fergus needed. They only had ten days left.

'Right. Let me just go fetch Grandmama and we can review the offer.' Fergus started for the door.

'We don't have to do this now,' Imogen said swiftly. 'Absorb the news and let's talk tomorrow, shall we?' He looked so unhappy, and she was desperate to help him.

'No, Miss MacLeod. Thank you very much for your consideration, but let's just do it now. Strike while the iron's hot, as they say. We've had quite enough of pride over prudence. I'll just be a moment.'

He left the room, and Lawlis and Imogen stared at the closed door for some moments.

'Well, that could have gone worse,' said Lawlis, then he started whistling softly. Imogen stared at her boss and slowly shook her head.

After a few minutes, Fergus returned with Lady Georgina in tow. She looked tired, thought Imogen. Very tired. The last few months had been disconcerting, to say the least. Was it only a few months ago they were happy and secure?

Happy. Was that the right word for this family? Imogen thought not.

'I understand you have an offer for us, Andrew. Shall I have Hudson bring us some tea while we discuss it?' Lady Georgina pulled the bell cord and looked around the room for a suitable chair. 'Let's move over here, shall we?' They nestled into a small reading nook under the spiral staircase. 'Now, what are their terms?'

Lawlis took them through the entire proposal, in detail, twice. It was generous enough, as he said, to pay the death duties, the debt on the Distillery, and the family debt. And there was money to keep Lady Georgina comfortable.

'But they want the contents of the entire house? All of it? Can't we at least keep some of it? That's very cruel.'

'I think there will be some room to negotiate. It's going to be a hotel, not a private home, so there are some items that naturally won't be of interest.'

'And they want Fergus to be the – what was it called, the manager? Is that like being the land agent? What will happen to him?' she asked.

'The agent will remain, and so will the gamekeeper and the staff, if they wish. Anyone being housed on the property will remain on the property, much as they do now. Essentially, nothing changes for the staff.'

'And the servants have agreed to this?' asked Fergus, marvelling at the generosity of the offer.

'No one's been told anything yet. It's up to you if you want to accept this offer or not. And once the new owners take over, it will be up to the staff if they want to stay. It's quite thoughtful, really.'

'Yes,' said Lady Georgina, looking annoyed. 'Thoughtful for the servants, but what happens to us? To the family? Where do we go?'

'That's a bit trickier. They've offered Fergus the Gatehouse, which is generous, and a salary. They are happy to offer you a small cottage on the property, near the edge of the Estate, or a suite of rooms in Drummond House, if you would prefer. But for the others, I'm afraid there are no provisions.' He had said it as delicately as he could, but how delicate could one be while evicting an entire family? After six hundred years of continual occupation.

'Well, we'll have to talk this over with the family, of course, particularly Angus—'

'No, Grandmama. We will not talk this over with the family.' Fergus leaned forward on the edge of his seat. 'You and I will make the decision and together, and then we tell the family what has transpired. Grandfather got us into this mess, Father and Angus did nothing to fix it, and here we are. Either we accept this offer, or we call in the bailiffs. Your choice. But we will not be discussing it with the family.' He sat back firmly in his seat but never took his eyes from his grandmother. She stared back at him. Imogen held her breath.

'Six hundred years, and a Gatehouse with a suite of rooms is the best we can do?' She sighed.

'Or a cottage,' said Imogen earnestly. 'It's very pretty.'

Lady Georgina stared at her for a long moment. 'Which cottage? I must have my roses.'

'They have accepted the offer,' said Hudson, setting down the tea tray.

There were gasps in the kitchen, and all work stopped.

'They have accepted the offer and Loch Down Abbey is going to be a hotel. Mister Fergus is going to be in charge and any staff who wish to stay may do so.' There was much to rejoice in with his statement and a cheer went up among them.

'It's firm? They've accepted it? Signed the paperwork?' asked Mackay.

'Yes. I watched it myself. It's a done deal. They're telling the family tonight over dinner. Loch Down Abbey has been sold.'

Mrs MacBain slumped onto a bench in the hall, breathing deeply. 'I never thought I'd see the day.'

She's clearly in shock, thought Daisy, the kitchen maid, newly returned after her illness. *Perhaps I should get her a glass of water.*

Lady Georgina commanded they attend dinner that evening, as they always had. One last time, thought Fergus – how sentimental of her. In truth, she felt it would be easier to break the news, hoping the formality of the table would keep them from another scuffle, like the day of the auction. Or the day they discovered Hamish's studio. Or the day his will was read. They scuffled quite a lot, she suddenly realised. Maybe splitting up was not such a bad idea. Plus, it would give the village far less to gossip about. Small mercies were not to be underestimated.

Lady Georgina had Hudson lay out the table carefully. There were place cards at each setting, which was unusual for a family dinner. As they settled into their seats, all were surprised to see not Angus and Constance at the centre of the table, but Lady Georgina and Fergus. She had surrounded herself with her children and tried to separate the main combatants. Iris sat at the end of the table with Auguste, whose parents were at the opposite end of the room. Once the consommé had been served, Lady Georgina would begin.

But where to start? And what to say? Of all the difficult conversations they'd had the past few months, this was the one she was least prepared for. Better to rip the plaster clean off, she decided. She tapped her wine glass with a fork.

'Now, as some of you may already know, Andrew Lawlis came this afternoon with an offer to buy the Estate. We have accepted that offer.'

There were some cries around the table, a bit of murmuring but she settled them and continued.

'It is not, however, complete salvation for us. The death duties and all the debts we owe will be paid in full. We may hold our heads high there. The family jewels will be sold at Bonhams and the proceeds equally distributed between Hamish's children Including you, Iris.' Angus started to object but Lady Georgina merely held up her hand. 'Angus, please. This is hard enough without a fight just now. And yes, Constance, I know you are the current Countess and the jewels belong to the Countess, but it is already arranged, so please don't start. Elspeth, you will keep the pieces Hamish left you but there will be nothing more, I'm afraid. Everything else in the house now belongs to the new owners.' She paused and took a long sip of wine. 'Hudson, I might need a lot more of this tonight.'

'Yes, milady.' He refilled her glass.

'Everything?' asked Angus.

'But for personal effects, yes,' said Fergus. 'The furniture, the art, even the battle-axes; they own it all now. We are to be out of the house by the end of the week.'

It deeply startled them all, including Ollie, the footman, who knew he'd have to pack for them. He glanced at Hudson, who simply nodded.

'By the end of the week? And just where are we supposed to go?' Angus was angry.

'I don't know, Angus,' Fergus said wearily. 'You can stay with Constance's parents in Edinburgh, I suspect. I'm sure Hugh's parents would be happy to have the children in the house, for a short while, at least. Grandmama is being given a cottage on the Estate. I'm staying on to run the place.'

'Run the place? What does that mean?' asked Bella.

'Loch Down Abbey is going to be a hotel.' A collective gasp went up around the table. It was so much worse than Americans.

Angus leapt to his feet, knocking his chair over, which Hudson discreetly righted. 'You did this. This was your idea! No one else believed it would work, so you must be behind all this! Everyone's homeless but you.'

'Oh, Angus, sit down,' Lady Georgina sighed testily. 'Fergus is not some evil mastermind, plotting our downfall. On the contrary, if you and your father had listened to him, our future would be far brighter than it is now. But no, no; both of you knew better. Everyone knew better than Fergus. And may I remind you that Fergus is the only one in generations to have made any money for this family? But no, you and your father knew better than anyone. And now we all must pay the price. Oh, the men in this family! I tell you, if women are not running the world in fifty years, more's the pity!' She took a deep drink of her wine and signalled for more. Iris had never seen her drink so heavily.

Angus sat down, looking much like a spoiled child who has been denied a really good tantrum. The table was silent. Hudson and Ollie glanced at one another, unsure if they should clear the consommé. It felt like the first course was over, but they weren't sure.

'And what will 'appen to Iris?' asked Auguste.

Oh damn, thought Iris. She had been hoping to be

unnoticed. The family turned to look at her, and Hudson nodded encouragingly.

'Well,' she started hesitantly, fingering the lace on her napkin. 'Um, I've decided to go to London.'

'What? You can't be serious. What will you do there?' Fergus was disturbed, as was Lady Georgina.

'It's far too dangerous for a young girl on her own. Where would you even live? No, you will stay here. Loch Down is your home. You need someone to look after you.'

'I was always going to leave the Abbey when I turned twenty-one, Lady Georgina, to be a governess,' she said simply.

'Oh yes,' Lady Georgina muttered uncomfortably. 'I'd rather forgotten about that. But . . .'

'And there is no home here. The Abbey has been sold. Fergus has a job. You have a cottage. Everyone else has a place to go to. This was all I had. I must make a life for myself, and it will be one of my own choosing.' She took a deep breath and gathered her courage. 'I'm going to London. I'm going to study art history and work with Mr Kettering.' Iris picked up her wine glass and took a drink. When she set it down, the entire table was staring at her in stunned silence.

'How modern! Well done, Iris!' Elspeth raised her glass to the girl and looked around the table. 'I'm very impressed by this. Oh, come on, people, the girl has a brain and, in this day and age, she can use it for more than table arrangements. The world is changing, and we must change with it.'

'Yes,' said Fergus supportively, 'well done, Iris.' He raised her glass and toasted her.

Iris blushed furiously, took a sip of wine, and murmured thank you.

Elspeth looked at Iris. 'You must travel down with us

when we leave for France, Iris. I'll write to friends in the morning and see who can give you rooms until you have yourself sorted. One needs all the help one can get when facing London. It can be such an unkind place.' She chattered on excitedly about shopping – Iris would need all new clothes – and of course, introductions to all the right people. Iris could barely take it in. Lady Elspeth – her aunt – wanted to help her.

'Shall we have the next course now, Hudson?' Lady Georgina felt the danger had passed. Angus had come out of his sulk with the news and was looking – well, not cheerful exactly, but not explosive, and that was more than she had hoped for.

Curious, is what he looked, thought Constance. What was her husband thinking? He was quiet through the rest of dinner, but not in his usual way. She could see the wheels turning in his mind and he kept looking over at Iris and then back at Hugh. Or Bella. She wasn't sure which. But something was happening in that brain of his, and it made her very nervous.

Fergus, for the most part, was feeling ambivalent. It would most likely be their last night together in the same room, and thankfully, thus far at least, there had been no fighting. Angus was subdued, but something was finally going on in his head. When Hudson leaned in to pour more wine, Angus declined it. It was a small gesture, but it didn't escape Fergus's notice. This might just be the first chapter of a good life for them all.

December

Fergus walked up the drive towards the Abbey, snow crunching under his feet. It was near Christmas and he had been summoned to meet the new owners, his employers, for tea. He still didn't know who they were. Was it odd to work for someone you've never met? He didn't know, having never worked in his life.

It had taken four months for the illness to loosen its grip on the Highlands, but things were finally, slowly, returning to normal. Not that Fergus knew what normal looked like. He'd spent the time in the Gatehouse, learning how to live there, without servants, without one hundred and twenty-five rooms, without family. The first few months had been blissful. After Imogen taught him how to make tea and scramble eggs, that is. But as the months dragged on and having only Imogen and his grandmother for company, he was yearning, actually yearning, to be among people again. The village had been largely closed, and it was only the previous week that the market had begun again. He hadn't known Loch Down had a weekly market. Other businesses were opening as well and last night the pub had pulled its first pint amid joyous cheers.

He passed the Old Chapel and waved to Reverend Douglas. He hadn't known how to cook either and the man was positively skeletal. Fergus wondered how long it would be before he was back on his eating rota. He needed a good feed-up.

Fergus walked between two ancient yew trees, now trimmed and shaped to frame the entrance to the forecourt. He looked across to his former home. It was so clean and tidy. Was that a flag over the entry? 'Loch Down Abbey Hotel', he could just make out, gold letters on a black background. How smart!

Mrs MacBain had overseen it all, of course. The woman should have been a field-marshal. After she had arranged everything for the family, including moving Lady Georgina into the cottage – that had been no easy feat – she had been tasked with readying Loch Down Abbey and Drummond House as a hotel. Fergus had watched as a steady stream of lorries and tradesmen went up and down the drive, removing, repairing, and replacing everything. Would it even look like home, he wondered?

As he passed through the stone archway, as he'd done countless times before, he didn't notice the sign, or the new lantern above his head. He didn't see the marble urns filled with flowers or the new doormat under his feet. No, he saw the doorman, in smart black livery, opening the large timber door for him, tipping his hat, and welcoming Fergus to the hotel. Fergus stopped to take a deep breath.

He stepped into the Armoury cautiously and stopped to look around him. It was so very different yet so very much the same. The vaulted ceiling, the battleaxes, the tartan carpet beneath his feet remained. But there were chairs and tables in the room now, places to gather. And a desk had been installed just at the foot of the guest stairs. A man he did not quite recognise stepped out from behind it and approached Fergus.

'Good afternoon, sir. Welcome to Loch Down Abbey. They are waiting for you in the Library. If you'll be so good as to follow me?' He led Fergus to the double doors of the

Library, as if Fergus didn't know where the Library was. As he stepped across the threshold, Fergus's eyes swept the room, cataloguing the changes that had been made. When the full room fell into view, he was greeted by Mrs MacBain and Hudson.

'Hello, Fergus.' She looked different, he thought. Hudson too. Of course, he'd never seen them in anything but the Abbey's Livery. And those awful tartan masks. He'd forgotten them until just now. It snapped him out of his musing.

'Hello! It is so wonderful to see familiar faces. It's all so different, and yet not.'

'Yes, I'd say it's quite a strange feeling for you.'

'Tea, sir?' Hudson gestured to the silver service, sitting in its usual spot.

'Um, no, thank you, Hudson. I'm here to meet the owners, actually.'

A voice from behind him replied, 'You just have.' Fergus turned around to see Mackay smiling at him.

Fergus felt the blood rushing to his ears. 'I'm sorry, what?'

'We are the owners, Fergus.' Mrs MacBain smiled kindly and sat down, offering Fergus a seat opposite her.

Fergus sat down slowly and stared at her. 'I don't understand.' Hudson put a cup of tea in his hand and sat down beside Mrs MacBain.

'It's a bit of a long story, so best you settle in.' Mrs MacBain started to explain.

Times were changing. Jobs were changing. They weren't going to be in service for the rest of their lives, that much they knew. But it wasn't until Mrs Burnside's aunt had been turned out by her employer, at the age of sixty-eight, and nearly ended up in a workhouse, that they realised just how tenuous their futures were. Mrs MacBain refused to meet that same uncertain future.

They needed a security net, so a plan was hatched.

Mrs MacBain recruited the senior staff to form a co-op. They agreed to pool their wages, thinking that a larger pot of money would equal better opportunities for them all in the future. What that would look like, they couldn't say. They just wanted something that would give them security.

And they went on that way for some years, until 1920, when Mrs MacBain read in the newspapers that America was outlawing alcohol. It was the opportunity they'd been waiting for, she decided.

Fergus shook his head, confused, and looked from house-keeper to butler. 'I don't understand.'

She nodded sympathetically and Hudson poured him a dram of whisky.

Still confused, Fergus took the glass and looked at the pale, honey-coloured liquid. Hudson nodded encouragingly. Hesitantly, he took a small sip. Surprised at the pleasure it brought, he nosed it again. 'This isn't Plaid.' Another sip. 'This is what Father was always drinking. His private supply.'

'That was our opportunity. The whisky you're holding was made by Ross,' she replied, looking very pleased.

'Ross? MacBain? The gamekeeper?' Fergus shook his head in disbelief. Clearly, it was going to be a very long afternoon of surprises. 'Of course, it's the Highlands; everyone makes whisky. But this is very good.'

Hudson preened behind the tea tray. 'Twenty years, aged in French Oak.'

'Did you say twenty years?' Fergus looked from one to the other and back again, dumbfounded. 'This is so much better than Plaid! Why am I only just learning of it?'

Mrs MacBain took a deep breath. 'When Ross came back from university, Old MacTavish taught him how to make whisky using the smallest still in the distillery. The hope was to have Ross replace him when the time came. It took years of hard work to get to something he wanted to start laying down. But eventually he did, and he's been making that whisky ever since.'

'I see.' He didn't. 'I'm sorry, but how is this an opportunity? And what does America have to do with it?'

'Well, that's where the Major comes in.'

'Uncle Cecil?' Fergus's eyebrows shot up in surprise. And alarm. 'He's involved in this?' Fergus held his breath, praying he wasn't.

'No! He hasn't a clue. But you know his special brandy from the Berry Brothers?' Fergus nodded. 'Well, one evening, he mentioned to your father that they were also buying and sending whisky to America, very quietly, and making a fortune doing it. Cecil suggested he and your father sell Plaid to the Berry Brothers. I gather there was quite a row about it. In those days, the Major was always involved in some dodgy scheme or another – this was before he married the Marchioness – but your father always steered clear of any business with Cecil.'

'How do you know all of this?' Fergus was riveted by the tale.

She looked at him a bit sadly. 'We do hear things, you know, as staff. We may be silent but we're not deaf.'

Fergus blushed. 'Of course not. But eavesdropping . . .' his voice was scandalised.

'When there was a row in this house, the staff had to spring into action,' she said stiffly. 'We woke you a bit later, delayed your bath slightly; anything to keep you behind the other person's schedule, so you're not in the same room

again for long. Our eavesdropping was what kept the peace
in this family.'

Fergus was stunned. He immediately thought back to all
the years of family rows, never realising they'd been separated
by Mrs MacBain until things cooled. The woman was a
marvel.

She shifted and smoothed her skirt, reminding him of
Grandmama. 'Anyway, after the footman told us about their
row, I remembered that MacTavish had a son in America
and I wondered if we could sell Ross's whisky that way. So,
we wrote to the boy and, as it happened, his job was guarding
the door at a speakeasy in New York. He set up the business
from that side.'

Fergus gaped. This was not the way he thought the afternoon would go. Secret whisky, bootlegging, distant sons
– well, that much he would have expected – but speakeasies?
He held his glass up for more, mouth still agape. Hudson
happily gave him a double. The boy was going to need it.

'So you've been doing this for, what, the better part of a
decade?' Fergus said. 'And no one in the family knew about
it?'

'Well, your father knew Ross was using the small still, he
just didn't know what we were doing with it. And Angus,
of course, was never very interested when he took over, so
MacTavish had free rein.' She looked at him, simply and
honestly. 'But then your father decided to sell the Distillery,
and we knew we had to act. Without it, we'd lose our income.
You were right about that; the Distillery has always been the
money-maker on this estate.'

Fergus grimaced and took a long sip.

'Mr Hudson's cousin is a solicitor in Fort William, so we
hired him to buy the Distillery on our behalf.'

'But why did Father never hire Ross to make this –' he

held up his glass – 'instead of Plaid? I begged him to replace MacTavish! For years, I begged him.'

'In fairness to your father, he never realised just how much whisky Ross was making. He presumed it was a few cases, enough for a personal supply for the three of them.'

'Three?'

'Lady Elspeth always takes several cases back to France with her.'

'I have so many questions.' Fergus stood and walked to the fire, leaning his arm against the mantle, head down. 'So, you've been making whisky, in the grandest of Highland traditions, on the sly.' Mrs MacBain smiled faintly and shrugged. 'And you sold it for what must have been a stonking profit, all to benefit your retirement.'

Mrs MacBain blushed a little and fussed with her skirt. 'We've done rather well, yes.'

'Rather well? You bought a distillery! Never mind that, you bought the Estate! "Rather well" is surely the under-statement of the century.' Fergus set his glass on the silver tea service and crossed to the window. It was too much to take in. All those years, he'd lobbied for change. All the sleepless nights, trying to find a way to make money from the estate, being told time and again how ridiculous he was being. And all the while, it was in his father's glass. Father and Angus, he thought bitterly, who always knew better than me. He took a deep breath and tried his hardest to put his feelings aside.

He turned back to the trio of former servants. He saw no malice in them. They had seen an opportunity for a better life, and they had seized it. Who could blame them? He'd been trying to do the same.

'I have to admit, I'm very impressed,' he said. 'It never occurred to me to sell the whisky abroad. That was a whale of an idea.' He returned to the sofa and was quiet a moment, lost in thought. 'So, why buy the Estate?'

'As you know, they're repealing prohibition.'

Fergus smiled. 'Yes, they've come to their senses finally. Oh!' he gasped. 'No more orders for you.'

'Precisely. We knew we'd need another income stream and one thing we know is service, so we decided to buy the Estate and run it as you suggested, as a hotel. But Lawlis refused our first offer, saying it wouldn't give the family enough to live on.'

Fergus had a sudden flash of memory that nearly floored him. 'That was you?'

She nodded. 'Yes. And in truth, it made us think about what we were doing. How could we possibly live with ourselves if turned out you and the family, just as Mrs Burnside's auntie had been? It wouldn't have been right. So we went back over the figures and tried to work out how we could take care of Lady Georgina, at the very least. And then it dawned on us: Plaid Whisky.'

Fergus's head snapped up. 'What?'

'One last sale.'

It slowly dawned on Fergus. 'You sold it all to the Americans?' Mrs MacBain nodded silently. 'All of it?'

'Every last barrel. We're not proud. Well, actually, we are. They never asked if it was the same whisky, so we never mentioned it. They paid us handsomely, we brought MacTavish's son back to Scotland, and then we bought the Estate.'

Fergus nodded, turning it all over in his head. It was a remarkable tale. But even more remarkable was that it had all happened without anyone in the family noticing.

The room was silent, waiting patiently for it all to sink in.

Finally, after some minutes, Fergus looked to each of his former servants and said, 'Thank you, all of you, for taking care of Grandmama. It was extraordinarily generous of you. And clearly, our family wasn't up to the task.'

Mrs MacBain blushed. 'Yes, well. . .'

He touched her hand gently. 'Thank you.'

They were silent for some minutes, Fergus trying to process everything he'd heard. It was not where he had thought the afternoon, or life, was going to go, by any means.

'So now I work for you. That's rather funny, isn't it?' Fergus said, grinning at them. 'Well, what happens next?'

'We get to work,' said Mrs MacBain brightly. 'Hogmanay is our grand opening, and we've lots to do. Come with me and I'll introduce you to the staff. I dare say you'll know most of them already.'

Fergus stood and looked around the Library. A good first chapter, indeed.

Epilogue

The Setting

Loch Down Abbey is a grand hotel near the village of Inverkillen, which sits on the shores of Loch Down, deep in the Scottish Highlands. On the hotel grounds runs the River Plaid, source of the famous Abbey Whisky and Inverkillen Smoked Salmon. It was home to the Ogilvy-Sinclair family for six hundred years.

The Hotel Staff

Director of Operations – Mrs Alice MacBain
Head of Food and Beverage – Mr Robert Hudson
Head of Guest Services – Mr Hamish Mackay
Head of Sales and Marketing – Mr Giles Lockridge
Head Chef – Mrs Eleanor Burnside
Head Housekeeper – Sadie Milne
Head Porter – Ollie MacNair

The Ogilvy-Sinclair Family

Dowager Countess of Inverkillen – Lady Georgina, who resides in Drummond Cottage on the edges of the hotel grounds. Her rose gardens are the pride of the hotel.

Her daughter-in-law – Lady Victoria, founder of the renowned Garvey Music Academy in East Sussex, England.

Her younger son – Major Cecil Ogilvy-Sinclair and his wife Eva, who live in London with her parents. They are rumoured to be divorcing.

Her daughter – Lady Elspeth Comtois, who lives in France with her husband, Philippe, Marquis de Clairvaux, and their children: Auguste, Hugo, Delphine and Florence.

Her eldest grandson - Lord Angus Inverkillen, who lives in Tangiers with renowned author, Hugh Dunbar-Hamilton, and his three children, who have a very strict Nanny. Constance, Countess of Inverkillen, lives in Edinburgh with her new husband and their first child, Rupert.

Her youngest grandson – Hon. Fergus Ogilvy-Sinclair, Manager of the prestigious Loch Down Abbey Hotel, his wife Imogen and their first child, Tessa. They have two dogs, Grantham and Belgravia.

Her eldest granddaughter – Lady Annabella Dunbar-Hamilton, who lives with her second husband, the British Consul-General of Shanghai, and their fourteen maids.

Her youngest granddaughter – Lady Iris Kettering, who lives in London with her husband Thomas, the Marquess of Drysdale, their twins Alice and Edward, and her mother, Flora.

Acknowledgements

This is the literary equivalent of the Oscars speech you give yourself while brushing your teeth. Who do you thank? What if you forget someone? Can this be used against me in a court of law?

Let me preface this by saying NONE OF THIS IS MY FAULT. The blame lies entirely with you guys:

To Monty, my dearest love, who listened to all my ridiculous plot lines and characters on our Covid walks throughout the lockdown. Thank you for listening, encouraging, laughing; for pitching your own ideas, correcting my history, and for chivvying me to write it all down. You make everything possible and I know how lucky I am to have you. Also, thanks for the first, but not the second, bottle of champagne when the news came this was going to be published.

To Honor and Iona, who listened to me bang on about this thing forever and never waned in their enthusiasm and excitement. There aren't many teenagers who care what their stepmother is doing, so I thank you for being amazing friends.

To Kate Rice, Jesse Czelusta, and Charlotte Edmundson, such tremendous friends! Thank you for reading early drafts, commenting and correcting, and encouraging me to continue. I look forward to returning the favour soon. Get writing.

To my sister, Melissa, who encouraged me, all those years ago, to write a blog. Turns out, it was the making of this version of me. So, this is mostly your fault.

To Dan, Jenn, and James, for sending all the care packages and junk food, throughout my lifetime, but especially as I was writing this. My family would have starved otherwise. Well, they'd have been deprived of the cultural highlight that is Hostess and Little Debbie.

To Clan Erskine, who accepted me with very few questions and a whole lot of love. Yes, one of your actual arguments is in there, but no, none of the characters are based on you guys. This time.

To Hunvey Chen, thank you for inviting me to France for your birthday and introducing me to Greg Messina, who is now my literary agent. None of this could have happened without that trip.

To Greg, for pushing me to write something and not laughing when I did. You've been superb. I appreciate everything you've done for me. I hope this makes you a ton of cash.

And lastly, to my editor Thorne. Thank you for believing in me and my story. This has been the most wonderful experience.